Mystery at the Rectory

By A. E. Fielding

Originally published in 1937

Mystery at the Rectory

© 2013 Resurrected Press
www.ResurrectedPress.com

Published by Intrepid Ink, LLC

Intrepid Ink, LLC provides full publishing services to authors of fiction and non-fiction books, eBooks and websites. From editing to formatting, to publishing, to marketing, Intrepid Ink gets your creative works into the hands of the people who want to read them.
Find out more at www.IntrepidInk.com.

ISBN 13: 978-1-937022-61-7

Printed in the United States of America

RESURRECTED PRESS CLASSIC MYSTERY CATALOGUE

Journeys into Mystery
Travel and Mystery in a More Elegant Time

The Edwardian Detectives
Literary Sleuths of the Edwardian Era

Gems of Mystery
Lost Jewels from a More Elegant Age

Anne Austin
One Drop of Blood
The Black Pigeon
Murder at Bridge

E. C. Bentley
Trent's Last Case: The Woman in Black

Ernest Bramah
Max Carrados Resurrected:
The Detective Stories of Max Carrados

Agatha Christie
The Secret Adversary
The Mysterious Affair at Styles

Octavus Roy Cohen
Midnight

Freeman Wills Croft
The Ponson Case
The Pit Prop Syndicate

J. S. Fletcher
The Herapath Property
The Rayner-Slade Amalgamation
The Chestermarke Instinct
The Paradise Mystery
Dead Men's Money
The Middle of Things
Ravensdene Court
Scarhaven Keep
The Orange-Yellow Diamond
The Middle Temple Murder
The Tallyrand Maxim
The Borough Treasurer
In the Mayor's Parlour
The Saftey Pin

R. Austin Freeman
The Mystery of 31 New Inn from the Dr. Thorndyke
Series
John Thorndyke's Cases from the Dr. Thorndyke
Series
The Red Thumb Mark from The Dr. Thorndyke Series
The Eye of Osiris from The Dr. Thorndyke Series
A Silent Witness from the Dr. John Thorndyke Series
The Cat's Eye from the Dr. John Thorndyke Series
Helen Vardon's Confession: A Dr. John Thorndyke
Story
As a Thief in the Night: A Dr. John Thorndyke Story
Mr. Pottermack's Oversight: A Dr. John Thorndyke
Story
Dr. Thorndyke Intervenes: A Dr. John Thorndyke
Story
The Singing Bone: The Adventures of Dr. Thorndyke
The Stoneware Monkey: A Dr. John Thorndyke Story
The Great Portrait Mystery, and Other Stories: A
Collection of Dr. John Thorndyke and Other Stories
The Penrose Mystery: A Dr. John Thorndyke Story
The Uttermost Farthing: A Savant's Vendetta

Sir William Magnay
The Hunt Ball Mystery

Mabel and Paul Thorne
The Sheridan Road Mystery

Louis Tracy
The Strange Case of Mortimer Fenley
The Albert Gate Mystery
The Bartlett Mystery
The Postmaster's Daughter
The House of Peril
The Sandling Case: What Would You Have Done?

Charles Edmonds Walk
The Paternoster Ruby

John R. Watson
The Mystery of the Downs
The Hampstead Mystery

Edgar Wallace
The Daffodil Mystery
The Crimson Circle

Carolyn Wells
Vicky Van
The Man Who Fell Through the Earth
In the Onyx Lobby
Raspberry Jam
The Clue
The Room with the Tassels
The Vanishing of Betty Varian
The Mystery Girl
The White Alley
The Curved Blades
Anybody but Anne

The Bride of a Moment
Faulkner's Folly
The Diamond Pin
The Gold Bag
The Mystery of the Sycamore
The Come Back

Raoul Whitfield
Death in a Bowl

And much more!
Visit ResurrectedPress.com
for our complete catalogue

FOREWORD

The period between the First and Second World Wars has rightly been called the "Golden Age of British Mysteries." It was during this period that Agatha Christie, Dorothy L. Sayers, and Margery Allingham first turned their pens to crime. On the male side, the era saw such writers as Anthony Berkeley, John Dickson Carr, and Freeman Wills Crofts join the ranks of writers of detective fiction. The genre was immensely popular at the time on both sides of the Atlantic, and by the end of the 1930's one out of every four novels published in Britain was a mystery.

While Agatha Christie and a few of her peers have remained popular and in print to this day, the same cannot be said of all the authors of this period. With so many mysteries published in the period, it is inevitable that many of them would become obscure or worse, forgotten, often with no justification than changing public tastes. The case of Archibald Fielding is one such, an author, who though popular enough to have a career spanning two decades and more than two dozen mysteries has become such a cipher that his, or as seems more likely, her real identity as become as much a mystery as the books themselves.

The books attributed to Archibald Fielding, A. E. Fielding, or Archibald E. Fielding, are quintessential Golden Age British mysteries. They include all the attributes, the country houses, the tangled webs of relationships, the somewhat feckless cast of characters who seem to have nothing better to do with themselves than to murder or be murdered. Their focus is on a middle class and upper class struggling to find themselves in the new realities of the post war era while still trying to live the lifestyle of the Edwardian era. Things are never as they seem, red herrings are distributed liberally through the pages as are the clues that will ultimately lead to the solution of "the puzzle," for the British mysteries of this period are centered on the puzzle element which both the reader and the detective must solve before the last page.

A majority of the Fielding mysteries involve the character of Chief Inspector Pointer. Unlike the eccentric Belgian Hercule Poirot, the flamboyant Lord Peter Wimsey, or the somewhat mysterious Albert Campion, Pointer is merely a competent, sometimes clever, occasionally intuitive policeman. And unlike, as with Inspector French in the stories of Freeman Wills Croft, the emphasis is on the mystery itself, not the process of detection.

Pointer is nearly as much of a mystery as the author. Very little of his personal life is revealed in the books. He is described as being vaguely of Scottish ancestry. He is well read and educated, though his duties at Scotland Yard prevent him from enjoying those pursuits. His success as a detective depends on his willingness to "suspect everyone" and to not being tied to any one theory. He is fluent in French and familiar with that country. He is, at least in the first book, unmarried, sharing lodgings with a bookbinder named O'Connor, in much the manner of Holmes and Watson, though O'Connor disappears in the subsequent volumes.

While the early books fall plainly in the "humdrum" school with Pointer appearing almost immediately and much of story revolving on the business of tracking down various clues, the later novels are much more concerned with the lives of the characters surrounding the mystery. Pointer is much less center stage, often arriving instead at mid-book to clean up the pieces and insure that the guilty do not escape justice. It is, perhaps, this lack of focus on the detective, which has caused the works of

Fielding to fade away while the likes of Poirot seem to attract the interest of each new generation.

One intriguing feature of the Pointer mysteries is that they all involve an unexpected twist at the end, wherein the mystery finally solved is not the mystery invoked at the beginning of the book. I leave it to the reader to judge whether Fielding is "playing by the rules" in this, but it does keep the books interesting up to the last chapter.

Mystery at the Rectory finds the good inspector caught up in the investigation of a death at that most English of institutions, the rectory of a small country village. The rector has been poisoned when his mushroom ketchup was replaced by a deadly toadstool extract. Only the inspector suspects the true nature of the death and can unravel the web of secrets that form the *Mystery at the Rectory*.

Despite their obscurity, the mysteries of Archibald Fielding, whoever he or she might have been, are well written, well crafted examples of the form, worthy of the interest of the fans of the genre. It is with pleasure, then, that Resurrected Press presents this new edition of *Mystery at the Rectory* and others in the series to its readers.

About the Author

The identity of the author is as much a mystery as the plots of the novels. Two dozen novels were published from 1924 to 1944 as by Archibald Fielding, A. E. Fielding, or Archibald E. Fielding, yet the only clue as to the real author is a comment by the American publishers, H.C. Kinsey Co. that A. E. Fielding was in reality a "middle-aged English woman by the name of Dorothy Feilding whose peacetime address is Sheffield Terrace, Kensington, London, and who enjoys gardening." Research on the part of John Herrington has uncovered a person by that name living at 2 Sheffield Terrace from 1932-1936. She appears to have moved to Islington in

1937 after which she disappears. To complicate things, some have attributed the authorship to Lady Dorothy Mary Evelyn Moore nee Feilding (1889-1935), however, a grandson of Lady Dorothy denied any family knowledge of such authorship. The archivist at Collins, the British publisher, reports that any records of A. Fielding were presumably lost during WWII. Birthdates have been given variously as 1884, 1889, and 1900. Unless new information comes to light, it would appear that the real authorship must remain a mystery.

Greg Fowlkes
Editor-In-Chief
Resurrected Press
www.ResurrectedPress.com

CHAPTER ONE

The rector got up from his writing table and laying his pipe down, stood a moment as though collecting his thoughts. A distinguished-looking man of around forty was John Avery, with his tall spare figure, his clever, scholarly face. He was frowning as he absent-mindedly straightened a yellow china jar on the corner of the mantelshelf. Then he returned to his knee-hole table, and, taking an apple from a plate which always stood on the corner, began slowly to eat it, still with a look of abstraction on his face, still with some inner discomfort marking a frown on his fine forehead.

The apple automatically disposed of, he drew out his watch and looked at it. Four o'clock. His sister-in-law would probably be in her own sitting room.

Stepping out into the rectory's big hall-lounge, he went up the stairs, broad and curving, and with a gentle preliminary knock opened a door giving on a room of blue and white harmonies. The rector's sister-in-law—Doris Avery, whom most of her circle, including the rector, voted a very beautiful woman—sat writing at one of the windows; the strong light struck naming gleams from the burnished hair that grew in a lovely crescent around her smooth white forehead. Otherwise, however, her features were just averagely good; the hazel eyes of no particular size or shape, their shade dependent, like most eyes of that colour, on the mood of the moment, and the mouth similarly neutral in its general placidity, though the mobile lips looked ready to smile on the least occasion. Her seated figure, too, revealed a length of slender limbs

that bespoke her tallness and fine proportions when up
on her smartly shod feet.

As she caught sight of him, she gave an exclamation
of pleased surprise. "Why, John! I thought of you as still a
captive in Damascus—or was it Ephesus? But since
you're free—try this chair."

The cheery invitation, although he seated himself in
accordance with it, failed to dissipate the troubled
expression on John Avery's face as he said with evident
reluctance: "My dear Doris, I'm afraid you'll think me
unpardonably impertinent for what I've come up to say to
you. But I feel it a friendly no less than a conscientious
duty."

At her glance of inquiry he said in a low but firm
voice: "It's about Anthony Revell." Adding gravely, as her
raised eyebrows and puzzled expression continued to
silently question his meaning, "Are you being quite fair to
him, Doris? *I* know your devotion to Dick, of course. But
Revell may not realise it so fully. It's not the first time
that something in his voice and look, when talking with
you, has given me the same anxious fear that he may
possibly misunderstand your quick sympathies. But it
has nerved me to say frankly that I think it would be well
for him to see less of you, my dear."

Doris Avery had a very charming laugh. It rang out
now. Then she stifled it to exclaim: "My dear John! How
deliciously nattering! But you should say it to Olive Hill.
Not to me."

"Olive Hill?" he repeated blankly.

"She would be pleased at your tone!" Doris spoke with
a spice of malice in her own. "Yes, Olive Hill. But don't
say a word yet, or you'll choke him off. He has intervals of
qualms. Olive may yet be sacrificed—but he is tempted."

The rector got up. His handsome face was all alight
now. Gone was the touch of austerity which showed when
he was grave.

"I confess I never thought of that simple
explanation." He did not add that it had never occurred to

him that any man would fall in love with Olive Hill when Doris Avery was before his eyes. Though Olive had an interesting face and really fine eyes. Olive was his sister Grace's companion. A slender brownhaired girl whose quietness had won her the nickname of "Mousie" as a child. She was an orphan. Her father had been a colonel in an Indian cavalry regiment and her mother a friend of Grace Avery's mother. Except for certain set duties, Olive was treated at the rectory exactly as a member of the family.

Grace came in now and sank into a chair with some compliment to Doris on how charming her room always looked.

"Wait till it gets its new covers," Doris said to that. "Olive's engineering them. Blue taffetas with black and white embroideries here and there. Awfully smart. By the way, Grace, I've just been confiding to John's well-known discretion—as now to your own—that Olive's the magnet responsible for Anthony Revell's increasingly frequent calls."

Grace looked perturbed. The news seemed unwelcome. "Surely you're mistaken, Doris," she said slowly, but was silenced by the smiling assurance: "I have it from Anthony himself, my dear. Only just now he was asking me whether I thought he had a chance with her. But this is in absolute confidence, remember, please. The secret's between us three until he musters up the courage to declare himself openly. But tell me how you like my new covers, John?"

The rector was, however, thinking only of Anthony Revell. Smart, well-groomed Anthony Revell, with a very large fortune and a beautiful old house.

"You really think he's in earnest," he queried doubtfully.

"Olive would be pleased to hear you," Doris answered dryly. "Oh, yes; he's very much in earnest, though I don't say I'm for nothing in the affair. He's a shocking flirt, of course. We all of us know his deserved reputation in that respect. But I've made it plain to him that he's gone too far, now, for further—

The rector's attention was suddenly caught by a door slightly ajar. It led into a sort of nondescript room which used to be one of the schoolrooms. Avery clearly remembered that this door had been quite shut when he began speaking to Doris just now. He was a man of shrewd perceptions and the wind was blowing from the other side of the house. As the door had opened, therefore, it had been opened by a human hand. Stepping to it, he flung it suddenly wide.

At the other side of the farther room stood a young woman doing something to a jar of flowers. But the tassel ends of a cushion between her and the door were still swinging. Evidently set in motion by her swift movement backwards.

Olive Hill—for it was she, looked round in well simulated surprise.

"Do you want me?" she asked with her faint surface smile, her eyes glittering as she turned them on the rector.

"There's a book on the hall table that's just come for you," he answered gravely.

"Really? Oh, thanks, I'll run down and get it."

And with another artificial smile she left the room by its opposite door. On which the rector turned back to Doris, shutting its nearer door firmly behind him.

"I'm afraid Miss Hill overheard us," he warned her as he did so. But Doris only laughed carelessly. There was a hard streak in her, as the rector knew. It was a pity. But, in his eyes, her devotion to his brother Richard outweighed it.

"She ought to feel flattered to learn that I'm trying to nerve a wavering lover." Mrs. Richard Avery lit a fresh cigarette. "For it will be my good deed when it comes off. I love matchmaking!"

"Then why not make one between him and Mrs. Green?" Grace asked, with a world of meaning in her tones.

The rector's face stiffened. He detested scandal, and there was a lot of talk about Anthony Revell and the woman artist staying at The Causeway who was painting his portrait and decorating his study for him.

Doris laughed.

"If you heard Anthony talk about her, Grace, you would realise that he looks on her as a sister."

"If you want to engineer a husband for Mousie," Grace went oil obstinately, "though I think she is far better off as she is, then why not Mr. Byrd? He and she are mutually attracted and would make an eminently suitable match. While Anthony! With his grandfather's fortune now in his hands there isn't a family into whom he might not marry! You let Mousie and Mr. Byrd manage their own love affairs."

"Mr. Byrd doesn't approve of marriage," Doris said coldly. "He goes about saying so. And I don't think that he's the least bit really in love with Olive. But surely that's enough discussion of her matrimonial possibilities," she finished with a rueful laugh.

Grace gave a nod that signified her complete agreement on that point as she rose and left her brother and sister-in-law to their own conclusions.

Doris's glance went to the table in front of her.

"I'm just writing to Dick," she said, tapping the paper softly as though the messages it carried made it precious. "I wish he weren't so mysterious about when he's coming home. It makes me dreadfully afraid that he's once more going to spend his leave out there. The Gold Coast isn't the health resort he tries to make me believe it. And oh! I do miss him so frightfully!"

Mr. Avery laid a sympathising hand on her shoulder. He was very fond of his sister-in-law who had kept house for him now for nearly two years. He hoped that Richard really was making his fortune, as he had hinted that he

was doing in a letter to himself nearly a month ago.
Richard was a clever chap with many irons in West
African fires. He had written in the highest spirits of one
of his investments. A banana-grove that he had bought
from a tired owner, and still more, some ore samples
uncovered when a torrential rain had washed away a
whole hillside, promised a bonanza. But, he added, it was
too soon to write with assurance. Which was why he was
not letting Doris in for a disappointment. But if his hopes
were realised, that month-old letter had said that
Richard would be back with Doris very shortly. And with
money enough to stay in England and comfort for the rest
of his life.

"Patience!" the rector encouraged her, therefore,
before saying that he must get back to Ephesus.

"To 'the Street called Straight'?" she asked. "The
street where you certainly belong, Jack," Doris said
gratefully as she turned to resume her letterwriting.

Descending the stairs thoughtfully, the rector caught
sight of Olive below. She was standing by the table on
which lay the book that he had mentioned to her, and he
looked at her with new eyes. If she married Anthony
Revell she would become a prominent member of his
parish. The Causeway, Revell's house, lay quite close; and
his father, the Admiral, had been a friend of the Averys
for years before he died. Anthony had a privileged place
in the community.

Studying his sister's companion with these
considerations as he came down, Avery was struck by the
intensity of the still figure. Will-power, concentration,
leashed-in energy, all were expressed by it. She suggested
a tautly-drawn bow, as she stood arched slightly forward
over her hands, spread out across the book. A drawn bow?
Or? Well, with a humorous twist of his lips the rector
privately thought that at this moment Miss Hill was
much more like a "Pussy" than a "Mousie." Her eyes were
staring straight ahead of her with a very curious light in
their depths. A light which the rector did not think had

anything to do with the beauty of the bed of Anchusas and Sidalceas lying directly in their line of vision.

Without speaking he went on into his study, and back to his beloved books, with a feeling that whether it was pussy or mousie just outside the study door, the lines had indeed fallen in pleasant places for all within the rectory; until he remembered Grace's suggestion that Olive was in love with Byrd. A most disquieting suggestion.

For Byrd represented to the rector the very spirit of evil in his parish. Byrd—Captain Byrd, to give him the rank which was his when he had retired on a full disability pension of thirty shillings a week—was a "Red" of the most vivid shade. He was not merely an atheist. Avery could have forgiven that. He was an "anti-God"; zealously and potently so. Able and quick-witted in debate, he was an everpresent thorn in the side of the Churchman. And the idea that, even though only through his sister's companion, his rectory could be linked to that man was intolerable.

Then he reflected that Grace might have no foundation for Olive's supposed sentiments. Doris did not take the assertion seriously, he had seen. Also—(and here the rector reached for his fountainpen) also, Doris, it appeared, had set her heart on strengthening Anthony's errant fancy for Miss Hill into an actual engagement. And what Doris set her heart on, she usually obtained. So that Olive's own happiness might be confidently hoped for, to the rector's relief on all scores.

Four days later a telegram came for Doris from her sister. Their mother, who lived with this married sister, was seriously ill. So ill that her life was in danger. Doris was off within the hour, leaving very careful instructions with Olive as to the running of the house. Such detailed instructions that she had rather the air of the Matron of a Home for the Feeble-Minded, when leaving one of her charges perforce in command. Mousie, however, listened with her usual air of careful silent attention. Her post as "companion" was now tacitly exchanged for that of

housekeeper, with special regard for the order to take
Mike, Doris's Irish terrier, for daily walks; though
"jumps" would have more accurately described his
favourite exercise.

The walks seemed invariably to end up by Mike's
joyous incursion into the gardens of The Causeway. And
as this necessitated catching him and leading him out on
the detested leash, the chase was apt to finish by his dash
into the house by any open door or french window.

All of which, of course, compelled Miss Hill to follow
apologetically for the truant's capture. This once entailed
explaining things to Mrs. Green on one of these
precipitate irruptions into a room where the artist stood
palette in hand, talking to her literally "model" host,
young Anthony Revell. An arrestingly handsome man,
with dark well-cut features, brilliant eyes and a merry
smile.

Anthony gave the intruder a laughing welcome. But
not so the annoyed artist, for Mrs. Green sharply shook
her brushes at him. The dog's sensitive nose received
some of the biting turpentine drops. Such an agonised
howl followed that Olive's apologies were cut short by her
cry of sympathy. While the victim's yelping dash into the
open, whence he streaked for home, was instantaneously
followed by Anthony's rush after the dog in a vain
impulse to apply some comforting first aid.

As the two women were thus left momentarily alone,
Mrs. Green said tartly: "Serve him right! That will teach
him not to come barging in here again in a hurry!"

"But the dog didn't harm anything!" Olive protested.
"And he does so love coming here!"

To which the answer was a sardonically significant:

"He loves to come?" With an insolent stress on the
pronoun that emphasised the personal implication.

Mrs. Green looked about thirty-five years old. Dark,
too, like Anthony, but with a vividly feminine face,
capable of exerting profound attraction. Perfectly dressed,
clever, amusing if not actually witty, Mrs. Green was

considered to be a social acquisition to the neighbourhood.

She had appeared in the district about four months ago, sending in her card to Lady Revell at The Flagstaff, and asking whether she might be allowed to copy the "Revell Morley." Lady Revell had given permission at once, had met her later at her work, and been struck by it and by her. A commission followed to paint a ceiling for the Chinese room, Lady Revell's pride. Mrs. Green's terms were ridiculously low, but she had explained, with seeming frankness, that she had been ordered by her doctor away from the North of Ireland where she lived, to the milder climate of England, and that the idea of idle hours filled her with horror. The two women had become very friendly. Lady Revell had insisted on her putting up at The Flagstaff, and there Mrs. Green had met Anthony on one of his infrequent calls on his mother. Anthony, twelve years older than Gilbert Revell who was his mother's idol, had been left a very large fortune when a boy of ten by his grandfather, between whom and himself there had been one of those warm affections that sometimes run between children and old people. Along with the fortune had gone The Causeway, a large house where Anthony had lived since coming down from Oxford. Mrs. Green, the well-read, the widely travelled, the splendid artist, had at once offered to paint some panels in his study for him. In other words, she had fallen head over heels in love with him, said local gossip, adding that she would not have been the first woman to find his very unusually good looks irresistible. Anthony flattered, and very much attracted, had at once closed with the offer. Mrs. Green had installed herself at The Causeway. Lady Revell had made no comment, though she had lent Mrs. Green her own maid to stay with her there.

Anthony must marry some day, the wonder was that he had not done so before. Mrs. Green was a widow, evidently of independent means, and might carry it off, though Lady Revell thought her foolish to risk a slip, for she did not think Anthony was at all in love with the artist; but that, Lady Revell decided, was the woman's own look-out, and certainly Mrs. Green was both keen-eyed and clever, though a good deal older than Anthony.

This was the woman then who now faced Olive with an appraising glance which was faintly ironic.

Olive said nothing, only looked at the little picture nearest her. Even she recognised the quality of the work being done.

"You're painting the steeple tile by tile," was her only comment. "It'll take a very long time at that rate, won't it," she added sweetly, "but I suppose you won't mind that."

This was the third time that the two had met. The other times Mrs. Green had shown an apparent friendliness, which Olive felt was but skin deep—if that.

Anthony came back now. He looked a mere lad, tall and rangy, though handsome as few lads are, as he jumped through the window on to the rug by Olive.

"Mike refuses to hear my explanations," he said, "you've wounded his feelings deeply, Mrs. Green. Outraged all his notions of hospitality. His last word was that he wouldn't come here again! Ever!"

"But that's the idea," Olive said brightly, "Mrs. Green doesn't like his coming. But, Mr. Revell, will you look out for me a good book on Euripides. You spoke of a Life of his—"

"Oh, I hope not!" came from Anthony in mock horror. He had taken a First in Classics. "When? Where?"

Olive only laughed, and had him take her to the big library. There she started him on his favourite Greek authors, and from them to philosophies of life in general. She talked amazingly well, he thought, rather revolutionary ideas—unexpectedly so—but very charming, and how charming too she looked. How her large eyes shone . . . She was so keen on hearing what he had to say—what he thought—especially about modern problems

The time flew—as it had flown before when talking with her, Anthony recollected. He said as much when begging her to use the library. She had just explained that she could not go to the rector's fine collection of books, as he so often needed to consult them himself. It was in the middle of his ideas on how to help unemployment, ideas which were like and yet interestingly different to those held, or at least talked of, by her, that she said she must be back in the rectory. They walked home there together. Anthony struck anew by some of the things that she said; things, had he but known it, that Mr. Byrd proclaimed at his weekly talks to any who liked to drop in at his little cottage which he had named, with his characteristic bluntness—The Hut. It too was not far from The Causeway, but on the other side from The Flagstaff.

CHAPTER TWO

Three weeks passed, and still Doris was not able to leave her mother, but Olive managed her affairs quite nicely without her aid, so nicely that one afternoon Anthony hurried after her as she was leaving The Causeway. He had been out when she had arrived "to return a book."

"I hope Mrs. Green didn't really annoy you," he said earnestly.

Anthony had not heard what the trouble had really been, he had only come on Mrs. Green looking quite flushed, and on Olive facing her with a look as though she were a little girl being scolded by her governess.

"She hates me," Olive now said. "She adores you," she added.

"Not adores," he said uncomfortably. "She's a very warm-hearted woman, and—well—very great friends at first sight—almost— " He plodded on, but Olive was not listening—apparently. Her face upturned to the trees, she was content to be now in the sunshine, now in the shade—apparently.

And then Anthony told her how he loved her, how he had fallen in love with her when he had seen her in Mrs. Richard Avery's sitting-room at the rectory only three weeks ago, and how he would never love any one else all his life.

"I wish I could say that I never had loved any one before," Anthony went on, "though in a way I can. That's the worst of not falling in love—true love—early. Had I met you before—other things wouldn't have happened. Couldn't have happened. But I can swear that from now on you'll be the only woman in my life. Had I known what love is, I wouldn't have been deceived by its counterfeit. Not I. But now"—and Anthony's arms went round her—"I love you, and you only, and do you love me?"

"Yes," she murmured, letting him kiss her.

Suddenly she drew away. "There's some one over there. I saw a shadow slip behind those bushes. They must have been behind this tree and heard every word we've been saying!"

"Who cares," he replied; and again forgot the world and other people.

Quite half an hour later, Anthony overtook Mr. Avery as he was walking home.

"I want you to be the first to know," Anthony began, and with that he went on to tell him of his engagement that afternoon to Olive. "We're keeping it to ourselves until I come back from my annual fortnight's rock climbing," he wound up.

Was the delay in order to get Mrs. Green to leave The Causeway, the rector wondered.

"And what about Mrs. Green?" he now asked gravely.

Anthony turned and faced him. "I told you before, Padre, that there was nothing between us—except friendship. I can repeat that. Honestly. She's a lonely woman," Revell went on, "a most charming friend. Very affectionate. But she might be a hundred, for all the love-making there's ever been between us. And on her side as well as mine," he added earnestly. "I know what people are saying, and she can be frightfully tiresome with her airs of —well—proprietorship," he flushed, "but it's only friendship, Padre. Only."

"Will the friendship extend to Olive?" Avery asked quietly. He was a man of few words, but he could cut in with the one question that went to the root of the matter under discussion.

"I'm afraid not," Revell said, "no, I'm afraid not. It's comical, but she doesn't think Olive good enough for me. Olive! Me! Me, why, I'm not worthy to breathe the same air with Olive!"

The rector liked the lover's hyperbole. He had had a romance of his own once.

"Mrs. Green's leaving The Causeway in any case," Anthony went on. "The paintings are finished, and jolly fine little things they are."

"So I'm told. Fairy tales from Grimm, I understand?"

"Yes. They're painted so as to seem just emerging from dreamland. Little house where the Seven Bears lived. Church, to which the hero rides for his marriage to the princess. Mountain peaks and bits of a blue lake far below, as seen from the window of the Sleeping Beauty. Landscape, such as Red Riding Hood ran through—all that sort of thing, but they're not nursery stuff. They're rather wonderful. Olive agrees about that."

"And your own portrait?" Avery had heard that Mrs. Green was painting one.

Anthony laughed. The rector liked his laugh. It was still boyish and unspoiled.

"That's too awful for words. Only equalled by the awfulness of the lines of the dinner-jacket in it. I've come out as a cross between Shelley, Byron, and the picture of Bubbles that hung in Gilbert's nursery."

"Olive seen it?"

"Yes. She thinks it stands for Mrs. Green's dream of what I ought to look like." And both men laughed.

"Mrs. Green's moving to my mother's. You know — apart from to-day, there was a horrid row yesterday," and suddenly he burst out. Mr. Avery had always been a sort of father confessor to Anthony. The two liked each other sincerely.

"Mrs. Green was infernally rude to Olive. She has been near enough to the line before, but she stepped over it yesterday—with both feet. Olive had dropped in to borrow books from my library. She's keen on books. Uncommonly well read, as I don't doubt you know"

The rector did not know.

"Mrs. Green seems to have taken a dislike to her —a quite ridiculous dislike "—Anthony looked furious—but also sheepish. "Every time Olive has come in about books, Mrs. Green made herself a fearful nuisance, and yesterday, as I say, we had it out. I told her she would have to apologise to Olive. She—she—oh, she was insufferable. Burst into tears and flung her arms around my neck. Poor Anthony looked so miserable that the rector stifled a smile with difficulty.

"One of the penalties of youth," he could not resist saying. "When you're my age, no one wants to throw her arms around your neck."

But Anthony was not listening.

"She's gone back to my mother's to finish a ceiling she's painting in the Chinese room there. And The Causeway will be shut up till I get back."

There fell another silence. "Though, mind you, till this happened, Mrs. Green has been the most delightful friend a man could find. She told me in the beginning that I reminded her of a son she had, who died years ago."

The rector made no comment. The Mrs. Green whom he had met did not look in the least motherly. Exquisitely dressed, charmingly pretty, with her air of ease and poise, she was the kind of woman who, the rector thought, played the part of friend to a handsome young man like Anthony at her own risk.

He asked Anthony to dinner, and the latter accepted with pleasure. Though he would have to leave rather early afterwards as he had a longstanding engagement in town which he could not break. He would be off next morning, in any case, for his fortnight's holiday in Derbyshire.

Olive showed a charming side of her at dinner that night. The rector had no idea there was so much hidden in Mousie. It was as well she filled the canvas, he thought, for Grace was no use at all. She kept glancing from one to the other of the young couple, but she talked very little.

When dinner was over and Anthony had had very reluctantly to tear himself away, she stepped into the rector's study, and stood a moment watching him fill his pipe.

"I haven't told you!" he said with a cheerful grin. "I haven't said a word!"

"Oh, it's plain enough. And yet, but for Doris's meddling, Olive would have married that horrid Byrd man, and I needn't have had this talk with you. Olive mustn't marry Anthony, Jack." Grace spoke with vigour—and anger.

The rector waited in surprise. He had to wait some time.

"That must be stopped," she said at last in a low voice, "for I've a dreadful thing to tell you. I suspect now that Olive had been pilfering from my things ever since she came," were her next and most unexpected words. "I can't otherwise understand—there's no other way of explaining—what has become of things that seem to vanish. Real lace—I had yards of it that I never wore-trinkets that I don't use—that gold-fitted dressing-case that you gave me. It was a frightfully handsome affair, but heavy as sin. They have all gone. I never thought of its being Olive till yesterday, when two one-pound notes were taken out of my purse—and could only have been taken by Olive. The purse was lying on a table in my sitting-room where I sat reading. She was in and out several times, and as it happened I counted the notes over when I picked up the purse, just as, by chance, I had when I laid it on the table, for I was half minded to ask you to give me a couple of five-pound notes for the lot. When I counted them the second time, I was two pounds short."

"You are absolutely certain it couldn't have been any one else. Or that you didn't make a mistake?" he asked very gravely.

"Absolutely." Grace's tone was very distressed. "I haven't spoken to her, for I don't know what to do about it." She looked as though she did not.

"It's a dreadful position. I loved her mother. I owe her a tremendous debt for her help when my mother died. And besides being Gertie's child, Olive is so quiet in all her ways, so amusing—always contented—marvellous memory—as a companion she's irreplacable. But she mustn't marry Anthony. You see how impossible that has become!"

The rector said nothing for a full minute.

Grace was his half-sister really. Born when he had been at Winchester, they had grown up with the unbridgable distance of years between them. She had married the year that he returned to his father's rectory as a curate. It was only on her husband's death a couple of years ago that she had made the rectory her home—at least for the summer.

She always spent her winters out of England. He did not really know her much better than he knew Olive, he was reflecting uncomfortably. Was this that she had just told him to be taken literally, or was it exaggerated? Was she so vexed at losing a companion that she had—the rector hesitated over the right word. He was aghast at what she had told him. Much too much so to talk the matter over at the moment. It would require the most careful thought... a sudden remembrance of some incident in her childhood came back to him. A nurse had maintained then that little Gracie had deliberately lied in order to get a governess whom she disliked out of the rectory. This extraordinary accusation, or series of accusations—made just now —the rector felt the ground underfoot to be very yielding.

"You must prevent the marriage," she said again. "It's absolutely impossible. Mr. Byrd—yes. He's always talking about people having no right to money and things they don't need, but not young Revell. The old Admiral would turn in his grave at such a daughter-in-law at The Causeway."

"But why have you left it so late to bring the accusation?" Avery asked, his face very grave.

"I hadn't an idea that Olive could get him," Grace said. "She's in love with Mr. Byrd really. I thought it was just some notion of Doris's."

"Doris's notions generally have something solid behind them," the rector spoke to gain time. "As for what you tell me about Olive—we must think out the best thing to do. The best thing for Olive as well as for Anthony. And meanwhile, not a word to any one else, Grace!"

"No one else, of course," she agreed, "though Lucy-May Witson or Mrs. Green would rejoice to know about it. Fortunately Anthony is going away for a fortnight. What is to be done?"

"No one must be told one word of it," the rector said sternly. "No one!"

Avery spoke with a sternness he rarely showed. He had great personality under all his sweetness. Where he thought the question one of right or wrong, he could crack the whip, and if need be use it.

Grace promised to say nothing to any one until they should talk the matter over—before Anthony's return from his holiday.

"And meanwhile keep your things under lock and key," he said. "Do not be the one ' by whom offense cometh.'"

She looked shocked.

"If only she can be cured. It must be kleptomania! I'm really deeply attached to her, but However, I shall say nothing to her or to any one for the present."

She left him, and the rector smoked his pipe and tried to see how to combine justice and mercy—that as yet unsolved problem. He had not solved it when next day Doris arrived back at the rectory. She was looking very fagged, and told him that though there was no immediate danger she might be summoned again to her mother's bedside at any time. There could be no question of any permanent improvement.

"But to talk of something happier," she went on. "I hear that Anthony and Olive have come to an understanding."

"Who has been indiscreet?" he questioned in his turn.

"I think it was Miss Jones when I stopped at the post office for some stamps. Or no. I believe it was Harmsworth the tobacconist—I was out of cigarettes."

The rector laughed at the idea of keeping anything from his villagers.

"I'm going up to have a word with Olive," Doris went on. "I do hope you will let the marriage take place from here, Jack?"

He made some non-committal reply at which she opened her eyes a little. Then she was gone and the rector heard her merry laugh overhead, and Olive's rather throaty voice replying.

Late in the afternoon he had to go some distance to see a sick parishioner.

He walked back by the oak wood whose last outcrop ran from The Flagstaff past The Causeway. There was there a glade that was none too easy to find, in which he loved to linger when he had the time to spare. Strolling through it he pondered on what could be done about Olive Hill. Her face rose before his mind.

Rather pale, heart-shaped, with big black eyes that could look like pieces of jet, or like rounds of velvet. It was not a sly face—exactly. Or was it? Subtle it certainly was. Trying to sum her up, the rector to his dismay realised that he had no fixed ideas at all about her. Yet he could not help her if he could not reach her. And you cannot reach a land whose latitude and longitude are unknown to you.

He walked on, his light footsteps inaudible on the thick soft turf. Suddenly he stopped. In a natural recess which nearly enclosed them stood two figures. Avery recognised the trim slight figure of Byrd by the erect carriage and the challenging tilt of the square chin, in the same instant he saw that the slighter, shorter figure beside Byrd was Olive Hill. Both had their backs turned to him. From her attitude, she was talking earnestly. Byrd was listening with head bent, poking the earth with the cane that he always carried. Something about his attitude suggested anger, but as he turned his face slightly, the light was on it, and Avery saw Byrd was smiling that saturnine, malicious smile of his. Meeting it, Olive threw back her head and with a quick farewell nod slipped on out of sight. Byrd stood a full minute before he took the same path, one which led on past The Causeway to his own little cottage farther down the road.

Avery was slightly disturbed. There had been a suggestion of intimacy—of secretiveness—in the place. But at any rate this meeting was no lovers' talk . . . there had been something very unpleasant in Byrd's smile. . . . Pondering earnestly on the right course to take about his sister's surprising companion, the rector made for his home by a short cut. He finally decided to do nothing for two more days. Then there would have to be a thorough clearing up of the position. But by that time he hoped to have come to some definite decision.

CHAPTER THREE

Next morning, Friday, the rector was in his study before breakfast. The waiting that he had imposed on himself was a strain. It did not seem fair to Olive either. She and Doris were making plans for the wedding—Grace had very sensibly gone away for the time being to stay with a friend who lived nearby, but who was tied to her room as the result of a car accident. She would come back on the Monday when, the rector had told her, he and she could thrash out what had best be done.

Doris had taken it for granted that Olive was no longer a companion, but was merely staying on at the rectory as a guest. This put the rector in a most uncomfortable position. But he could not alter it at the moment.

He pulled some papers towards himself, and took up his pen. He was busy bringing out a Life of Saint Paul. In another moment the machine began to work, the wheels to turn, the wings to lift, and then he was up and away; far away from the problems of ordinary life. In short, he was that enviable thing a writer in full swing.

Fraser, the butler, came into the study, and stood in the door which led into the library. The two rooms opened out of each other.

"Major Weir-Opie to see you, sir."

Major Weir-Opie was the Chief Constable of the county. He and the rector were old friends.

"Put them on the writing table," murmured Avery without looking up, "and I hope they're riper than the last lot."

"It's not fresh apples, sir, it's Major Weir-Opie to see you, and I've shown him into the study."

Avery came to earth. Rising, he went into the next room and greeted a short, thick-set, straightbacked, man warmly. Weir-Opie had a red face with keen eyes, and a business-like expression.

"I've called on very tragic business," he said at once, "but I wanted to let you know immediately, and I hoped to find you alone. Anthony Revell has just been found shot dead at The Causeway. Apparently he had an accident with his revolver. It was lying under his fingers."

Mr. Avery was profoundly shocked. "But I thought— we thought—that he was away in Derbyshire."

Weir-Opie agreed. "We thought so too. We had entered the name of The Causeway on the list of houses on which to keep an eye during the owner's absence. Well, he evidently returned late last night.

"One of our constables patrolled all round the house at ten last night and it was shut up then, he says. Yet a milkman, who called there at half-past seven this morning for some bottles that the cook had promised to put out when she left, and which he hadn't had time to fetch before, saw that one of the ground floor windows was standing wide open. He went to the back, to ask if he should leave any milk, and got no reply. He tapped on the open window and got none either. Meeting P.C. Marsh a little later, he spoke about it to him. The constable went to investigate, and found Revell's sports car in the garage, and his dead body stretched out in the drawing-room."

Avery was astounded. Why had Revell returned home without a word to any one, or had it been without a word?

The other continued:

"He lay in the drawing-room beside a table on which was a box of cartridges. Close to one hand was the revolver, beside the other a cleaning cloth. He must have been cleaning the revolver and possibly caught the cloth in it. The shot went through his temple—the right temple. Death must have been instantaneous. Absolutely."

"What a dreadful affair," Avery repeated slowly, "does Lady Revell know yet?"

"She heard of it with fortitude," Weir-Opie said rather dryly. "I went there before coming here. Gilbert is now the heir, I suppose, and he has always been his mother's idol."

"What about that lady artist—Mrs. Green, though I understood that she wouldn't be at The Causeway any more."

"Nothing to keep her there, you mean?" Weir Opie asked in the same tone. "No, she was with Lady Revell. Returned Monday evening, it seems. Gilbert spoke of fetching her to hear the news. Lady Revell sensibly shut him up. She says she has no idea why Anthony was at The Causeway. We think that he came back for something forgotten, heard some one prowling around; we've had a good few housebreaking jobs lately that we can't account for —opened his drawing-room window so as to hear or see better—got out his revolver, he bought one some months ago for just that purpose, and then as nothing happened and time began to drag, he began to tinker with his revolver—was careless and killed himself. The doctor thinks he must have shot himself around about one o'clock."

The telephone rang beside them.

"That'll probably be for me. I told my men I should come in here next."

It was for Weir-Opie, who listened, murmured "Good!" and hung up.

"We've got into touch with the couple with whom Revell was climbing. They say that he told them early yesterday morning that he must go back to London to see his dentist about an aching tooth. He drove off around nine. That accounts for his being able to drop in at his home last night. He evidently came on here after having had his teeth attended to, to fetch something he wanted while away. Now to the next step, Padre. Lady Revell told me that she had just had a letter from Anthony —she's been away till Tuesday and so didn't see him when he left—saying that he was engaged to a Miss Olive Hill, who, she tells me, is Miss Avery's companion, and that she was on the point of coming over to see Miss Hill and get up a dinner-party for her, when I brought her the news of this. That's why I came on at once from The Flagstaff to you. It's a terrible thing to have happened. Is the young lady in?"

The words were a fresh shock. Avery had forgotten Olive for the moment. What an appalling piece of news for her. Whatever her faults, what a dreadful blow!

Avery rose and with a word of excuse went up to Doris's sitting-room. Some one was on a couch, her head buried in the cushions. As he stood a moment he heard a sound as of an animal in agony. It was too late to withdraw. Doris, for it was she, had sensed a presence in the room. She sat up with a jerk.

"I locked my door," she began in a harsh sort of whisper.

"My dear Doris!" came from the doorway. It was Grace just entering. "I had no idea that you cared for poor Anthony like this"

"Anthony?" came from Doris in a sort of screech. "Who cares about Anthony! It's Richard!" There was no mistaking the lack of affection in the one case, the agony in the second. "But what's happened?" Grace was aghast as Doris staggered to her feet.

"I've had no letter, and I told him I should count the days," Doris said wildly.

"But there was a letter for you that came yesterday. I sent Olive to you with it at once. She wanted to ask you about some dress or other."

Grace was speaking to Doris.

"She didn't give it to me. I haven't had a line for ages—I thought—I thought "Without finishing, Doris, with a travesty of her usual grace, fairly swept the two from her room under the plea of a frightful headache.

Grace stepped into her own.

"She's been worrying lately. Something that Violet-May Witson said started it, I think," Grace whispered.

Lady Witson was a dreadful gossip as they both knew. And one of her brothers was a fellow Commissioner out in West Africa.

"But what does she mean about not having had Dick's last letter? As I met Olive running down with some patterns that Doris had promised to help her with yesterday, I handed her the letter. She went on straight into the room, I'm sure."

"Well, we can't ask about it now," remarked the rector.

Grace nodded and gave him a meaning look. "No need to worry about telling poor Anthony now, and you would have had to tell him—"

"How did you know that something had happened to him?" he asked.

"The milkman, of course! He told cook. Cook told Margery who brings in my tea. Well, I wanted the engagement broken off, as you know, but hardly like this! I can't understand it! Poor Anthony!"

She stopped as Doris, looking herself again, came in.

"Where's Olive?" she asked. "I want that letter from Dick that you gave her, Grace."

"And John wants to break some bad news to her."

"Bad news? Is Anthony ill? Was that what you meant just now? I'm afraid I was too wrapped up about Dick to care what had happened to any one else." She was facing the rector.

"It'll be a shock to you too, though," he said now. "Revell is dead, Doris."

She stared at him open-mouthed.

"It seems that he has accidentally shot himself," he explained. "Weir-Opie has just told me. He thinks Anthony was cleaning his revolver and did something awkward—a bullet went through his temple."

"How awful!" breathed Doris. "What will that poor girl do? What a dreadful thing for her!"

"I want to tell her at once. Weir-Opie wonders if she knew that Anthony was back last night."

"Back? But he's away rock-climbing surely. How could he be back! You don't mean—" her tone grew more shocked still—"that it happened at The Causeway?"

He nodded gravely. "In the drawing-room there. I don't know more myself."

"I'll find her," Doris volunteered. "And I'll let the letter stand over for the time being."

For a moment the rector wished that he could also let her break the news to Olive. But with all her attractiveness, Doris was not a religious woman at all. And in moments such as this, the only consolation was that which religion had to offer. It might, probably would, fail, but there was no other.

The two women left him, and a minute later Olive came in, looking very confident and smiling. Avery stepped forward and took her hand.

"My dear girl," he said in a very kind voice, for after all she was engaged to the dead boy. After all a smile and a pat, or even a jarring laugh might mean little. "Prepare yourself for bad news. Very bad news. Sit down here—" and then he told her just what the Chief Constable had told him. It seemed to turn her to stone. Before her pallid silence Avery was at a loss, for it had some unexpected quality in it that he felt, but could not name. Of personal grief, as he expected to meet it, there was practically none.

Had she not loved Anthony then? Had she only accepted him as what he was, in one sense, a marvellous stroke of luck? The rector had had his doubts on that score since yesterday, but he had told himself that it was not fair to probe too deeply into her motives.

"Major Weir-Opie wonders whether you would let him ask you a few questions," he went on.

She made for the door without a word. The Major turned at her entry with some apprehension. But a glance at her tearless face relieved him. He looked at her with secret curiosity. Anthony Revell was a young man who could have married any one, and he had chosen this girl, Olive Hill, a companion here at the rectory. True, Anthony Revell had always seemed quite unconscious of his position as fortune's favourite, a country life and books had always seemed to attract him more than the smart world, but even so, he was a prize in the matrimonial market, and this white-faced girl had won it. She was, he saw, quite pretty, but still—and then she raised her eyes.

"Any thing's possible with those eyes," he thought, meeting them full on. They were so intelligent. They seemed to be asking something of him. . . or trying to suggest something to him. . . The Major felt touched. He expressed his sincere sympathy with her in her great loss. Then he asked if she knew about Revell's return to his house some time last night after ten o'clock?

She said that she only knew what the others knew, that Anthony was joining a friend and his sister rock-climbing, as the three had arranged months before. Anthony's engagement to her was to be publicly announced on his return. The delay in doing this was her wish.

"Now, Miss Hill," the Chief Constable went on, "had he any valuables in the house? Anything that would especially attract thieves?"

"He had lots of cups," she said, after a long silence.

He cocked his head to one side. Cups nowadays, with silver at the price it was—not much temptation, besides Major Weir-Opie had an idea that Revell sent his silver to the bank when he left his house for any length of time, and he was leaving for a fortnight, wasn't he?

Except for the cups, Olive seemed to have no suggestion to make.

"You're wearing no ring," he went on a little anxiously. Tears must be near, he did not want to start the flood. "I wondered whether by any chance he would have the ring he meant to give you at the house? Would that be possible?"

She said that she did not think it likely. He intended to bring her the ring on his return. A London firm was setting it.

And then, since she could not apparently help him with any information, Major Weir-Opie left. Olive, palely composed, held out a hand which he found icy to the touch. She turned at once and went up to her room, locking herself in.

Weir-Opie hurried away.

The rector walked up and down his study. No need now to raise the question of Grace's terrible accusation. No need for him to prevent the marriage now. He felt the sincerest pity for Olive, and yet she baffled him.

He had his car sent round; he must call at once on Lady Revell. But when nearly at the flagstaff he had his man take the turning to The Causeway, where the tragedy had happened. The house, a large one, lay isolated but for one cottage on the winding road, the cottage where lived the unsatisfactory Captain Byrd, or Mr. Byrd as he preferred to be called.

The door of The Causeway was standing open. A policeman rose from his chair in the hall and saluted as the rector stepped in. Jamieson, the young butler whom Byrd had got Anthony to try, and who was doing well, came forward, his face working.

"They sent word," he explained. "I came up at once, sir—not that I can do anything now—but at least I'm here."

"The other servants?"

"No need for them to come back, the Major says, till the inquest to-morrow, sir."

The rector stepped into the room, the drawingroom which had been turned by Jamieson and the gardeners into a sort of chapel. It had a raised part at one end and there, on a draped bed, lay a long, motionless figure covered with a beautiful Chinese rug.

The rector spent a quarter of an hour beside the dead boy, then he let himself out and continued along the road to The Flagstaff. This was a big house which stood behind high walls. It had, unlike the homely Causeway, regular entrance gates, and a lodge beside them. There was quite a sweep up to the front door, of a size that suggested that nothing under a Rolls or a Bentley could ever stop here. There were footmen. There was a butler. There was a general air of exalting the fussiness of life, that had always amused the rector, for the Admiral had considered anything less than a dozen servants as squalor. Small wonder that Gilbert lent a discreet ear—when his mother was out of the way—to some of Byrd's stinging words, Byrd whose theory was that no man should serve another, except the latter were a cripple or over the age of ninety. Anthony, with the excuse of attachment to his grandfather, had early escaped to The Causeway, where life was more to his liking.

Lady Revell, dressed in pale blue, rose to receive the rector. She flung her cigarette into the fire and motioned him to a seat beside her. Her face wore its usual thick coating of white, on which level black eyebrows were beautifully drawn above her eyes, which were small and close-set.

She had strange eyes, had Lady Revell. Green as the sea, and of an infinite melancholy unless she were laughing, when they could glitter like cut glass.

"I was just thinking, as you came in, Mr. Avery," she said in her rich deep voice, a voice with an enormous amount of verve and "go"in it, "that one doesn't trust Providence half enough."

The rector was surprised. Piety had not been a quality which he had ever found in Lady Revell.

"I've been a pig to Anthony," she continued in a remorseful tone, "because Gilbert was so obviously better fitted to have all that money that it made me wild. And, after all, in the end, it's Gilbert, and not Anthony, who is to have it."

She had been a pig indeed. The rector knew how the elder boy had felt the frost that seemed to grow harder and more severe with each year after Gilbert was born. Lady Revell might well feel remorse now. She had acted as though she hated Anthony because his grandfather had left him his vast fortune. But for the genuine sweetness of Anthony's nature she might have ruined his temper. As it was, she had saddened the lad. Still, it was something to find that the mother had come again to the surface, the mother who used to be so fond of little Anthony, before Gilbert came to sweep all her affection up to himself.

They talked a while of the death. Lady Revell asked warmly about Olive, and, just as Anthony had thought, did not seem opposed to the match.

"She might have steadied him," she said finally, "and he needed steadying. His looks were too much for most women. I know of two at least around here who would have gone any length."

"Mrs. Green for one," murmured Gilbert, who had just come in. "The silly woman was really off her chump about him."

"Mrs. Green for one," agreed Lady Revell. "But scandal bores the rector"; and they talked of the dreadful accident instead.

Gilbert was only eighteen years old, and though to the rector, as to his father and grandfather, he had none of the charm of Anthony, Anthony the sunny who never lost his temper, never complained, never blamed others, Gilbert was not without his friends. Spoiled he was, but he had unexpected grit in him which had refused to let his mother turn him into a pet. He had insisted on going to Rugby, and that breezy and robust school had liked him, while Anthony was a true son of Eton. The two brothers had been fond of each other, which spoke well for both. And now all that had been meant for the one would go to the other, with probably a good slice for Lady Revell. She was Irish, a sailor's daughter, and had no settlements, the rector knew, and from certain signs at The Flagstaff he was sure that she was hard pressed for money lately. The Admiral had had no idea of retrenchment, and there were hair-raising tales told of the extravagance that still went on in the servants' hall.

The rector drove away feeling that his dislike of Lady Revell had been mistaken, that in spite of her biting tongue to Anthony, she had really loved her first-born.

CHAPTER FOUR

Lunch next day was a painful meal. Olive sent word that she was going for a long walk, and would not be back till late in the afternoon.

The rector seemed to see still before him that handsome young face which had turned to him at this very table so short a time ago.

Grace had returned and was very silent.

"When is the inquest on Anthony to be held?" Doris asked after a long interval of silence.

"This afternoon," Mr. Avery said. "It's a foregone conclusion—the verdict I mean. Poor Anthony, I should have thought, was the last man to be awkward in handling anything, let alone a gun!"

"I suppose it couldn't have been suicide?" Grace asked in a low voice. The sweet was on the table and the servants were gone.

"Suicide!" Doris stopped helping her sister-inlaw to the tart. "What on earth?

"What put that idea into your head, Grace?" the rector asked gravely, "or rather what made you say it." He wondered if Grace were developing a tendency to wild statements.

"Well, it's all so funny," Grace said irritably. "Olive was out last night; no one knows this of course, but it's a fact. I went to her room for some toothache drops I knew were in that wall cupboard in there, and she wasn't there. That was nearly midnight. Her bed hadn't been slept in. She says she was up on the roof watching the stars, as she does at times. But I'm wondering whether she met Anthony and told him that she didn't want to be engaged to him—that she didn't love him"

"But she did!" broke in Doris imperiously.

"You chose to think she did," was the tart reply, "and so engineered that ridiculous engagement, but Olive didn't care for him. That was her charm for Anthony, I think. Such a contrast to most of the women he'd met. No, Doris, you spoilt a girl who was in most ways one of the best companions I shall ever have and all to no purpose. She was quite happy here with me."

Doris helped her brother-in-law to apple tart, and passed him the cream with an expression that said that she considered Grace's words not worth a reply.

"What do you say?" he now asked turning to her.

"Of course she was in love with Anthony!" she said with certainty. "Why, the two were all eyes and sighs for weeks past. Violet-May suspected Anthony of being in love with Grace," she said maliciously—Doris could say very cutting things in her light easy way—"you believed he wanted to flirt with me," she added as Grace's face flushed—"but it was Olive all the time—from first to last."

"Except when it was Mrs. Green!" Grace said.

"Mrs. Green!" scoffed Doris. "Mrs. Green is an artist, Grace. She adored Anthony's good looks and she liked him personally as well. But as to the garbage that people talk about her being in love with him—" Doris made a sweep of the sugar sifter do duty for her opinion of that.

Remembering Anthony's own words about how irksome he had himself found Mrs. Green when Olive came into his life, the rector felt uncomfortable, but the two young women were not looking at him.

"You're bound to take that view, as you engineered the whole affair," Grace said in a very unconvinced voice.

"No, Cupid did that," laughed Doris. "I simply arranged with you to let me get Olive to design and engineer those chair covers for me," and Doris, with an excuse to the two, rose from the table with her usual air of swift decision, which suggested the brisk alert mind which she turned to everything. Just as Grace's slow languid way of getting out of her chair suggested the uncertainty that was an integral part of her nature too.

The inquest was soon over. At no time was it interesting except to the local people who crowded the room. Lady Revell, looking almost indecently cheerful, was there with Gilbert who wore a very sober expression. Near them sat Mrs. Green. Some of those present refused at first to recognise the middle-aged, badly dressed woman with the deep pockets under her eyes.

"If that really is Mrs. Green and not her mother, she must have made-up well up to now," was the general spoken or unspoken comment.

First came the evidence of identification, which, as the Coroner was also the Revells family solicitor, was purely perfunctory. Then came the evidence of the police as to how the body had been found.

Then came the evidence of Anthony's manservant, who spoke of his master's high spirits before he left and coyly admitted, when pressed, that he had told him, Jamieson, about his coming engagement to Miss Hill. He identified the revolver found on the table as one which Mr. Revell had bought a month or so ago, when there were so many cases of housebreaking around them, saying that as The Causeway was so isolated and so hidden in trees, it might be as well to have one in the house. The revolver was kept in an unlocked drawer in Mr. Revell's bedroom. He had no idea, he said, as to what brought his master home last night. Mr. Revell had apparently touched nothing in the house but some mixed biscuits and the whisky and soda.

As to why he should have gone to the drawing-room —Mr. Revell liked that room of an evening. But as to why he should have had his revolver with him, the servant professed to have no idea—beyond the obvious one of Mr. Revell having seen some suspicious person loitering about, or heard footsteps.

The doctor gave evidence next. He described the wound which had been made by the entry of the bullet in the right ear. The scorch marks showed that the weapon must have been practically touching the head, and the passage of the bullet had been on a dead level; it looked to him as though Revell had had his head turned sidewise down over the revolver, as though to look along the table top at the moment when the fatal shot was fired. Dr. Black did not insist that he shot himself in that position, but the course of the bullet suggested it.

Dr. Black went on to say that Revell was a most casual young man, and while holding the revolver in his right hand, might very easily have made some incautious movement with the cloth in his left hand which had sent a bullet through his head. The doctor showed just what he meant. He thought that Anthony had been about eight hours dead when he was found. Which meant that he had been killed around one o'clock in the morning. Black was a young man, also a Cambridge graduate, and he and Revell had been very friendly. He spoke of his certainty that there was no reason whatever for Revell to have taken his own life. He too had been told of the engagement which was to be announced on his return from the climbing holiday. The doctor had happened to pass him on the road as he started off, and Revell had said that he was the happiest man in the world.

The two friends with whom Anthony had been climbing were called next. They were a brother and sister of the name of Gartside. The latter, a plainfaced, very resolute-looking young woman of around thirty to thirty-five, the former a little older, with a taciturn expression. Both were very short in their replies, but both told how on Thursday morning, two days after they had started their climbs, Revell, who seemed in excellent spirits, came down to breakfast with a very worried look and said he that must go back to London at once to his dentist to have a tooth put right that was worrying him badly. He expected to be back on Friday in the afternoon. Revell had suffered agonies from toothache once before when climbing a rock exposed to the east wind.

In answer to a question by the foreman, the jury learnt that the dentist to whom Revell usually went, was away on holiday just then, but the secretary said that at least two people—men—had rung up Thursday in the late afternoon, and on hearing that he was away had declined to make any appointment.

Revell might have been one of these.

The police gave further evidence of the undisturbed appearance of the body, the room, the house and the garage, of Revell's fingerprints on the revolver, and, in answer to a question of the Coroner said that they had no reason to think that death was other than due to misadventure.

The jury brought in a verdict accordingly, and expressed their profound sympathy with the family and friends of the deceased. The inquest was over.The funeral would be next day. Gartside and his sister were staying for it.

The little group from the rectory had listened with the closest attention. Seeing how white Olive looked, the rector told himself that he must be wrong. That she must have loved Anthony, but that her feelings were evidently of the kind that burrow deep. And yet, as he met her eyes on helping her into his car when it was over, he was struck by their expression, so secretive and yet so fierce. Again he felt sure that here there was no grief as he knew it. A strange girl this. . . .

As Doris put her foot on the step a telegraph boy jumped off his bicycle and handed her a cable.

"From Las Palmas," Doris murmured as she tore it open. She read a few lines and gave a cry of joy. Without speaking, quite heedless of the others, she turned and set off for the rectory at a pace that suggested a desire to be alone.

Grace, unlike her brother, had no clue to Las Palmas, but Avery guessed that Richard had already started for home. He had written him that he would probably fly from Ashanti—his nearest town—to Las Palmas, there to wait for a friend with some papers which would need signing before he could proceed to England.

Lady Revell came out towards her own car. She stopped and gave Olive a warm handclasp. The rector thought that but for the ramrod stiffness of the girl she would have kissed her. "I want you to come to us," Lady Revell said softly, "I want you to come and stay at The Flagstaff, Olive, and let us get to know each other. Gilbert here feels just as I do"

"Oh, rather!" said Gilbert awkwardly, but with emphasis. His eyes were very friendly as he looked at the girl who, but for this unexpected tragedy, would have been his sister-in-law. Olive did not look at either mother or son.

"I don't think I can... I can't leave Miss Avery at once"

Lady Revell was very sweet and soothing, and let the invitation drop for the moment as she moved away to speak to a very smartly-turned-out young woman, thin as a rail, whose expensive perfume filled the air, whose paint lay like plaster on her cheeks, and yet Lady Witson was good-looking in her own way, with a very intelligent face under all its make-up. And she was quite young— well under thirty.

As for Grace and her brother, they drove to the rectory in silence, each busy with their own thoughts.

On the rectory steps, they heard Doris's laugh floating out through the open window. Joyous and happy. Free and clear. Looking into the morningroom Grace and the rector came on Doris radiant, hugging a letter to her heart.

"I've found it behind the hall table. And the cable is its postscript. He's coming home! He's left the Service! He's going to buy a place near you, Jack! He's at Las Palmas!—" Doris was almost incoherent with sheer joy.

"You sound happy—" Grace said almost reprovingly. "It's not a very happy day for most of us—" she looked after Olive who had run on up the stairs.

"I know! I know!" Doris's tone was remorseful for a second only, "But I'm too happy to live!"

The rector thought of Anthony's words to Doctor Black. He could not but be pleased at the joy shown by Doris after her agony of Thursday morning. It might not indicate a high degree of unselfishness, so to forget Anthony and Olive, but who could be vexed with a wife looking as Doris looked now at hearing that her husband was on his way home?

"Well," Grace said, closing the door, "did you think that Olive acted to Lucy Revell as to her all-but mother-in-law? You can see now that I was right. Olive didn't care for Anthony"

"I have no way of guessing what goes on inside Olive Hill's heart," the rector said, "presumably she has one, but only presumably."

"I think it's given to young Byrd."

The rector frowned. "You said that before. I hope not, I sincerely hope not. How could she have got to know him sufficiently. I should have thought that you would have seen to it that Olive did not see much of him," the rector said in a tone of some warmth. "She's in your charge. An orphan girl—"

"My dear Jack—" Grace only called him that when she was very annoyed, "you know as well as I do that Olive has all along done what she liked—apart from her set duties I mean, and whom she saw, or when she saw them, are things no one knows but herself."

"Then what makes you persist in thinking—" began the rector.

" I saw her kissing Byrd about a fortnight ago. Lost to the world, my dear."

"A good-bye perhaps," the rector said shortly.

"Oh, probably," Grace agreed, "Olive is very thorough. She would never try to play a double game. But that's what I meant by wondering if Anthony might not have shot himself. He was spoilt, passionate, and really immensely in love. And if she told him that after all she loved Byrd—and he knew he had lost her—she's a most fascinating person, John."

"Really?" he asked dryly.

"Oh, quite inexplicably so. You notice her absence, you notice her all the time. I don't know what she's going to do now"

"I hope not marry Byrd," the rector said gravely. "Putting aside what you told me about her, you must do your best to prevent that. Byrd has no standards, no health, no morals, no desire to work—nothing that would mean happiness if he had to provide for two. His temper is proverbial—it's won him the nickname, of Blackbird. As for the rest, he told me that he had thirty shillings a week to live on and not a hope of a penny more. He bought that cottage he has called The Hut with money he won on a bet. He can just manage to live on his lordly income—somehow. But a wife?"

"Funny," Grace now said, "I was just thinking that no one seems to care much for Anthony's death, and yet a month ago one would have said that every one would be awfully grieved. I except that artist woman—she is all in."

"And you can except me, and yourself too, and Gilbert, and Lady Revell, and many many other people, Grace," the rector said firmly. "But as a matter of fact, I don't think that most of us can realise yet that Anthony is gone. That we shall never see his handsome face again— nor hear his eager voice and real emotion made the rector stop for a moment, before going on to his study.

On the Monday, Doris woke with a vague feeling that some sound in her room had wakened her. She sat up and looked at the clock beside her bed. It was only a little past five, when as a rule she was in her soundest sleep. Could the cat have got in?

Bending lithely over her bed, she called it. Nothing stirred. Then she saw that one of her slippers was lying on its side and had evidently been stepped on. Not by Doris. She had put them as usual side by side ready to thrust her feet into. That was what had wakened her. She lay back and tried to think out what it meant. She had nothing in her room worth stealing. Nothing of any interest to any one. Yet some one had stepped on her slipper, which meant that they must have been very near her bed, been bending over it, or over her . . . But she was very sleepy and, turning over, she fell asleep again on the instant.

After breakfast, Olive stepped into the morningroom. She wanted to know whether Doris could use her services as a secretary "or anything of that sort." From things Doris had said, Olive thought that there might be a great deal to do just now, before her husband got back home. . . .

Doris was puzzled. It seemed to her an odd request. What about Grace? she asked, for since Olive's engagement the three women called each other by their Christian names.

"I want to get work as a secretary rather than a companion," Olive said," and I can't do that without having a reference for my work. If I could stay with you for a while—it would be a help"

Doris fuzzled the cat's ear and thought hard. Something lay behind this request, or rather this plan. What? Curiosity was always strong in Doris.

"But you have to know shorthand to be a secretary," she said finally.

"I'm fairly good at it," Olive replied, "I've been having lessons in it. I've taken down the rector's last sermons quite easily. He speaks fairly slowly of course, but I shall improve, I know."

Doris laughed. "So that's why you have taken to coming to church, is it?" she said easily. "I wondered at it when I heard you had been there. Grace and I have to go, of course, in common decency whenever the rector himself preaches, but I wondered—"

She had thought that Olive had merely gone to show that she knew what would be expected of her after her marriage. So, Olive had only gone to practise her shorthand. But surely, as Revell's wife, Olive would not have needed shorthand. Doris's eyes spoke for her. Olive read them correctly.

"I began to learn shorthand months ago. And I always hate to lose anything I have learnt how to do, don't you?"

Doris agreed that she did. But it was odd . . . just as it was odd being wakened this morning by some one tripping over her slipper. Doris was puzzled by Olive. She wondered what she was up to.

"Wouldn't you rather go quite away for a while," she asked in a kindly voice.

Olive shook a decided head. "It would make it worse. I would very much like to stay on here until I can make up my mind what to do next."

"If you've really made up your mind to leave Grace, and if she doesn't grudge me you," Doris said in her pretty and flattering way, "I shall be only too glad to have your help," and on that Olive went on up to her own room. Doris looked in on Grace, and told her of what had just been arranged.

"That is, if you don't mind?" she wound up.

"Now perhaps you'll believe me that she's in love with Byrd?" Grace said, laying down a letter she was reading.

"I confess I'm beginning to think you may be right — about whom it was she really cared for. Though, mind you, all I was certain of was that Anthony was in love with her. I never pretended to be sure about her feelings."

Grace let this pass. She looked very uncertain about something.

"She wants to earn a good reference for her work," Doris said after a little pause. "Rather pathetic considering how near she was to being a wealthy woman."

"I understand Lady Revell and Gilbert intend to settle The Causeway on her for life, and a sufficient income to keep it up," Grace said.

"Yes. And Violet-May says that Mrs. Green is doing her best to put a spoke in that wheel. She wants to buy The Causeway herself it seems."

Doris did not pay any attention to any speeches of Lady Witson's. She was notoriously inaccurate, to put it politely, though there were those who called her plainly an awful liar.

"You have no objection to my taking on Olive?" she asked, "frankly she would be a tremendous help just now. It would save my having to find a secretary who knows my ways, and is as clever as Olive is."

"She's very clever," Grace said hesitatingly, "very capable. You never have to tell her anything twice. And her loss makes one terribly sorry for her. I mean merely her loss of position and wealth. I really don't know what to say, Doris. Try her by all means—but—I'm not sure whether I ought not "she stopped uncertainly. "You might ask John—"she suggested.

Doris was glancing at some letters. She had only heard the first words. She looked up.

"Well, I'll try Olive, partly because I want to see what's her object in staying on in the house. Oh, I know what she says. But what's behind her words?"

"To be near Byrd," was Grace's confident reply. "I don't think that you understood the position at all, Doris. Anthony may have been in love with Olive, but she was, and is, in love with Byrd, who in his turn doesn't care in the least for her. To make the circle complete, of course, he ought to be in love with Mrs. Green," she wound up regretfully.

Downstairs in his study the rector was talking to Mr. Smith, the Coroner.

"I was sorry you weren't at the reading of the will this morning," Mr. Smith was saying. "We couldn't get it out of the bank in time on Saturday." He had invited the rector to be present. "Everything was left to Gilbert. Bar a few legacies. There was one for you. I've dropped in to tell you of it."

"His stamp collection?" Avery asked.

"No, his Vauxhall. Insurance paid to the end of the year. A very lively car apparently, judging from the time he drove her here from Derbyshire the day before yesterday, stopping in at town on the way too. I understand she does a hundred in the shade. Anyway, it's his fastest car."

"It was a kind thought," the rector said gratefully. "My own car is very slow. He told me years ago that he was going to leave me one of his cars in his will, but I thought that that was only a joke. Who gets his stamp collection?"

"It's not mentioned specifically. The Gartsides may, since they're to choose as souvenirs any four articles which are in his house at the time of his death—bar furniture or family portraits. Is his stamp collection a good one?"

"Not as far as I know. But he was talking of it when he dined here a week ago—only a week ago, Smith!—I have some boys in the clubs I run who collect—what they can. Unwanted stamps are always welcome therefore, and he said he'd let me have his albums to distribute when he got back, as he'd given up collecting years ago. As a matter of fact, the very last thing he did was to leave some stamps that he had mentioned, here at the door, before he drove on up to town."

The two talked very kindly of the dead young man.

"I suppose," Smith said finally rising and reaching for his hat, "I suppose—eh—you were at the inquest —eh— strange affair, that death!"

"Terribly," Avery said.

Mr. Smith still lingered, pinching the crown of his felt hat in quite a spiteful way. Then he seemed to decide that there was nothing more to be said, and held out his hand. He himself looked rather troubled as he walked away after telling the rector that the car would be sent around when certain formalities were completed, which would probably be in about a month's time.

Grace looked in on her brother when he was alone. "Olive wants to become a secretary, and Doris is willing to try her out. I haven't said anything. I've missed nothing more. I don't know what's the right thing to do?"

"Olive's to have a fresh chance? Good," said Avery kindly. "I sometimes think that interesting work could cure any criminal, Grace. And a companion's life is not a normal one for a girl. . . . We'll see how she shapes with Doris."

The rector did not add that there would be no question of stolen articles not being instantly missed by Doris. Olive must know this. Supposing Grace to have made no mistake—of which the rector did not feel at all sure—it looked as though—if a pilferer in the past—Olive meant to go straight now, or she would not have asked to work for keen-eyed, business-like Mrs. Richard Avery, who had no old ties of friendship to blind her.

CHAPTER FIVE

Two weeks passed and apparently left no trace of their going except that by a tacit agreement Anthony Revell was rarely mentioned. His ending was too sad for his name to be spoken easily, and the result was that to a stranger it was as though he had never been. The Causeway still belonged to a Revell, only the first name of the owner was Gilbert instead of Anthony. But Mrs. Green never came to paint in it, and Olive avoided it after a week of daily visits.

It was when coming away from the last of these, that she almost walked into Mrs. Green, who was standing by a stile with folded hands staring straight before her. At Olive's startled exclamation, she turned slowly, and looked at her from between narrowed lids.

"Some one told me to-day that there is and always has been some talk of your marrying Mr. Byrd," she began. Her voice was harsh and threatening.

"There is no question whatever of my marrying any one—now," Olive said tersely. "Don't agitate yourself again—needlessly."

Mrs. Green's face worked. Then she continued with at least outward calm. "In that case, I should agitate myself, as you call it, and not needlessly. For I know something that I haven't told the police, nor the Coroner, about the death of Anthony. But I will tell it you now. I know that you met Anthony Thursday night, the night that he—died."

"Never! burst vehemently from Olive.

Mrs. Green looked as though she could have rent her limb from limb. "He told me so himself. I met him driving into The Causeway late that night. I wanted to get a sketch of the house by moonlight, and had no idea he was anywhere near. He told me that he had hurried home to see you about something tremendously important—to you. And he was never seen alive again! I don't claim to understand your motive. If I had, I should have told the police my story at once. You never loved him, never!"

"Told them what? That you were up, and at The Causeway the night that he was shot?" Olive asked, and there was venom in her tone too. "They would have been interested, Mrs. Green, much more so than in the ridiculous story you are telling me. It was not to my interest to shoot Anthony, whether I loved him or not. I didn't as it happened. You're right there. But he loved me. And that would be quite enough to make a revengeful woman who wouldn't believe that he was not attracted to her, shoot him rather than let him marry some one else. Or rather than let him finish telling her what his real opinion of her was!"

Olive stopped. Mrs. Green looked as though she were fainting, but jerking herself away from Olive's very perfunctorily steadying hand she gave her a terrible look, and turned down the lane beside them. For a long moment Olive hesitated. She looked worried and undecided. Then with a very unmouselike set to her jaw she walked on back to the rectory. She went no more to The Causeway.

By the end of fifteen days it was shut up, with the butler in charge as caretaker. Lady Revell still spoke occasionally of offering it to Olive Hill, since Gilbert said that he would never live in it himself, but nothing was done in the matter. As for Lady Revell, she refused point-blank to go over it with the solicitor.

One Saturday, a month after the inquest, Major Weir-Opie was sitting in his comfortable bachelor quarters talking to Chief Inspector Pointer of New Scotland Yard. A pleasant though very reserved looking man was the Chief Inspector, with something in the gaze of the fine grey eyes that was unusually unemotional, lucid, and resolute. It suggested a very well-balanced mind behind it, and yet there was that about the mouth and chin that spoke of a secret store of dynamic energy. It was a rather stern, very grave face, but the eyes could twinkle, and the face could change in the instant into a really merry one.

He had come down in person to make some inquiries about a missing girl, and the deductions made by him from a couple of seemingly idle facts as supplied by Superintendent Shilling had just resulted in the swift finding of the damsel in question, and her restoration to her family, much to her own indignation. Pointer had but this moment had a telephone talk with the mother, and blandly agreed with her that no matter what the doctors said, darling Gertrude evidently had quite lost her memory as the result of a recent attack of influenza.

"This finishes the job," Pointer said contentedly. But the Chief Constable promptly asked him to stay on over the week-end none the less, promising him some good trout fishing. Pointer cheerfully agreed to borrow his host's fishing tackle and relaxed in his arm-chair with the air of a man enjoying a slice of unusual good luck.

"Perhaps I had better warn you, though, that I'm due to dine at the rectory to-night," Weir-Opie said suddenly. "Shall you mind coming too? The rector, Mr. Avery, is the most delightful of hosts. I'll ask if I may bring you."

He picked up the telephone, and in a moment a warm invitation was extended to Pointer. Weir Opie hung up with an affectionate smile, and then he and his guest talked shop for a solid hour.

"And now about a spot of lunch, and then we'll have a try for a fat old trout, whose continued existence is a disgrace to us fishermen," suggested the Major. "It looks like rain," he added gleefully.

They spent a wet but cheerful afternoon, which "the fat old trout" enjoyed as much as they did, till finally, with some younger members of his family whom the old gentleman, fanning himself with his fins at the bottom of his favourite pool, thought could very well be spared,

Weir-Opie and Pointer presented themselves at the rectory at eight punctually.

The dinner was a pleasant affair. Olive was not present, but Mrs. Richard Avery was the gayest of hostesses. Her beauty shone like a lamp lighting up the room and all in it. Grace Avery too was a handsome addition to the board, if rather a quiet one. But there was a cut to her mouth which made the Chief Inspector think that when really roused, she could be as "alive" as her slender, laughing sister-in-law.

The next morning, rather to the Major's surprise, Pointer accompanied his host to church, where the Major went, as usual, from a feeling of duty.

"I will say that for Byrd, he's made us join up our ranks. He's a ruddy 'Red' who lives down here. Though, mind you, Mr. Avery's a capital preacher," he said as they drove off.

The little church showed a mellow growth. A tablet to a crusader, a Tudor window, Stuart carving, Hanoverian organ pipes. . . . The choir sang well. The congregation, far larger than it would have been if any other than the rector himself was to preach, followed valiantly.

Mr. Avery mounted the pulpit and gave out the text in his clear resonant voice. "The third verse of the second chapter of the First Book of Samuel. 'Talk no more so exceeding proudly; let not arrogancy come out of your mouth: for the Lord is a God of knowledge, and by Him actions are weighed.'"

He opened his own pocket Bible at a place marked by a folded paper, repeating again the second half of the text, "For the Lord is a God of knowledge, and by Him actions are weighed."

Pointer was all interest. This sounded a verse after his own heart. His mother was a crofter's daughter from the Hebrides, and a good sermon delighted the Scotland Yard man. Mr. Avery had now opened up the paper, he always jotted down the headings for his sermon on a half-sheet of letter paper, and beginning "Our text to-day—"

suddenly stopped. His eyes were riveted on the slip of paper. He bent forward, reading it with an attention that seemed breathless. All colour left his face, he stretched out a hand, not in rhetoric, but to catch hold of the pulpit edge.

Then he looked around and down at the puzzled attentive faces and once more he repeated "For the Lord is a God of knowledge," in a strange, awestruck whisper. He replaced the slip of paper, folded up as before, in his own Bible and laid them both on one side. Then, for a long minute, he stood in what was evidently silent prayer. His hands which were clasped tightly in front of him, trembled as Pointer saw.

Then only did he begin his sermon. Never had any of those present heard a better. Pointer doubted if they ever could. It was short, not quite ten minutes, but no one shifted an eye from the speaker, no one noticed the time, until Mr. Avery, with a deep sigh let his head fall a moment on his breast, and then turned to the East. The sermon was finished.

"Well," the Major said as they left the church, "I was afraid at first that Avery was unwell, but if that sermon is the result of ill-health I'm afraid few of us who heard it will want him well again. Magnificent!"

Pointer nodded in silence.

"And extempore," the Major continued getting into his car. "Evidently some mix-up occurred, and he had come off with notes that didn't fit the text. He looked very ill for a moment before he got really started. I thought he was going to have to leave the pulpit. He may have got a chill driving back from Sir Hubert Witson's—I happened to meet him late last night just leaving there—" Weir-Opie went on to talk of chills and his own rheumatism.

There followed a silence. Apparently Pointer was not interested in Avery, thought the Chief Constable, when the other suddenly asked him:

"Have you had many cases sent up to the Assizes from here of late? I don't seem to remember any."

"Not for months and months," agreed the Major.

"And the magistrates' bench?" Pointer rambled on—" any difficult cases? I mean ones that seemed as though they weren't quite as plain sailing as the accused made out?"

"No, nothing interesting. But there was a funny little affair of a purser and his extra wife—" and the Major launched himself into this story with gusto.

It was duly laughed over, and capped, and recapped, and then Pointer asked whether lately there had been any mysterious happenings or unsolved mysteries in the neighbourhood.

"Mysterious? Unsolved? What, are you a psychic investigator? No. Nothing whatever."

After dinner that evening, the two played chess. Very much to Weir-Opie's surprise, for he had played with Pointer before, he won the first game.

"Your mind wandering to the fair damsel you've sent home to her parents?" he asked.

"I was thinking of the sermon this morning," Pointer said truthfully. "Mr. Avery didn't preach to-night, or I'd have gone to hear him make half his congregation uneasy again."

Weir-Opie grinned. "Fine effort. By the way, I phoned him up this afternoon before we went fishing again to ask if he is all right again. He said he was—quite. But he seemed in a great hurry, and hung up before he had really finished. Very unusual. I guessed he must have a bit of a throat coming on," and with that the two settled down to another game of chess. Pointer finally won it, for he gave his mind to it, deciding that the—to him—significant affair in the pulpit was none of his business.

Next morning Pointer was down to breakfast at eight. Weir-Opie had to be off very early about a missing car, and the Chief Inspector had to get up to town as soon as possible, and report for duty.

The two talked of their fishing, and the Major was just recounting how he had first missed Colonel Spots, the trout in question, when the telephone rang. The Major still talking, still with his mouth full of devilled kidneys, reached for it. As he listened, the amused reminiscent look was wiped away as though by a magic sponge, and his face grew rigid. His eyes told Pointer as they lighted on him that what he heard concerned him too, but he hung up before he turned to his guest.

"The rector's been found dead in his study about two minutes ago. That was Dr. Rigby on the telephone. He lives almost next door. A case of toadstool poisoning, he thinks. Care to dash along with me? Unofficially? It's not likely to be anything but a genuine accident. Avery hadn't an enemy in the world. Avery! Best of parsons! Best man I ever met!"

A quick affirmative, and Pointer ran upstairs three steps at a time for the small attache-case which he always had with him. The Chief Constable sent word to his Superintendent to be at the Rectory to meet him, then he hurried out to his car. Pointer joined him, and the two were off at top speed.

"About the likelihood of its being a case of toadstool poisoning," Weir-Opie began at once, "I must explain that. Some months ago three children in the village died from eating what they thought were mushrooms. The parents nearly went mad with grief. The rector was with the children when they died, and brooded on it a bit. Finally, he got the idea that it might be possible to find out something which if cooked with the damned things would make them harmless. We have a very clever chemist called Ireton who believes he can do the trick. The rector is—was—tremendously keen on it." The Major could not immediately get used to speaking of John Avery in the past. "He's financing it. As Ireton's a family man with half a dozen kids, the toadstools are boiled down at the rectory, and Ireton fetches the resulting extract in a bottle whenever he needs some fresh stuff for his experiments. Here we are. There's Shilling on the steps!"

A moment more, and the three stepped into a large sunny room beside the front door. There on a couch that ran across one corner from wall to wall, lay the twisted, contorted figure of the rector. His face was dreadful to look at, bearing as it did every sign of his having died in torment. The doctor looked shaken as he straightened up and nodded to the two newcomers.

"Been dead for some hours. About eight, at least, I should guess. Just as I think I can guess what happened." His eyes rested for a minute on a door facing the one by which the Chief Constable and Pointer had entered. "People were saying only last Saturday that Ireton had found what he was after—the antidote, or rather the nullifying agent. I hope the rector didn't believe this too implicitly, and try it on himself with this result."

The three police officers, to include Pointer in a section where he did not strictly belong, had moved away from the body to a tray on a table by a window. On the tray was a plate with remnants of cold beef and smears of dark brown liquid on it. A bottle half full, marked as a well-known brand of mushroom ketchup, stood beside the plate. There was, besides, some bread and butter, what looked like the remains of some sort of a sweet, and an empty quarter-bottle of a good Australian wine.

The doctor came over and looked down at it too. "That stuff on the plate must be toadstool extract. See how it has blackened the fork? That wouldn't be true of the ketchup. However, plate and bottle will be analysed, of course. Not that it will bring Avery back to life! He'll be terribly missed. Terribly! And to have died in such torment! I can't think why he didn't ring one of the bells in here."

The Chief Constable went to the mantel and lightly touched both. Two distinct rings could be heard.

"Now I must see to the housemaid who found him. She's had a shock, poor girl! That face will give her nightmares for weeks!" The doctor went on out.

Pointer stepped into a room that opened out of the study. The library as he saw that it was. It had no other entrance or exit. Going to the fireplace, he touched the bells there with his gloved finger. Nothing happened.

"Don't they ring?" asked the Chief Constable who had followed him in.

"Oh, yes, sir, they ring all right," came the voice of Fraser who had been summoned by the study bells.

Pointer pressed again.

"That's queer!" the butler was surprised. "They rang all right yesterday afternoon. All the other bells are all right. Must have these two seen to," and then his automatic, professional interest dropped away, and he turned back to the other room and the body of his master. Weir-Opie and Pointer followed him.

"What about the ladies? Are they up yet?" Weir-Opie asked.

To his relief he heard that the early morning cups of tea had only just been brought them. Breakfast at the rectory was at nine.

"Too bad that Mr. Richard Avery isn't back yet," murmured the major. "But failing him, I ought to see Miss Avery first."

Fraser, a shortish man with an honest and conscientious face, just now pale and tremulouslooking, only nodded.

"The rector! To think of him being gone!" he said, staring in horror at the couch.

"I know!" Major Weir-Opie said sympathetically, "it's a terrible business. But now tell me exactly how he was found."

"Margaret, the second housemaid, came in to open up the room as usual, sir. I was outside having a look at the front door varnish when I heard her scream. I rushed in to find she'd fainted dead away—she had touched the rector, sir. Cold and stiff and all screwed up as he is. I carried her out into the lounge and telephoned for the doctor. He got here before I had more than hung up. Then

I took her downstairs to my pantry and told cook and the maids to stay that side of the baize door. I locked the door as well, in case—and I've just let the doctor through—and locked it again."

"Quite right, Fraser," Weir-Opie said approvingly, "though the ladies must be told shortly, of course."

"What was it, sir? He looks awful!" Weir-Opie and Shilling had covered up the body on the sofa with a rug. "Maggie thinks it's heart," the butler said, "but I know that it's worse than that from the questions the doctor asked me."

"Let it be thought to be heart at first," Major Weir-Opie ordered, "it won't be such a shock to the ladies that way. But between ourselves, the doctor thinks he may have eaten some of those toadstools of his by mistake. Who brought in that tray there?"

He learned that Fraser himself had. The rector, every now and then, liked to work late at his writing, in which case he would skip the regular dinner, and have a tray instead. After he had brought in the tray Fraser had as usual on Sunday gone off for a walk, got back by ten, and went to bed, after locking up at eleven.

Had he looked in on the rector? asked Shilling. Fraser had not. As usual, he had taken every care not to disturb him, for the rector was writing in the library. He had closed the shutters both in the library and the study when he brought in the tray. He had opened them this morning after telephoning for the doctor. In reply to a question of Pointer's he said that no bells had rung after ten last night, or he could not have failed to hear them. No, he would not have heard the rector calling, not if the study door had been shut, but he would at once have heard the opening of the door in question, as, unless done with the utmost caution, it jarred the house, and he slept on the ground floor, at the back of another wing.

"Were the lights on?" Shilling asked him.

"No, they had been turned off, or I should have noticed them this morning, for the study door shows a ridge of light under it. The rector must have turned them out so as not to dazzle his eyes when he felt queer, and lay down on that sofa," the man volunteered.

Fraser answered all the questions put to him very carefully and helpfully. Pointer, for instance, learnt among other things that the rector kept the library exclusively for religious work—even to the talks in there, even to every book and paper in the drawers of his writing-table. Worldly—in which he included friendly—affairs were transacted in the study, where he wrote all letters that came under that heading. Fraser said that the dead man did not like him to come into the library with a message, let alone with a tray. In short, the library was really consecrated ground to the rector, a sort of chapel, but one in which he wrote on religious subjects.

Weir-Opie's nod said he knew of this, but he let Fraser talk on, to give Shilling time to think out his questions for the servants' hall. Then he cut the butler short, and told him to prepare the women servants.

"The Superintendent and I will come down to the hall now and see the housemaid, and cook, and so on, and ask questions about that tray. Remember, Fraser, that indigestion often leads to heart attacks.

"Care to come with us?" Weir-Opie asked Pointer. The latter said that he would prefer to stay where he was, and look about him. "Much obliged if you will," said the Major, "for I don't like to leave the body—though as things are, I'm sorry I bothered you to come. Distressing sight, and nothing to be done. By the way, before we have our talk to the servants, I'll show you where that toadstoolstuff was brewed."

The Major and Shilling opened a door opposite to the one by which they had entered the study. It led into what had evidently once been a small fernery. But it now held a fitted basin, and a small kitchen table on which stood a gas-ring, the gas turned down to the merest sparks. On it was a covered red-enamelled saucepan, half full of what looked like brown rags which gave out an acrid smell even though the ventilators in the roof were wide open. A funnel stood beside the saucepan, and four bottles which had once held some sort of sauce, but on each of which a label had been pasted showing a skull and cross-bones and the word POISON in capitals. Around the neck of each a small bell, such as is used for kittens, was fastened with a wire. Even in the dark the bottles could not be mistaken for anything else. There was further a small trowel, and garden fork, and a basket half filled with repulsive toadstools beside which lay a thick pair of gardening gloves. A door—locked—led down into the garden by a couple of steps.

"And the rector always locked the one into his study when he was out of the house, I know, for he told me so," Shilling added. "Very careful always he was."

"And Ireton and he were the only persons to have a key to this garden door." Major Weir-Opie looked with a shudder at the toadstool basket. "That was so that Ireton could come in for fresh material any time."

The Major wheeled as the door of the study opened. It was the doctor. He came across to them.

"Those toadstools weren't worth the rector. Not by a million miles. Nothing was worth losing him. You'll let the Coroner know, of course. I've given the girl a sedative," and with that the doctor hurried away—before Grace and Mrs. Richard Avery would have to be told of the tragedy.

The Chief Constable and Shilling left the room for the servants' quarters.

Pointer went back to the study. Standing in front of the closed door into the lounge, he studied the room. Going round the walls, clockwise, there was first a table with books on it, then the couch on which the dead man lay. At his foot was the fireplace with a wide marble mantelshelf on which stood a clock in the middle, and a bunch of honesty in a white alabaster jar at the end nearest to the couch. Then the wall continued with the door into the library. Then, facing Pointer, was the east wall with a big window in it, and, where another window to match would be expected, was the door into the little glassroofed fernery where now stood the apparatus for the toadstool broth. Then came the south wall with two big windows in it, one of which was beside the front doorsteps, and then the wall with the door where Pointer was standing. Besides many easy-chairs, there was a table by the east window, on which stood the tray brought in by the butler. Apparently it was a table used for books and oddments. Between the two south windows stood a kneehole writingtable, like one in the library itself. It was tidy and seemed to be used for occasional writing, Pointer fancied. There were several bookshelves and a few more occasional tables. It was a cheery room, with its light cream walls, parquet floor and green covers and hangings. The library beyond was very like it, except that Mr. Avery had completely covered its door into the lounge with fitted bookshelves. So that there was only the one door into, or out of, the two rooms. On its writing-table lay the small Bible which the rector had taken into the pulpit yesterday morning. But neither in it, nor beside it, was the folded half-sheet of paper which had so disturbed him.

CHAPTER SIX

In about a quarter of an hour Major Weir-Opie stepped back into the study with a "Well, that's done. Nothing fresh learnt. I've left Shilling taking it all down. Now there's nothing to detain us after I've had a word with the family—" He stopped and looked hard at Pointer.

The Chief Inspector, when on the hunt, was a formidable-looking man. The swiftness of decision, strength of will, and powers of endurance that were integral parts of him at all times showed then.

"What have you found?" Weir-Opie asked sharply.

"For one thing, why those bells in the library didn't ring."

Pointer led the way into the inner room, and stepping to the fireplace again, still wearing the gloves that he had not pulled off, unscrewed the bellcover. He showed the puzzled Major a scrap of paper inside, slipped in where it would break the contact.

"This has the same," he unscrewed the bell on the other side of the fireplace.

Weir-Opie looked puzzled. "Odd," he agreed. "Apparently the rector didn't want them to ring"

"There's a sheet missing from yesterday's Observer. The rest is lying by the waste-paper basket in the other room," Pointer said quietly. "These two scraps are torn from the missing front page. See these bits of the name? That means that these bells weren't put out of action before yesterday morning at the earliest."

Major Weir-Opie's face altered. It stiffened. He gave Pointer a long steady look.

"You suggest that the rector's death wasn't an accident?" he said slowly.

"Come back into the other room and look at what's recorded on the door in there," was Pointer's reply.

The Major watched while Pointer puffed some fingerprint powder over the panels. He took the little rubber puffer from his attache-case to do so. For a moment the Major was puzzled at the semicircular marks that came up first. These weren't prints of fingers at all. . . . Then he gave an exclamation under his breath. He saw what they were. The marks of where a man had pounded on the door with the sides of his clenched hands. One palm had a deep cicatrix in it. The right hand. Just such a scar as showed on the right hand of the dead man on the sofa.

Pointer was now busy around the doorknob. Fingerprints innumerable showed there. Among them were long, dragging prints as though hands had groped and missed, had fumbled, and fallen away.

"His?" the Major asked with a backward sweep of his head towards the couch.

"They are," was the reply. Pointer now was working on the lower panels. He was puffing his powder almost at the ground level. The Major looked inquiringly at him.

"Sunk to the ground," was the reply, "on his knees here, groping for the handle and not able to get it. Then here, fallen full length—still trying to open the door— which had been locked on the outside, I'll swear."

The two looked at each other. Each tried to keep an official mask of composure over his own private feelings, each face was the face of a man who was seeing red.

"But the bells rang in here—" muttered the Major thickly.

"I'm sure they didn't!" came from Pointer. "Only, in their case, the murderer, male or female, single or plural, remembered to take out the bits of paper that they had slipped in. Though, even so, they screwed the covers on only half, and that half crooked. They didn't remember the ones in the other room, the room that hasn't been searched. Whatever they were after, they knew, or felt certain, was in this room. For this room, sir, has been hunted over until they had no time to tidy the cupboards again, as I'll show you."

"But Avery! What on earth did he own that could be worth a hunt, let alone a murder?" Weir-Opie asked the question half of himself.

Pointer looked at his shoe-tips. He saw, not them, but a man—John Avery—staring in horror at a folded slip of paper that he had just taken from his Bible.

"Did they get away with whatever they were after?" the major asked.

"I don't think so, sir," Pointer said promptly. "More and more desperate, as the time passed, less and less careful. For instance, the rector's pockets have all been searched."

Weir-Opie, who was no detective, looked his question.

"He isn't lying on anything—keys, money, papers pocket-knife, note-book," Pointer explained. "All are free of the body."

"Which wasn't the case when he dropped down on that couch," agreed Weir-Opie.

"Yet everything was replaced with the greatest care so as to look natural, and, I fancy, into the pockets from which they came. Time was taken to do it all very neatly. After his body, the obvious places in the room where papers would be kept were taken next. That bureau—this writing-table. With them, too, everything was taken out, even to the lining paper of each drawer, and put back again very much as it had been—only a lot tidier. But when they got to those cupboards under the windows,"— Pointer looked at the cupboards along the south, the front wall of the room—" time was running short, and more and more the contents were thrust back anyhow, in a desperate hurry—but everything was taken out all the same, to the last corner. Which is what makes me hope that they didn't find what they wanted."

"I hope to God you're right, and that they slipped up on it!" breathed the Major, and no prayer was ever more fervent.

Pointer now stood looking down at the writingtable. A fountain-pen lay there poised on a spectaclecase.

"Anything here?" asked Weir-Opie hopefully.

"That's just the trouble, I fancy. Nothing is here now, but that fountain-pen looks to me as though the rector had written something, some accusation, some explanation, and left it here on the table. When he was so ill—found himself locked in—when no bell rang."

"Yes," Weir-Opie said at last, "certainly the rector would keep his senses about him to the last, if any man could. But of course if he did write anything down, it's been taken and destroyed. Look here, Pointer, I shall insist on the Yard letting you take on this job. You must take it on! Shilling's a good fellow, but he's not a trained detective, or he'd have been wasted here all these years."

Pointer said promptly what was so ardently expected of him, to wit that, if it was turned over to him, he would certainly do his best.

"And damned good that best is!" replied the Major, drawing a deep breath of relief. "My hat, to think I saw nothing out of the way here; that Shilling saw nothing out of the way! Any other discoveries?"

"No, sir. But I can't properly search the room till the fingerprints and photographs have been taken."

They stepped into the fernery. Pointer puffed some grey powder over its door also. Similar marks to those on the door into the hall came up, but the upper ones were smudged and blurred. Pointer examined them through his magnifying glass.

"Some are the light smears made by contact with the shoulders of any of us just now, but these marks —I think Mr. Avery tried hard to burst this door open with his shoulder after pounding on it." Pointer looked slowly around him, and at the floor. "I take it that the murderer—there may have been more than one, and 'he' may have been 'she'—didn't dare lock the door in between the study and this, for fear of the rector noticing it, but relied on what I think happened, that he wouldn't try this outer one and notice that the key was gone from it, until too late, or even if he did notice it, would think that the chemist, Mr. Ireton, had taken it by mistake. Mr. Avery hoped to break it down and get out. I wonder why he didn't succeed." Pointer opened the door, hardly touching the knob, though he had his gloves on.

"Nothing like locking the stable door" murmured the Chief Constable. Both he and Shilling had used that knob several times since they had come, and neither of them wore gloves. Pointer stepped outside. Three shallow steps led down to the gravel path, on the other side of which was a line of shrubbery hiding the east wall of the garden. There was a small railing, too, for a handhold in slippery weather. An ugly affair originally, creepers twined around its close-set uprights had turned it into a low and quite decorative green wall. But Pointer was chiefly interested in the outer side of the door itself. "See those marks, sir?" he pointed to two places, and then looked down at the base of the creeper-clad railing. "And these two places where the branches have been badly pinched? That door was wedged with two planks of the kind gardeners use when working on flower-beds, I fancy." He stepped down on to the gravel and went round the nearest corner. There leaning against the side of the house he found what he was looking for. Carrying the two boards, he and Weir-Opie tried them. They fitted exactly. Pointer initialled them and leant them against the railing.

"They can be taken away when the stretcher comes." The Chief Inspector thought that that was the best chance of getting the boards away without being noticed.

He closed the door again, he had scrutinised the floor of the fernery before. There was some gravel on it, which the rector himself might have brought in yesterday during the morning or afternoon. Speaking literally, the planks were of course an outside job, and obviously done after dark. That meant now, in early June, about ten at the earliest.

Doris Avery waked from a profound sleep with the feeling that a hand had touched her face. With a suppressed scream she sat up, and peered around her room. No one was to be seen. A tea-tray stood on the table beside her bed. The curtains were drawn back. It was just past eight. It could not have been the maid. Then who had been in the room? Why had some one been so close to her? She was very drowsy, but she forced herself out of bed. After dipping her face in cold water she was able to look about her carefully. Her things were still folded up as neatly as when she had left them, and Doris was exquisitely tidy, but they were not in the order she liked to place them. Her keys lay on the dressingtable, not exactly where she had left them. She unlocked a Wellington in the window. Every single drawer, she thought, had been searched, even to under the white lining paper. She dressed quickly and went downstairs. The morning-room looked at sixes and sevens. The breakfast table was but half-laid. She rang the bell peremptorily. There was no such immediate answer as a ring in that well-ordered house usually received. After a moment, as she was about to ring again, Fraser came in. His face as composed as he could make it.

"Madam, I've something dreadful to tell you," he began, going across to her.

She interrupted him.

"Hampson's given notice? After having upset all the rest of the staff," she suggested in a tone of worried conviction.

"It's the rector, ma'am," he said in a low voice.

"The rector!" she repeated in a tone of incredulity, "how can it be the rector, Fraser? He never interferes in the housekeeping"

"Stop, madam!" he almost shouted at her.

"He's"—he choked—"had an accident—" he finished wildly.

Within two seconds she got it out of him. Rushing to the study she burst in.

"Oh, no! NO!" she caught sight of the covered body on the couch and put her hand to her mouth as though to check a further cry. "Was it in his sleep? Was it his heart.?"

"Yes, heart failure," said Weir-Opie promptly.

"As to seeing his face, I wouldn't, Mrs. Avery," he counselled kindly. "He evidently died in great agony. Evidently. The doctor wonders whether it's possible that he made some mistake about that toadstool extract of his."

She turned mutely and surveyed the table in the window with a look of horror. "I told him it was frightfully risky, but he was certain there could be no danger since he was the only one to touch it. Is the doctor still here? Is it certain?" she faltered, her hand half outstretched towards the couch.

"Quite," said Weir-Opie sadly. "And I can't say how sorry I am at this tragedy."

"And you think his heart may have been affected?" she asked again.

"The doctor hasn't settled that for certain," the Major said at once—and meaningly.

Ah!" Doris went pale. You couldn't look at Doris's beautiful crescent of a forehead without realising the logic that had shaped it so smooth and so white. You could not look into her ardent eyes without seeing that she had a character that could withstand shocks. "Of course! The autopsy!" she murmured under her breath. "And to-day of all days I overslept!"

A bell could be heard pealing through the house.

"Will you let me have a word with you in another room?" Weir-Opie asked.

Shilling coming up at that moment stayed in the room.

Pointer caught sight of Fraser and spoke a word aside to him in the lounge. As he did so, something made Pointer look up. He saw a slender, darkhaired girl looking down on them.

Now yesterday in church Pointer's attention had been attracted by the faces of three women in the congregation. All looked as though the sermon to which they were listening held for them some special and terrible meaning. This was one of the three.

He now guessed her, rightly, to be Olive Hill. Quite a pretty little thing. Then he met her eyes. For a long second they stared into his, and Pointer realised that there was will-power in those eyes. Something in their depths suggested—to him—that there was very little their owner would shrink from, once she had made up her mind to attain a certain object or goal. There was a hard kernel to this young woman. Cold, clever, hard.

Then she turned and, instead of coming on down, disappeared with a noiselessness and a speed that spoke of muscles in good training.

Pointer went into the room where Weir-Opie was asking Mrs. Richard Avery about any visitors at the rectory yesterday evening. He learnt that a young couple quite well known locally had been in to dinner and stayed till about ten o'clock or later.

No, the rector was not at dinner, he never was of a Sunday night unless particular friends of his own were in the house. He had had a tray sent in to his study. Had any of the visitors of last night had a talk with him? No, they had not asked for him.

In the afternoon the rector had had some parish calls to make. On his return he had been in his study all the time. Was that unusual? It would have been, but for the fact that he was very keen indeed on finishing his Life of Saint Paul as soon as possible; it was very much overdue. She knew, they all knew, that the church magazine in which it was being published had begged him to let them have the next part as soon as possible.

The bell rang again. A deafening peal this time. Doris put her hand to her head, a very unusual gesture with her, as Pointer rightly guessed, and said she must now tell her sister-in-law the dreadful news—and there's Miss Hill, of course," she went on. "And I must have a moment to myself to realise—to grasp." Doris squared her shoulders quite unconsciously, with the air of one girding herself up for a piece of work, unpleasant but necessary, and therefore to be done promptly. But before she left them Weir-Opie asked her when she had last seen Mr. Avery. She said that she had stepped in after her visitors had left to read him some bits out of a letter which she had received from her husband. That was around a quarter-past ten, but he had been deep in his writing, and after staying perhaps a quarter of an hour helping him with some references which he wanted looked up, she had gone on up to bed. Before falling asleep—about an hour later—she had heard his voice as though talking to some one in the study which was below her bedroom.

Again the bell rang. She moved to the door. "I must let Miss Avery know" and this time she left the room.

The ambulance came a few minutes later. The stretcher was swiftly carried into the rectory and as swiftly out again, this time covered, and the ambulance drove off immediately with the two planks inside as well. They were all glad to get that part over without attracting notice. That horrible part—Weir-Opie set his teeth as John Avery had to be virtually smuggled out of the home which owed everything to him—to his great heart, to his scholar's brain.

Pointer went in search of Fraser, and found him as requested in his pantry with the door shut, fairly holding a tray in his arms, a tray on which stood a silver coffee-pot, a milk jug, demerara and white crystal sugar, and some half-dozen used coffee-cups of different colours and patterns.

"Not washed yet? Good!" Pointer felt relieved.

"The rector didn't use these, sir," explained Fraser needlessly, "he didn't have any coffee last night. When I took in the supper tray he said as he wouldn't be wanting it."

"Even if the rector didn't drink any of this, I think the Major would like it saved," Pointer said, and taking a cardboard box large enough to hold it all, set the tray inside, and corded it, carrying it himself into the study and writing on it that the cups were to be especially analysed for any narcotic.

As he passed through the lounge he met Olive Hill full on. Pointer could have sworn that she knew what he was carrying so carefully, more, that she knew why he was carrying it—to find out if any coffee had been drugged last night. She had speaking eyes, had Miss Hill.

In the study he found Shilling, who was listening to what the Major had to tell him.

"Of course, it's unofficial yet," Weir-Opie was saying, "but I think we can take it that the Yard will let Pointer carry on what he has begun so well—"

"Begun so well!" Shilling gave Pointer a congratulatory look. "Though I don't say that we would have taken the death of the rector lying down. I felt something was wrong, but I couldn't light on what. To have let him die in here like a dog! But what's to be done first, sir? Mr. Madden, of Madden and Weybridge, claims that their shop was broken into last night and then fired. Arson, they report. Now shall I send Inspector Green—"

The two were lost for a moment in names and numbers.

"You'd better go yourself, Shilling," was the final recommendation. "Send up a couple of men here, one of them Tracy. Tell him to bring his fingerprint powder, we'll wait for him. Who's to analyse this stuff on the plate? Ireton, I suppose."

"Send it with the other things to be tested to Hendon," Pointer said promptly. "One swab to Mr. Ireton, if you think he's safe, but not more."

"Ireton had nothing to do with any hanky-panky that's gone on here," Weir-Opie said firmly, "he thought the rector a saint from heaven. But have it as you think best, by all means."

A few minutes later first one policeman and then another, and then another, slipped unobtrusively into the rectory. One was to stay on duty in the study itself. One was the photographer and one the local fingerprint expert.

"Now that's all well under way," Weir-Opie went on, "suppose you and I go back to my house for breakfast. I can't get into touch with the Yard yet, but I probably can before that's finished. I must just look in on Madden with Shilling here—"

Pointer wanted a word with the gardeners. He found that there was only one, a youngish man with a careworn honest face, of the name Higgins. After expressing his sorrow at the dreadful news about the rector, and his opinion that you couldn't be too careful with a weak heart, he let Pointer lead the talk to the planks. Evidently they had been standing where the Chief Inspector found them, on and off for the best part of a week, as Higgins had been setting out some Canterbury bells to fill up a few unexpected gaps in the borders.

Pointer asked Higgins where he lived, and learnt that it was in the village; that being so, for the moment he was of no further interest to Pointer, for Higgins said he had not been near the rectory since he stopped work on Saturday till he came this morning at nine.

Shilling was to investigate the whereabouts of the rectory servants last night, and look into their characters. The superintendent had said that he was sure that the latter would all prove to be of the best if they had been engaged since Mrs. Richard Avery had taken over the reins, a matter of four years now, for she had promptly put an end to the rector's way of helping down-and-outs to start afresh.

Pointer had finished at the rectory for the moment, until he had a regular position in the inquiry, and until the doctors were absolutely and officially certain of the cause of the rector's death.

He walked on now to the Chief Constable's house, and as he strode along, lithe and erect, he thought over the case as a whole. Taking the doctor's certainty as justified that the rector had been poisoned, then he wondered if a clue to the crime might not lie concealed in the sermon that he had heard yesterday morning.

Mr. Avery had preached to Pointer's ears not so much a sermon as an exordium to some member or members of the congregation to realise that no deception would avail them at the last, that they might have hoodwinked men but not their own souls. It went much further than that, it seemed to Pointer to be a pleading to some one not to mind the judgments of men, but to come forward at once, to speak out now. And the night after preaching that sermon the preacher was dead—poisoned. Shut away in a locked study, where no bell would ring, where no cry of his had brought help.

Pointer thought it very likely that Mrs. Richard Avery, who had her rooms over the study and the library, had had her coffee drugged, so as to ensure her sleeping through any sounds from below; the height of the rooms on the ground floor of the rectory would also have helped to deaden the rector's moans, but as she had recognised his voice she might otherwise have heard them.

And that folded paper that had, Pointer believed, caused the sermon to take that particular course, was possibly, he thought, the object that had been hunted for so desperately, and apparently so fruitlessly. That folded paper! . . . Avery's almost perfunctory glance at it had changed to a look which Pointer had thought, even then, to be one of sheer horror. But if that folded paper stood for the centre of this puzzle, then it looked as though, even so, Mr. Avery had not quite grasped its character, nor the character of the persons whom he had tried to reach in his sermon.

The rector, Pointer thought, had had in his mind some one who had kept silence—who had concealed — who had lied possibly, but Mr. Avery had not realised that the paper which he had seen was not so much a link as a proof. But if he, Pointer, was right in his ideas, then whoever it was at whom the sermon was especially directed had known better,had known at once that both that paper, and the rector because he had seen it, must cease to exist.

Pointer roused himself from his deep reverie as to what that paper could have been. . . . Some crime committed in the past for which the wrong person had been punished? . . . Or some unguessed crime? . . .

He was on the steps of the Chief Constable's house.

He shook himself, and rang the bell.

CHAPTER SEVEN

The breakfast was a silent meal. Weir-Opie was beginning to feel the shock of his old friend's death as a personal, not merely as a professional matter. Pointer was secretly amused when, half-way through, who should be shown in but Superintendent Shilling.

"I've left Inspector Green to carry on, sir," he said with defensive speed as he came towards the table. "Uncommonly good is Green. Deserves a chance to work a thing out on his own!"

Weir-Opie looked at him in silence for a minute, then with a twinkle in his eye, he invited him to join them, and as Shilling had had but the merest sketch of a breakfast, he was only too glad to shove his long legs under the board.

"Do you think this affair at the rectory was an inside affair, Pointer?" asked Shilling.

Pointer thought that it was impossible to say so far—with that door into the garden. The rector might have given some one an invitation to come in by it and see him last night.

"There was no second tray, so, if so, it would be some one the rector wouldn't expect to have eat with him?" queried Weir-Opie.

Pointer thought one could not tell. It might be a member of his own household who had already dined, or it might be a friend of whom the same was true.

"Now as to the women at the rectory, what did you think of them?" asked the Chief Constable with interest.

"Mrs. Richard Avery seemed a radiantly happy woman, and that is not the description of a murderess as a rule. Miss Avery—I took her to be a woman hard to stir but capable of being as selfish and as energetic, when really roused, as her sister-in-law, which I fancy is saying a good deal. Who is Mr. Richard Avery, by the way, sir?"

"He's an Assistant Commissioner in Nigeria who's just struck something lucky, left the service, and is coming home to live. Mrs. Richard is in the seventh heaven as you noticed, at the idea of his joining her so soon. Nice chap Richard, rather like the rector."

"What did you think of Miss Hill?" asked Shilling with interest. "Or haven't you come across her yet?"

"Yes—from a distance. I thought her very keen on seeing all there was to see this morning," Pointer said. He did not add that he had a strong impression of some purpose, some very absorbing purpose in her; and Shilling, who had been about to tell him of the tragic end to the man to whom she had been engaged, forgot to pass on that piece of information as his eyes followed the Chief Inspector's stare at Weir-Opie's mantelshelf.

"I wonder if anything stood there," Pointer said quickly. "I meant to ask before. In the rectory study," he explained, "there are only two things on the mantelshelf. The clock in the middle, and on the left-hand end, a white jar of honesty. Did anything usually stand on the right-hand end?"

Weir-Opie thought back. "Yes. Bright orange tobacco jar. Empty. I tried to dip into it once, and the rector said it had too clumsy a lid for everyday use, but he liked the colour and shape. The study tobacco jar—a wooden barrel—stands on his writing-table."

Pointer remembered it.

"Then where's the orange jar?" he asked. "I didn't see it in either room.

"It had no real value," Weir-Opie said. "I take it it's been put somewhere else."

He stopped at that, for just then the telephone bell for which they were all waiting rang. The Major had asked the Yard to let him know as soon as the Assistant Commissioner should have arrived. A brisk conversation now took place over the wire. Weir Opie found it none too easy to get his way, but in the end the Assistant Commissioner promised him the loan of the Chief Inspector, provided the latter could make time to come up for a couple of important meetings due this week. Pointer then received his orders over the telephone which would be confirmed later. He was to stay down, officially to advise the local police, but in reality to take the real, if not nominal, command of the case.

The little party broke up. Weir-Opie himself had to drive off to a neighbouring town, as well as drop in for a word with Inspector Green, and for the moment Shilling had to accompany him, however much the superintendent pleaded that it was only fair to Green to leave him an absolutely free hand.

"What will be the first thing you do on returning to the rectory?" asked Shilling, as Pointer stood up ready to go.

"Question the butler more closely about the tray, about yesterday's visitors, and find out if anything fresh has been shown by the photographing of the fingerprints."

"What! Before you look for the missing tobacco jar?" chaffed Weir-Opie. Then he looked keenly at the other. "I believe you've got some sort of an idea in the back of your mind," he said at once. "I mean, about the rector's death. You have an idea what papers the murderers were looking for in his study."

"I have just an idea," Pointer agreed.

"But what papers could the rector have that were of any interest to any one but himself?" Shilling asked of the world in general.

"Were you at morning service yesterday?" was Pointer's counter query.

The superintendent shook his head. "My wife went. Never misses the rector's sermon, she doesn't," he said proudly.

"Did she say anything about the sermon?" Pointer asked.

Shilling considered. He was a young man for his post, with a fine crop of red hair, keen blue eyes, and a tight-lipped mouth. He might be lacking in imagination, but he would have great driving power, and looked as keen as mustard.

"You mean about the rector's having brought the wrong notes for it?" he said shrewdly. "Yes, she said he seemed to get a fearful jolt when he opened his slip of paper and evidently found he'd brought one that didn't fit his text, but she said he went on from memory and did better than ever. She came home quite full of it. As to the mistake, he was shortsighted, and without his reading glasses couldn't tell any one paper from any other."

Shilling broke off to stare at Pointer, as his superior was doing.

"But surely you don't think the murderer was after the original notes!" came in a tone of stupefaction from the Chief Constable.

"Notes for a sermon?" Shilling echoed his tone. "The rector was a wonderfully learned man, we all know that, but surely a sermon can't be valuable!"

Pointer was amused at the way in which both had gone off the rails.

"I don't think they were after notes for any sermon," he explained, "but I think it's just possible, barely possible, that they were after that folded slip of paper which the rector had thrust into his Bible in mistake for his notes, and which was something quite different, as he knew the moment his eyes fell on it in the pulpit. I thought at the time that its contents stunned him."

"Gosh!" was Shilling's contribution to the argument.

"By jove!" came in a breathless whisper from the Chief Constable. "When you said last night that you were thinking about his sermon did you expect this?"

"Not murder, no, sir," was the instant and truthful reply. "But I thought it suggested some trouble in the place. I thought that that folded slip of paper had been picked up by him, or handed him by some mistake, and that it referred to, or meant, something shady coming off in the future, or threw some light on something in the past."

"And you think the rector's death?" Weir Opie was groping his way.

"Looks to me, sir, as though the rector may have been mistaken in thinking that whoever it was only needed a little bracing up to speak out. That would suggest that the whole affair was much more serious than the rector guessed. And that the person concerned, or persons, knew that he or she couldn't come forward, and also realised that if that paper were to be shown to some one else, or passed on, his or her fate would be sealed. Irrevocably."

"And pass it on the rector would have," muttered Weir-Opie, "if it was the right thing to do. Nothing could have turned him from his duty. There was steel under all his kindness. Finest character I ever came across, or ever shall." Then the Chief Constable heard a clock striking somewhere and grasped Shilling as though he were a straw about to be swept out of reach by his interest in what Pointer was saying. "Later, Shilling, later!" commanded his superior, but in a tone that suggested there would be a hereafter for himself too, and with a wave to Pointer they jumped into a waiting car and were off.

At the rectory, Pointer found that the ladies were upstairs in their own rooms, but on the ground floor Tracy, the local fingerprint expert, was just finishing his work. He was looking at a tumbler on the tray which had held water and was quite empty.

"They're his, sir. Pretty well the last he made, I fancy. The glass was slipping from his grasp as he set it down. Poor Mr. Avery!" Tracy's voice shook a little. "Very different prints from those on the dessert knife, sir," he hurried on, "there the grip was firm, however many times he handled it. But this tumbler—"

Pointer too saw the loose streaks half around the sides of the glass that showed where it had almost fallen out of the fingers so loosely holding it.

As for the bottle on the tray marked "Mushroom Ketchup" which they thought had last night held pure toadstool extract for a time, the marks were very smudged, but many of them were undoubtedly Mr. Avery's. The same was true of the bottle in the fernery from which in all probability it had been filled, one of the bottles with bells on it, a bottle marked POISON which was almost empty.

"Tremendous number of prints on that," Tracy said, following Pointer's eyes. "But the last were Mr. Avery's, though very smudged. Very smudged indeed."

"By another hand which was wearing a glove?" Pointer asked meaningly.

"Ah," said Tracy, "that's just it, sir, isn't it!"

Which apparently meaningless string of words was received with an emphatic nod. After which Pointer had him cover the inside of the door with sheets of paper. The photographs might not be as clear as the real prints of Mr. Avery's hands. Then the Chief Inspector allowed himself a free hand in examining the room, or rather rooms, for he went first into the inner room, the library, where Tracy had found only Mr. Avery's fingerprints and those of Fraser. On the writing-table was a manuscript page half-filled by the beautiful handwriting which Pointer by now knew as Mr. Avery's. The last sentence of all was one in which the writer deplored the lack of space which would not let him linger over that most difficult phrase to translate, "Through a glass darkly"

He turned away. Yes, Mr. Avery had apparently seen things through a glass darkly. If he had seen clearer. . . .

Pointer looked around him. He had never been in a room which so suggested peace and freedom from the friction of daily life. He went over it inch by inch, then he stepped back into the study, and did the same there, beginning with the couch. When he came to the books, he felt sure that they had been searched already, by the same hands probably that had turned over the papers in the writing-table drawers and cupboards. Suddenly he stooped. He was beside the east window, the one near the door into the library. From a novel lying on its side he lifted up a stamp. It was Italian, very faded and thin, and apparently quite old. He and Tracy hunted for others but found none.

He passed on to the window seat beside it. Lifting the frill he saw something lying like a glittering snake. It was a necklace of oxidised silver with hand-cut beads of crystal. Fastened, it would hang down to the waist of the wearer. The catch itself opened easily, he saw, and was not strong enough for anything so heavy as this necklace. Two of the links were sharply bent almost at right angles.

He now helped Tracy to pack up the "exhibits," not including the necklace, as such things should be packed. Nothing amused Pointer, and incidentally Tracy, more than the light-hearted way in which amateur detectives in books stowed away, in pocket or bag, articles with fingerprints on them. These ones were each wrapped in special paper, slung in special rubber slings and carried as though the cases contained bombs.

Tracy finally got into a police-car, and the various boxes were stacked around him. He was going straight to Hendon with them. Just then, a short, pleasant-faced, middle-aged man came up the drive.

He hurried up to Tracy. People were saying that the rector had died in his sleep—heart failure—was there any truth in the dreadful rumour? he asked breathlessly.

"It's quite true, Mr. Ireton," Tracy said, and then introduced him to Pointer.

Ireton was quite overcome, now that the report was confirmed. Pointer could get little from him at the moment, but that little bore out what he had heard about the way in which the chemist obtained fresh supplies of the boiled-down toadstool brew.

Mr. Ireton had been in only yesterday afternoon around three o'clock for some. He had filled a small bottle which he brought, and had left the bottle in the "fernery" as he still called it, half full. The bottle was undone for him to see, and he stared at it.

"Have you spilled some out, or what?" he asked.

"We're wondering whether he took some to try, trusting too much to your having found an antidote or whatever you call it," Major Weir-Opie said from the rear. He and Shilling had just got back.

As Ireton stared in horror, the Major continued:

"It's said that you told the rector you had found something which would cancel out the poison in the toadstools, if cooked with them."

"*I* say such a thing? Never! I'm on the way—yes. But I haven't got there yet—not yet! You see it's a new line, quite different from Pasteur's antiphallinic serum which they use in France."

"Could the rector have misunderstood you?"

"Impossible!" Ireton poured forth a flood of details showing how impossible it would have been for Mr. Avery, informed of every step in the search, to have jumped to any such error.

Pointer asked if Mr. Avery was ever absentminded in handling the stuff.

Ireton said the rector was exceedingly careful. He looked quite overcome at the turn the questions were taking. How could there be any idea that the toadstools were responsible for Mr. Avery's death, he asked, with tears on his cheeks which he was too agitated to wipe away.

Weir-Opie reminded him that until the autopsy brought more definite knowledge, every question that could clear up such a death had to be at least talked over.

They let him open the side door and go in as usual. Nothing in the little room was altered, he said, except for the absence of the bottle that Tracy had with him.

"Did you go into the study at all yesterday afternoon?" Pointer asked.

No, Ireton said that he had not. He had walked up the drive with Byrd about three o'clock. He had overtaken him by the gate. Byrd had gone on to the front door. He thought that he heard his voice later on in the study, but he had only stayed in the little fernery long enough to fill his bottle. He could not say if the door between had been locked or not. That would depend on whether the rector was in. He always locked the door and took the key if he were going out.

With that Ireton was allowed to go home. He looked quite ill. As well he might. As far as opportunity went, he was in the first rank of suspects. The three returned to the study and rang for the butler.

"When did Mr. Byrd call yesterday?" Pointer asked him.

"Around three, sir. Just after Mr. Gartside and his sister."

"Gartside!" echoed the Chief Constable, and Pointer noticed that Shilling wheeled about as though he too were particularly interested in that name.

"Yes, sir, Mr. Gartside and his sister both called to see the master yesterday afternoon. I showed them in here first, then Mr. Byrd.

"But the rector had a call to make which kept him out all afternoon."

"Mr. Byrd knows the Gartsides, doesn't he?" Shilling asked.

Fraser said that the three had shaken hands and chatted as though they did.

"He climbed once for a week with Revell and them," Weir-Opie said, "two years ago."

Fraser went on to say that the three visitors had left together, after waiting only a very few minutes.

"Mr. Gartside and his sister are staying at Hamble's farm," the butler added. "I heard them say as much as they went out. Come down here to see about something that Mr. Revell had left them in his will—like the car he left the master, which the rector only got on Saturday, and only drove it Saturday evening, and now won't want ever any more!" At this point emotion overcame Fraser.

Pointer gave him a moment in which to recover himself, then he asked for a list of all the people who had visited the rectory yesterday. Fraser said that, apart from Mrs. Richard's friends who had come in to dinner, and stayed until a little after ten—he had been back when they left—there were only the three visitors of the afternoon, and Lady Revell, who came about nine. She had telephoned in the afternoon asking if she could have a word with the rector, who, when at last he had got home about six, had told Fraser to ring her up and ask her if nine o'clock would be too late. Lady Revell had said that nine would suit her perfectly. She had not yet arrived when Fraser had brought in the tray, as he had reminded Mr. Avery, who said that he was on no account to wait in for her or hurry back, as he would be on the lookout for her himself. Fraser did not know when she had left, but she must have been gone by ten, as he did not hear the front door open after he shut it on Mrs. Richard's friends.

For the moment, Pointer asked no further questions about the standing of the visitors. Instead he inquired as to what had happened to whatever it was that stood on the end of the mantelshelf nearest to the window.

Fraser looked at the mantel and then round the room. "The orange tobacco jar with the stamps in it?" he spoke as though greatly puzzled. "The rector must have taken it into the library, though I never knew him to do that before. . . ." They went through into the inner room, but the jar for which they were looking was not to be seen, as Pointer knew.

"The rector liked a wooden one for tobacco," explained Fraser, "but he used to drop any stamps he got into the china one, till he had time to put them in his albums."

"Did he collect stamps?" Pointer asked.

"Not himself, sir, but he had lots of boys at his clubs who did. I'll see if I can find the jar."

"Don't worry any one with questions about it," Pointer said, "use your eyes, but don't ask about it. Some people might think it heartless, under the circumstances."

"Leave it to me, sir," Fraser said promptly, and vanished.

Weir-Opie looked puzzled. Pointer showed him the stamp that he had found, and where he had picked it up. Weir-Opie and Shilling looked still more puzzled.

As for the necklace, the Chief Constable felt pretty sure that he had seen Lady Revell with just such a thing hanging round her neck when he had dropped in a week or so ago. "Lady Revell," he began, but stopped as Fraser came back to say that he had looked everywhere for the jar without seeing it, and adding that he knew it had been in its customary place last night, as he had all but knocked it off with the end of his tray.

"What stamps were kept in it, do you know at all?" asked the Major.

"Some Mr. Revell left for the master the very last time I ever saw Mr. Revell, sir," the butler said solemnly. "Some people would say ill-luck went with that gift, wouldn't they?"

"Revell?" the Major repeated curiously, and Pointer noticed the quick intake of Shilling's breath beside him. "When was that? And how did Mr. Revell come to be interested in stamps? I never heard he was a collector."

"He wasn't, sir. I happened to be waiting at table when he first spoke about the stamps. That was the day before he went off for that climbing holiday of his. He dined here. You remember at the inquest that was spoken of, sir?"

Weir-Opie nodded.

At the inquest! Pointer's gaze flicked to Shilling's face. It was very rigid. The Chief Constable, too, was sitting far forward on his chair.

"Quite. But where did the stamps come in?" asked Weir-Opie.

"Mr. Revell, sir, said he had come across some old letters of his great-grandfather. Written while on a tour of all the places that Garry"—Fraser hesitated —"Garry Baldy, I thought he said, had been to."

Shilling looked puzzled, so did the Major for a second, then he nodded understanding. "Revell's great-grandmother was a Trevelyan, I remember. Distant kinswoman of an aunt of mine. She would be interested in anything to do with Garibaldi."

"Well, sir," relieved that the name seemed to be accepted without more ado, Fraser went on, "Mr. Revell asked the rector if he would like the stamps off the envelopes. He said that there were only about twenty and probably of no value. The rector thanked him, and said he would be very glad to have them, if Mr. Anthony didn't want to keep them himself. And after Mr. Revell had left he drove up again, on his way to town that was, and handed me an envelope for the rector, saying that he wouldn't come in again, but there were some stamps inside, would I hand it to Mr. Avery in the morning. Mr. Avery was still up, as it happened, so I took them in to him at once. He was reading the newspaper in that arm-chair there, sir." Fraser indicated the one. "He opened the envelope, said that Mr. Revell had been kind enough to make out a list, and dropped the lot into the jar on the mantel. It was empty then."

"I wonder if they were of any value after all," the Chief Constable said in a casual tone.

"No, sir," was the prompt reply. "None whatever. Mr. Byrd was in only a few days afterwards about some tithes protests which he is backing, and the rector, who never bore no one any malice, had tea brought in, and was showing Mr. Byrd the stamps as I came in with the tray.

"'N.G. all of them,' Mr. Byrd said, hardly looking at them. That's Mr. Byrd's way, that is. But he knows about stamps all right. He's a fine collection, he has, nearly as good as Sir Hubert's, some say it is."

"What did the rector reply?"

"Oh, he didn't mind one way or another. He had only shown the stamps so as to be polite. Same like ordering tea. Mr. Byrd didn't take any interest in either of 'em. Pearls before swine was the rector's politeness to Mr. Byrd."

"What sort of paper was the list written on?" Pointer asked, "did you notice?"

Fraser said that he had, for a very good reason. Mr. Avery used a special linen letter-paper of a peculiar off-grey colour. The list was made out on the same paper. Mr. Revell had evidently torn off the back page of a letter from the rector and used that, as his things were more or less locked up by Monday night."

"Same paper in fact as the rector makes out his sermon notes on?" Pointer asked, as though trying to get the item clear.

"That's right, sir."

Pointer showed him the necklace that he had found in the room when searching it just now.

Fraser recognised it instantly as belonging to Lady Revell. "She must have worn it when she came to see the rector last night, and it evidently dropped off, as it did the night she wore it to dinner here—just dining with the rector and the ladies. It dropped off then. She said as how the catch was weak and she would have it seen to." And with that the bell rang, and Fraser had to go.

CHAPTER EIGHT

"And who was Revell and why was there an inquest on him?" Pointer asked as the door closed on the butler.

The Major tossed a cigarette away. He glanced at Superintendent Shilling.

"I don't mind owning it's queer," he said in the tone of a man saying something very handsome. "Stamps, eh? I don't believe objects can bring bad luck."

"But they do bring criminals after them—if they're valuable," finished Shilling, his eyes very bright.

The Major pulled out his watch and said he would have time to give Pointer a brief summary.

"It's quickly told. Anthony Revell was a young man who lived at a house, not far from here, called The Causeway. His grandfather's house it had been. The Lady Revell we spoke of is his mother. His father, a K.C.B., is dead. Anthony was at Eton and Cambridge. Handsome as a film star. No end run after by women. Lady Witson for one. She's the wife of the man—Sir Hubert Witson—whom the rector had been calling on when I last saw him alive —Saturday evening. At one time it was supposed that Anthony was going to marry Miss Avery. She has a thousand a year of her own, and expectations of more still when the rector should die, and she's a handsome enough woman, though older than Revell. Then instead of Miss Avery we hear that it's definitely to be Miss Hill, Miss Avery's companion, and that it's to be announced as soon as Revell comes back from a fortnight's climbing holiday in Derbyshire, which for years he has always taken with a brother and sister called Gartside. Then three days after he starts on his fortnight's holiday, Anthony is found dead in his own drawing-room at The Causeway.

Shot through the right ear. His revolver on the floor by his foot, a cleaning rag on the table, a box of cartridges beside the rag. The revolver had been fully loaded, only one bullet had been fired, and that was dug out of the depths of his head at the autopsy. Now there had been a good many cases of thefts from houses around. It was thought that Revell, coming back for some reason or other—toothache, said the Gartsides—heard some suspicious sound, or saw some suspicious person loitering about, got the revolver ready, and while doing so caught the trigger in the cleaning cloth. He was quite unaccustomed to revolvers, so said the gunsmith from whom he had bought it in case of burglars. But Shilling always has believed that there was more in it than that— though what, he couldn't say. Gartside had a note from Revell to show at the inquest—all quite simple and clear—raging toothache—be away for two days and back on the third. Plans for the climb on the third.

And the dentist's secretary—" The Major ran over the case. " There was some talk of giving the house to Miss Hill, but apparently that was only talk," he added. "And who inherited Mr. Revell's money and estate?" Pointer asked.

His brother Gilbert, bar a life-interest for Lady Revell. "Nice boy, Gilbert," added Weir-Opie.

"Oddly enough he was by way of being a friend or disciple of Byrd's, our local communist. But that's sure to be off now—naturally! Nice woman, Lady Revell, too, though she never tried to hide her preference for her younger son as she should have done. Now, mind you, Pointer, don't be misled by the way that Revell died, though Shilling here didn't like it."

"Well, no, sir, I can't say as I was over pleased about that affair," Shilling said quaintly. "Couldn't prove anything though. Nothing whatever to go on. Nothing!"

"Ah, but that was only because you wanted something to get your teeth into," said Weir-Opie. "The feeling you had, Shilling, was that here was a fine chance for a murder inquiry all lost in the dead end of an accident."

"And what about these missing stamps, sir? Don't they link the two deaths?" Shilling asked almost exultantly. "The paper in Mr. Avery's Bible could have been the list of stamps. The rector wore what he called street-glasses, and as he had to change them to read, half the time he would put a paper away in his pocket without troubling to make the exchange of spectacles."

"So that if the list of stamps had strayed out of the jar, and been picked up by the rector Saturday night or Sunday morning, and been thought by him to be the jottings for his next sermon, he might easily have folded the paper into four lengthways and placed it in his Bible, to be opened out in the pulpit and read with his reading-glasses—yes—that's possible, Shilling. But to explain the shock Pointer here thinks he got, and to explain the subsequent sermon—as Pointer evidently thinks it should be explained—there would have had to be on the list one or more stamps of such value that it—or they—had immediately shown the rector a dreadful possibility about the death of young Revell." Weir Opie was quite pleased with his perspicacity.

"Would the rector recognise the value of any rare stamp he found on the list?" Pointer asked the question now. "And is there any stamp of great value to be found among Italian stamps?"

"I don't know," Weir-Opie said thoughtfully. "I don't know—but I'll tell you who would have known and been able to tell him, and that was Witson. And don't forget that Avery was driving away from Witson's house when last I saw him about ten on Saturday night. Witson has a marvellous European stamp collection. Best in England, bar the Royal ones."

"But that visit would have been before Mr. Avery opened out the list in church," Pointer reminded the other, "and whatever he saw on that paper came as a complete surprise to the rector, sir. I'm sure of that."

"True "Weir-Opie frowned, "true! But I'll tell you what. Witson never talks of anything but his stamps. It's quite possible that he told Avery about some exceedingly rare stamp, and, in that mysterious way in which new names always turn up after being heard for the first time, Avery saw that very stamp on the list that he looked at in the pulpit on Sunday. His logical brain would see at once that here was a motive for Revell's so-called accident. Yes, Shilling, I'm coming round to your opinion. This stamp business—Pointer's way of taking that sermon of the rector's—I do agree that Revell's death may not have been an accident. May not have been only, mind!"

"That's all I say, sir," Shilling said immediately. "May not have been."

"I'll have a guarded word with Witson," went on Weir-Opie.

"What is his reputation in the neighbourhood, sir?" Pointer asked.

Weir-Opie made a face. "One of Carson's Dublin knights. And not one of the pure patriots. That's the trouble with his wife, they're not popular. Certainly Sir Hubert isn't."

Pointer wanted to get to the police station telephone at once. The three drove off in the Chief Constable's car.

Over the station telephone Pointer had a talk with one of the great philatelists' emporiums of London. He learnt that the rarest European stamp known was a five centisme grana cobalt stamp from Sicily. "Few, even of the best collectors, have ever seen an example. We bought one some years ago from Count Spingardi, the purchaser of the famous Ferrari collections. We sold it at once to a member of the Royal family."

"May I ask what the value of another example would be? At the present time?"

"If it's in perfect condition, I would be pleased to take it off your hands for five thousand pounds," came the voice at once. "I'll make you the offer in writing, if you like?"

"Please do," Pointer said. "But above all, will will you let me know the instant such a stamp should be offered?" And with that he hung up.

'There we are!" said Shilling gleefully, when he heard the result of Pointer's inquiry.

"I must say——" murmured Weir-Opie. "It all fits together. . . I'll see Witson at once."

The telephone bell rang. It was for the Chief Constable. From Doctor Rigby. Mr. Avery had died from a dose of almost pure toadstool juice—cooked—and from nothing else.

So, now the death was officially labelled as due to poison.

And a moment later there was another message—in code—from Hendon—the fingerprints yielded nothing unexpected. All the important ones were made by the rector. As for the dark fluid over the remains of cold beef on the tray, it was almost pure toadstool juice such as was in the bottle marked "poison," with a small amount of the genuine Mushroom Extract, such as was in the bottle so labelled, to give it a harmless flavour. The rest of the food on the tray was quite as it should have been. So were the coffee grounds in the cups.

"I thought, and still think, that Mrs. Richard Avery's coffee may have been drugged," Pointer explained.

"That would account for her saying that she had overslept herself this morning," murmured Weir Opie.

"But it also would have stamped it as an inside job," said Shilling. "Or partly inside. As it is, we're left to find that out for ourselves."

A constable came in to say that Mr. Byrd would like a word with the Chief Constable.

"Show him in," was the reply. Weir-Opie got up and stooped to Pointer's ear.

"One of the people we would like to be sure was in his bed all last night—and the Thursday night that Revell died." Then he straightened to greet a slim, trim, figure that was shown in.

"Captain Byrd, sir," said the constable. "Plain Byrd, very plain Byrd," corrected the visitor.

And very plain he was. But it was an interesting face. Hawk-like nose, hawk-like eyes. Thin flexible sardonic lips. Lantern jaws, blue shaven. Unexpectedly thick curly hair which gave the lie to the cold mouth, for it suggested hot blood and impetuosity. Around five feet six in height, Mr. Byrd was an army man by the neatness of his well-worn clothes, and by his straight back. There were lines on his forehead and around his mouth which suggested a man who had been through great suffering, and something in the eyes hinted that they had once looked on terrible things. Pointer put him down, correctly, as about thirty-eight years old.

"I've come to ask you why my meeting to-night is to be stopped," Byrd demanded of the Chief Constable.

"Too red," was the laconic reply. "Why must you rail at the Royal Family as you do? I think it's deuced bad form in a man who's once worn the King's uniform, and has a pension."

Byrd laughed, a real, but unpleasant laugh. "How can you know the hue when it's still some hours off."

"From the tint of the last one."

"Well, you're wrong, Major. I was going to talk about my island, instead."

"Umph," the Major grunted.

"Is it true that the rector's dead?" Byrd continued. "Poisoning, some are saying. This gentleman here come down already about it?" He looked at Pointer. "Oh, don't trouble to say that he is a friend of the family. He's a man from Scotland Yard or I'll eat my new hat, the one I wear in church when the rector preaches."

Weir-Opie gave a vexed grin.

"Have I the mark of the beast on my forehead?" Pointer inquired.

"You have the mark of brains on your forehead," was the retort.

"Supposing the rector has died from toadstool poisoning. Can you help us clear up how it happened?" was Weir-Opie's question.

"So he's gone!" Byrd said under his breath. His lips pinched together after the words.

"You were here yesterday afternoon?"

"Dropped in for a moment. Found the Gartsides here and we all walked back together as far as the turning to my cottage."

"What did you talk about?" asked Weir-Opie. "Politics?"

" Religion," said Byrd blandly. "Chiefly. And a word about the weather probably. And another about Anthony Revell. Well, Major, I won't detain the hounds straining on the leash." He turned to the door.

"Can't you help us clear up the mystery—for there is one—about how the rector met his end?" persisted Weir-Opie.

"Haven't the time. Haven't the sources of information that you can tap," was the rejoinder.

"Which ones would you tap if you had them?" Pointer asked in his turn.

But Byrd took his leave without replying.

"That's Byrd all over," grumbled the Chief Constable. "You can't pin him down to anything. The regular demagogue. Though I will admit he believes in sharing what he has, as well as in insisting on his right to share in what others have. The rector and he were at daggers drawn, as I told you, though he never failed to turn up when Mr. Avery preached. He appreciates a good thing, does Byrd, in men or —according to Fraser—in stamps."

"Why do you want to know where he was on the night that Mr. Revell was shot?" Pointer asked.

"He's Gilbert Revell's great friend. Lady Revell has no idea, as I happen to know, that the only son now left her is one of Byrd's most fervent perverts. And with Gilbert a wealthy man—Byrd's position may have undergone a tremendous change. Shilling would tell you, besides, that

Byrd and Miss Hill were supposed to be very interested in one another. Personally I don't think that's a motive worth considering. I watched the two more than once at one of his meetings. She acts as secretary for The Dawn, as he calls his society. She may have been in love with Byrd. I thought she was. But not Byrd with her, though he was doubtless quite willing to use her. She put her name down as one of his island refugees. Another name of his for any one willing to plunk down a hundred pounds, and go out with him to some island—latitude and longitude unknown—where all are to live in complete idleness, and yet in comfort. I forget how it is to be worked."

Weir-Opie gave an impatient snort.

"But that island has come a lot nearer now that Anthony Revell's dead and Gilbert Revell reigns in his stead?" Pointer queried, and got a nod for assent.

There was a short silence.

Then Shilling had reluctantly, and very temporarily, to remain at his station, but Weir-Opie and Pointer drove back to the rectory where the Major told Fraser that the rector's death was due to toadstool poisoning, and that since Chief Inspector Pointer of New Scotland Yard happened to be staying down here, he was taking charge of the investigation into how the rector could have taken the poison, or had it given to him. And with that he too had to hurry off.

Fraser needed a second repetition before he understood what was being said. He refused point-blank to believe it at first, then he grew very pale and very agitated indeed. He took him upstairs, opened the door into Mrs. Avery's sitting-room and shoved the Chief Inspector in as though he were a parcel, and the room a post office counter, then he went slowly downstairs, feeling numbed by the dreadful turn that the tragedy had taken.

Both Doris and Grace were in the room, Grace had evidently been crying.

On being shown the crystal necklace they recognised it immediately as belonging to Lady Revell. The finding of the necklace in the study did not appear to have any significance, but as Pointer went down to the lounge he almost ran into Olive Hill. He introduced himself, explaining the reason for his presence in general words. Then he showed her the necklace. She looked at it with an apparently indifferent glance, and said that she did not think that she had ever seen it before, but then, she added, she was dreadfully unobservant. If so, she did not look it. She next said that she must have some fresh air after the shock of the dreadful news about the rector. Pointer had no right to stop her, even had he wished to. Pulling on a beret with a careless hand, she hurried on out, just as the Gartsides were announced. Their greetings were of the coldest and briefest, he saw. He was expecting the visitors, for he had got Shilling to telephone to them as soon as he, Pointer, had left with Weir-Opie, telling them of the rector's death from toadstool poisoning, and asking them to go up at once to the rectory for a word with Chief Inspector Pointer.

The Gartsides explained that having been asked by Revell's solicitor to come down and choose some souvenirs left them in Anthony Revell's will, they had arrived on Friday, taken rooms for the night at a farmhouse which the solicitor had recommended, collected the souvenirs on Saturday, and called at the rectory on Sunday afternoon. After waiting in vain for the rector's return, they had asked for a word with Miss Hill. She, too, was out, and being at a loose end, they had stayed on till to-day, Monday. They wanted to meet Mr. Avery, of whom Revell had often spoken—and above all, to meet Revell's fiancee, Miss Hill.

Mary Gartside's jaw seemed to set as she said this. She was a tall young woman. Big-boned—very thin and very proud of her thinness—with a good complexion, well-waved russet hair and a strident voice.

She did not make a good impression. She looked a thruster. Nor did he care for her brother's face either. But liking or disliking meant nothing to him. He told them that the doctor said that Mr. Avery had died from the effects of toadstool poisoning; there would be an inquest therefore to-morrow—Tuesday afternoon, and would they kindly stay for it?

They would stay for it and for the funeral on Wednesday, of course, they said instantly. Pointer led the talk to Mr. Revell, and asked about his stamp collection. Had that been one of the things left them? Gartside said that Revell had left them any four souvenirs they liked to take. As a matter of fact, among the things they had chosen, such as a pair of field-glasses, and so on, he, Gartside had added a stamp album which Revell had started, or more likely had had started for him, when a boy. It was the typical schoolboy's lot, of no value whatever. But it was a jolly good album, and Gartside's young brother would like it.

As to Byrd, they confirmed his account of the short talk yesterday. It had turned chiefly—what there was of it—on the rector's sermon which seemed to have impressed Byrd. They themselves never went to church.

Pointer finally had a few words about Anthony Revell. The Gartsides were not over willing to talk of him, but Pointer could be as dense as the next man when he wished. After they had left, he went carefully over the rooms at the rectory. The books of each inmate interested the Chief Inspector. A man's friends are not always of his choosing, but his bedside books are.

Grace's were chiefly scholarly works. Olive had novels of a bitter tinge. The House of Mirth seemed to be a prime favourite. Pointer did not think that Olive Hill would fail through any of Lily's faults. Did she keep it by her as a warning not to let opportunity slip? Mrs. Richard Avery had a few books from the circulating library in the place of honour. Chiefly travel or autobiography. Nothing subtle for her. In a cupboard above her washstand he found a nearly empty bottle marked "Sleeping Mixture."

She was in her sitting-room as he went downstairs, and he asked her about it. She explained that she was always a poor sleeper and that every now and then she took a dose to give her a good night, and that, most unfortunately, last night had been one of these. Indeed, as she had had a very hilarious though small dinner party, she had felt so wide awake on going up to bed that, to ensure a sound sleep, she had taken an unusually full dose.

Was any one with her when she took it, he asked as casually as he could make it sound, explaining that had she, say, been talking she might have taken even more of a dose than she had intended.

He was told that Miss Hill was in the bedroom at the time. She chanced to come in to ask about some library subscriptions which were overdue and stepped in just as she, Doris, was pouring the stuff out into a table spoon, but Doris scoffed at the idea that that, or anything else, would make her overdo a drug.

Pointer left her with the riddle of last night's deafness explained. Given a strong sleeping draught taken late, and Avery might indeed have called and pounded in vain. That problem disposed of, he had a talk with Fraser. He wanted, first of all, to know the hour when he had last seen his master alive. It was around half-past ten, Fraser could not give it precisely, but it was when Mrs. Richard Avery left the study after seeing her guests off. Mr. Avery was holding the door open for her. Fraser thought that the master had looked more cheerful than he had earlier in the day. Fraser, who happened to be passing, had wished him good-night, closed the door for him, and gone on to his own room and to bed.

As to the position of the tray, Fraser showed exactly where he had stood, how wide open the door between the two rooms had been—and other details that must be entered among the facts of the case, but which in

Pointer's opinion had little real bearing on this murder. For the two rooms were thickly carpeted, the door between them was often shut, and rarely wide open, and it was only when open to its fullest extent that it was possible, from where Mr. Avery sat writing, to see the table on which the tray had been placed, the table between the east window of the study and the fernery door.

It would have been quite possible for any one who knew the place and knew that the rector was busy in the library and who had the necessary coolness and nerve, to have come in by the door into the fernery, watched their time, stepped into the 'study, slipped the papers into the bell-pushes, lifted off the bottle of mushroom Catchup from the tray, all but emptied it in the fernery basin, filled it up with toadstool extract from the bottle standing there, and replaced the so-called ketchup on the tray. After that there would be nothing to do but to lock the study door on the outside after they heard the rector busy at his supper, take the key and quietly place the boards in position.

Then, when all was still inside that dreadful room, they would unlock the door, make sure that their victim really was dead, and start the search which Pointer believed had lasted—unsuccessfully—until close on the time for the servants to start Monday's work.

He now had the housemaid in for a talk. Maggie, as she preferred to be called, gave a rather hysterical account of how she had gone in as usual and opened the window and the shutters of the study.

Next Pointer had to run over the list of visitors yesterday with the butler and try to find out if there were any oddities about their stay in the house. Weir-Opie had already vouched for the harmlessness of the young couple who had dined at the rectory, they were an army man and his young wife. Neither of them likely to be the least interested in poisons. Fraser seemed to have nothing to add to the few details which he had already given.

Pointer next decided to have a word with the Revells' solicitor about the Gartsides and their recent legacies. An inquiry at the office told him that the firm's junior partner, Mr. Merton, was at the moment away at The Causeway seeing to some details.

Before setting out to walk the short distance, Pointer stood a while looking at his shoe tips, as a crystal reader might consult her crystal.

He thought over the sequence of events as so far known to him. If such a stamp as that priced to him could have lain unknown at The Causeway, and if, in making the list for the rector, Revell had let it be seen by some one who knew the value of stamps, and who did not know that the stamps in question were to be given away, that person might have come to The Causeway to hunt for it. Come more than once, because drawers and cupboards would be locked. The thief might well have tried place after place. That would explain the odd fact that it was in his dining-room that Revell's dead body had been found, with no sign of any effort having been made to get a room ready for the night. Supposing, as the jury at the trial had, that Revell at once, on entering his home, had seen signs that the house had been entered during his absence, and found those signs most noticeable in the drawing-room. . . .

He walked up to The Causeway. It was only ten minutes away.

As the front door was opened to him, Pointer saw a young man with some papers under his arm just ready to come out who stood aside for him to be shown in. As he heard the name he wheeled.

"Chief Inspector Pointer? My name is Harry Merton. I'm the junior partner of the Revells' solicitors, and the Averys' too. I've just left the senior partner—Mr. Smith—talking to Major Weir Opie about the rector's dreadful death."

He opened a door, motioned the detective officer in and closed it. Harry Merton had a humorous round face, covered with freckles, and an air of being very much entertained by life, though his mouth hinted that, if not entertained, he might get bored. His way of greeting Pointer suggested that he looked upon him as a short cut to a good deal of interest.

"Want to look round here? Why here? I understand that you're making sure there wasn't anything funny about the rector's death. But what brings you here?"

"I'd like to know what the Gartsides chose to take," Pointer said without answering the question. "They told me, but I would rather like to check it."

"They seemed to me reliable enough," Merton said, "but of course you have to be suspicious, I suppose?" he added questioningly.

"Oh, very," was the reply.

"Here's the list of what they took," Merton began to look bored. He held out a slip of signed paper to the other. Pointer looked it over.

"Stamp album" he seemed to ponder the choice.

Merton gave him a swift glance and nodded meaningly. "Just so. Miss Hill thought it was to go to her. She assured me that Revell had promised it to her the last time he dined at the rectory, when the talk happened to turn on stamps. But of course—if the Gartsides wanted it—and as he hadn't made a new will"

"Some Italian stamps she wanted, I believe?"

Merton looked as though he would stifle a yawn in another minute. "I only know what she said to me," he explained. "I'm not interested in stamps myself."

"Unlike the rector, or as I understand, Mr. Revell," threw in Pointer.

He was in the drawing-room and looking about him as he spoke. On each side of the fireplace, arched recesses had been turned into china cupboards as far as the top halfs were concerned, but the lower halfs were cupboards, and locked. Facing the fireplace was a very handsome old chiffonier. Its three divisions were locked. There was a smallish walnut tallboy in one corner. Its drawers were all locked. A bureau bookcase—also locked—was at one side of the window. Pointer asked if these had all been locked when Mr. Revell left for his climbing holiday. Merton nodded. He looked quite sharply at the detective officer, but there was something about Pointer, for all his simple manner, that did not encourage people to take liberties with him. Pointer asked if he might have a glance round the other rooms now he was here, but Saunders told him they were all absolutely empty. The furniture had just been removed to The Flagstaff, but nothing from this room had been taken. Lady Revell and Gilbert were agreed on that.

By this time the young man was talking quite freely about Anthony Revell. "Handsomest chap I have ever seen. Easily."

"And knew it?" Pointer asked.

"The women knew it," was the reply. "How they ran after him! Not Miss Hill though. I will say that for her." Merton seemed to be able to convey a whole sentence by what he did not say.

His last might have stated in so many words that there was nothing else he could, or would, say for her.

Pointer saw that if any one had wanted to search The Causeway's drawing-room for those stamps, it would have taken a long time. He asked to have a look at the fastenings of the back doors.

"Look here," Merton said, "you don't think—you're not here to go into Revell's death, are you?" His tone told the other that, if so, Merton would not be absolutely surprised.

"Well," Pointer said, "I don't feel as certain as the Coroner seems to have done that everything was as he thought it."

"Oh, him!" was the disgusted one word which spoke volumes. "He's my senior partner," he added glumly. "My father died two years ago and I was just down from Oxford. There was nothing for it but to buckle into his old harness." Again a volume was compressed of vain

longings and dreams, and straitened means. "Old Smith
is all right, Merton went on, "but he's slow and dense.
And never can see beyond the length of his nose." By this
time they were at the back door. It would have been
difficult to open from the outside, but Pointer saw that it
would be quite easy to slip back the catch of the pantry
window.

Pointer asked Merton what he thought of the
Gartsides.

Merton had not liked either of them. He thought
them too keen on getting the most expensive of the
objects from which they could, choose. "Did they look for
any length of time before selecting their souvenirs?"
Pointer asked.

"They did!" Again Merton's tone spoke volumes. "In
fact I'm afraid I left them to make their own choice at the
end, they were so slow. Everything of importance had
been inventoried, you see. Besides, they were chiefly
interested in papers. She wanted a chance to get back
some of her letters, two of his cupboards are chock-a-
block with them, and I didn't see why not. She did take
them. All!"

"Was she, too, interested in Mr. Revell?" Pointer
asked.

"Very much so. Underneath. That's why he came
home, in my opinion. Only in my opinion, Chief Inspector.
But she struck me as hot stuff—and I never did believe in
that about Leland—that's his dentist, for Mr. Smith had
a talk with him, and learnt that Revell had had all his
teeth put in perfect order only a month before. But any
port in a storm! He fled—in my humble opinion."

"And you say she wanted all her letters? Well, that's
natural. I wonder if you have any specimen you could let
me have of her and her brother's handwritings."

Putting his papers down, Merton obligingly hunted
until he found two short notes, one from the brother, one
from the sister, which he lent Pointer against a receipt.

"By the way, did either of them ask specifically for any of the things?"

They had not, he was told.

He next asked Merton if he had any idea how Mr. Avery had left his money.

Merton knew all about the rector's will, and very simple it was. Five thousand went to Miss Avery, who was already amply provided for. Richard Avery was left an equal amount, and for the same reason. Mrs. Richard Avery, to whom the furniture at the rectory went, also got five thousand—free of death duties in each case. The bulk of the estate went to charities.

Grace and Richard Avery shared the pictures, and the silver, between them. The will was drawn up a couple of years ago, and its contents were known to all the household, said Merton.

Pointer thanked him and drove on to The Flagstaff.

CHAPTER NINE

At The Flagstaff, Pointer was shown at once into a room where a tall slender woman rose to meet him, and he saw the second of the faces which had shown such uneasiness during the sermon yesterday. Lady Revell seemed to feel the rector's death very much, quite apart from the manner of it. Pointer asked her about her visit to him yesterday evening. There was just an infinitesimal pause, then Lady Revell said that she had not gone to the rectory last night. She had intended to, but a headache had come on, and she had countermanded the car almost as soon as she had ordered it. She had meant to telephone as much to the rector, but her headache had made her forget that too. She was without a personal maid at the moment, and such things were apt to slip her mind, she said, with a very charming smile. Pointer found her altogether charming, but she had, none the less, he thought, the face of one who would not care the snap of one of her manicured fingers for law as law. It would simply not exist in any reckoning of hers. He felt sure that Lady Revell considered herself as being outside it, not so much by birth, for it was an attitude that Pointer had found equally in the very lowly born, as from some attitude of mind that made the person concerned only see what they wanted to see, and as they wanted to see it. A dangerous character to find on the scene of a crime, or near it. He asked her about the necklace which he drew out of an envelope. She opened her eyes wide.

"Where did you find that? I could swear it was lying upstairs in a little cabinet I keep for such stones. Why, I showed it to Miss Hill not long ago, and I haven't worn it since, I feel sure."

Pointer told her where he had picked it up. She seemed puzzled.

"I know I wore it when I was there last. But that's weeks ago. Surely it was after that that Miss Hill called? I know it was. How odd! However, I suppose I must have worn it and forgotten about it. Thank you for finding it and returning it to me." She extended her hand, for Pointer had the necklace back in his own fingers by now. At her gesture he said at once that unfortunately this must remain in his custody until the inquiry was over, as it had been found in the room where the rector died.

"As you like," she replied, with what seemed indifference.

"For, forgive my bluntness, but the presence of this necklace in the rectory study last night must be explained. Had you been to see the rector at nine, and had then been wearing it, there would, of course, be no difficulty whatever."

Pointer now added that the police had to be quite sure that the poison had not been given to Mr. Avery deliberately—by another person.

Lady Revell looked incredulous horror.

"But who could have done such a thing? He hadn't an enemy in the world! We all loved the rector. We all set our moral clocks by him, as it were. Oh, you can't really believe such a possibility."

"We do," Pointer assured her very gravely with something very stern in his face. "We do. And so everything in that room last night, Lady Revell, must be accounted for."

She seemed unable to help about the necklace which was by now back in an envelope in his pocket.

"I will have a word with the Chief Constable," Lady Revell said, a touch of hauteur in her tone. "Major Weir-Opie knows me well—and may be less keen on red tape."

Pointer bowed, apologised for troubling her, and was shown out.

He was not happy as he drove away. Women were the devil in a serious investigation, he thought. So often their actions, which looked so suspicious, were so innocent, or at least so trivial. But here?

Pointer did not feel sure either that Lady Revell was lying, or that she was telling the truth. But of one thing he did feel confident, and that was that, given provocation, the woman whom he had just seen was capable of having flung that necklace to the floor and of having left it there, damning the consequences. She was the type to cut off her nose *con brio* to spite her face, once she was really angry. But surely Mr. Avery would not have put her, or any woman, into a passion? But against that was the fact that three faces that Pointer had noticed yesterday during the sermon remained in his mind as having shown signs of very intense emotion. Miss Hill, Lady Revell, and a woman whom he had not yet identified. A woman dressed in violet, with deep rings around her eye's, and a general unkempt look. Not one of the three had glanced at the other. On the contrary, he believed from their expressions that each had felt herself alone with the rector and with some terrifying knowledge of his. He thought of Olive Hill hastening to The Flagstaff. She had had the opportunity, he felt sure, of taking a necklace off Lady Revell's dressing-table had she wished to do so, and had such a necklace lain there. . . . But why? Then she too was put on one side, until further facts should throw added light on her.

Near the rectory gates he passed Dr. Rigby who promptly stopped his car for a word.

"Yes, it was toadstool poisoning all right, to give it its homely name, and in a concentrated form which could only have come from that bottle of his in the little fernery." He went on to give technical details.

"How long would it have taken to kill him, do you think?" Pointer asked when these were over.

"An hour of agony would see the end, I think," the doctor said with a gruffness that hid real feeling.

"And his supper was eaten when?"

"We've worked everything out very carefully and in detail, checking one thing with another. I don't think I'm far out, if at all, in saying that he took that hell-brew some time between ten and midnight, and that everything was over in an hour. But why didn't he call for help or ring a bell? Or stagger into the hall? That's what beats me." And with a groan the doctor drove on.

Pointer was met by Doris who was very pale and looked very sad as he entered the rectory. There was nothing of her old spring left in her step. "I wonder if you have found a letter I left in the library," she began, "a letter from my husband, stating when he would be back and giving me all sorts of directions as to what he wanted me to do meanwhile. It was the one I wanted to read to the rector last night when I stepped in after dinner."

Pointer said that he had not as yet seen it. Would she care to come in and have a look for it? She said that she would very much like to, as the dreadful shock of the rector's death had driven all remembrance out of her mind of what her husband had asked her to do.

They went in together and she hunted for her letter. It looked for a long time as though it were lost. And it was Pointer who found it at last, underneath a lining paper in the back of a drawer in the library.

"The rector must have thrust it in here. I suppose I left it on the table top, it was in his way, he dropped it in here and then it got pushed to the back of the drawer under the paper," she said as she took it from him.

Pointer thought that the place where it had been found was odd, seeing that all the rest of the drawers and shelves in the room only held papers or notes connected with the rector's religious writings. It looked to him as though the letter had been deliberately hidden.

"There are no directions in it, I suppose, that any one would want postponed?" he said now tentatively.

She looked startled. She hastily skimmed through it again. Then she held it out. "You are quite at liberty to read it," she said quietly, "though it's very affectionate, for it's only meant for my own eyes. But perhaps you had better read it through." He apologised for the necessity and did so. It was the letter of a man to a very dearly loved wife, one moreover whose judgment the writer evidently valued highly.

Richard explained that, owing to his hurry to get home to her, he had omitted certain legal formalities in the deed of sale of his West African property, which must be put right at once or it would be invalidated. It would be at least another month before he could be in England. Most of the letter referred to this. Finally came an allusion to Miss Hill. Mrs. Richard had written that she wanted to stay on with her, as her secretary. Richard Avery did not want this, that much was clear. He suggested that they should have their house to themselves for at least a year, unless she could make some arrangement for Olive Hill to live outside. He wrote sympathetically of her loss, spoke of Revell as though he had liked him, and wound up by asking whether the Revell treasure had been found yet. Then came a most affectionate conclusion full of happy hopes for a future in which neither need be parted from the other for more than a few hours.

"The Revell treasure, what is that?" Pointer asked as he thanked her for letting him read the letter, and handed it back.

She had not noticed the phrase and had to read it herself again.

"Oh, some idea of Anthony Revell's grandfather that there was a treasure hidden in the house. Of course there isn't. The dear old man was quite in his second childhood, and whenever he thought he was being left on one side by his children, he would let some allusion drop as to a treasure at The Causeway whose whereabouts he alone knew.

"As a matter of fact, the rector did find that where The Causeway now stands an old manor belonging to the

Fettiplaces had stood, who have all long died out. He fancied at one time that there might be something in old Mr. Revell's maunderings. Though I oughtn't to call them that, for he only very rarely spoke of the treasure. Anthony thought that he tried to say something to him about it on his death-bed, but the rector, who was present too, was sure that he was speaking of a good conscience . . . that sort of treasure."

"I wonder what he really said?" Pointer spoke lightly. "I mean the old gentleman . . . when he was dying."

But Doris knew no more than what she had said. She was looking around the room as she talked. For her husband, she said, had enclosed a message for the rector about the kind of house which he hoped to be able to find near the rectory. This was written on a separate half sheet, on paper such as the rector always used, and such as Richard Avery had sent out to him regularly.

"It's so odd to lose it when the rest of the letter is here. It must be close at hand," she insisted.

They both set to work to hunt for it.

"I had both letter and it in my hand," she went on, "when I stepped in here."

Searching and talking, she explained that she had gone to the library as soon as her visitors had left her last night to hand it to the rector, but he had been writing and was so busily engrossed in his work, that she had put it off for a better time. There was nothing pressing in her husband's message. The rector asked her to look up a reference for him, and she must then have laid down her letter. The rector was working against time, and she had stayed about a quarter of an hour jotting down which editions he had consulted, until she had finally gone to bed.

"I could have stayed much longer," she added in a tone of deep grief, "and if I had known—"

She turned away for a minute and tried desperately for composure. By this time they had finished their search, and she sank into a chair, with her face working as she covered it with her hands.

"I miss the rector so frightfully, and so will my husband! He doesn't know yet—I don't want him to know till he gets here." She jumped up after a moment, realising, Pointer thought, that she would be sobbing aloud in another minute, and fairly ran from the library and up to her own room.

Standing by the door as he closed it behind her, he felt some one try it gently. Pointer opened it on the instant. Miss Hill looked a little taken aback, he thought.

"Mrs. Richard was looking for something, wasn't she?" she began rather breathlessly.

"How did you know that?" Pointer asked with a smile, holding the door wider open for her to come in.

"I heard the unmistakable sounds of something being hunted for," she said easily. "I was waiting for her up in her bedroom," she continued in answer to the question in his eyes, "and you hear everything up there. That's what makes it so difficult to understand that she didn't hear anything last night.

"I wish I could find whatever she has lost," Miss Hill went on swiftly, "she's sobbing her heart out in her bedroom. She says it does not matter, but I would so like to find it for her. It must be something very important to upset her so. It's a letter, isn't it?"

Pointer did not tell her what it was, he only said that he, as well as Mrs. Avery, had searched the two rooms carefully, but if Miss Hill thought she would have better luck—he indicated that the room was at her disposal.

A plain-clothes man entered and without a word to Pointer went to a table in the window and sitting facing the room began to fill a sheet of paper with writing. As Pointer explained to Miss Hill, Jackson would not be in the way, as there were no drawers in the table at which he would be writing down some facts for the Chief Constable. Nor would he be long, he added.

"Oh, don't let him hurry away on my account," begged Miss Hill as Pointer left the room.

A moment later Mrs. Avery, restored to her usual outwardly calm self, was now coming down the stairs. She did not look in the least as though she had been indulging in any such wild grief as Miss Hill had reported.

Pointer motioned her into the room on the opposite side of the broad lounge.

"Miss Hill is trying to find the enclosure for you," he said easily.

She stared. "What do you mean? She doesn't know that it's lost," she said.

She was out of the dining-room and crossing to the study door as she spoke. Then she paused. He saw her shudder.

"I hate more and more to go in," she said frankly, but she turned the handle before he reached it and stepped inside. So did Pointer.

Jackson was just helping Miss Hill get down an etching off its nail.

"What are you doing?" Mrs. Richard asked with her quiet directness, but in a manner that softened her words.

"This young lady couldn't reach it, ma'am," explained Jackson.

"I want to find the paper you've lost," Olive Hill said sweetly to Mrs. Avery.

"But I haven't lost it," was the reply. "I've only mislaid it. Besides, unless you have second sight, Olive, how could you know anything about it?" Mrs. Avery spoke with something of sternness in her voice.

"I heard a hunt going on—among papers—so it could only be a letter that you had lost," Olive said stubbornly. "I've lost one too, as it happens—about a month ago."

"Oh? Was it for that you hunted through my room this morning before I was up?" Mrs. Avery asked coldly.

Olive said nothing. She had turned pale. "Come, Olive," Mrs. Avery went on sharply, "be sensible, and tell us what you are looking for? Then we could help you. I'm sure it's for something of your own—not mine."

Olive did not speak for a moment, she stood staring down at the etching which lay on the table now.

Christopher Byrd was shown in just then. Pointer had given orders that whenever he or a constable was inside the room, people could come and go in it as they liked. The room was to seem unwatched.

Byrd had a few words to say to Mrs. Avery of really very well expressed regret at her brother-inlaw's death. Then he turned.

"What's wrong with the etching?" he inquired.

"Ask Miss Hill," came from Mrs. Avery. "She's hunting for something, and we want to help her."

Olive Hill turned a very inscrutable look on Byrd, on Mrs. Avery, on Pointer. "It's something of Mr. Revell's that I'm looking for," she said at last very quietly.

Byrd gave an exclamation. It was under his breath, but something in the quality of the voice registered with the Chief Inspector as a man who had had a most unexpected jolt, and one that went deep.

He said nothing, however. Only with narrowed eyes he stared hard at the girl. Olive did not look at him now.

She was very plain to-day. Her face was white. There were circles around her eyes. And never had the Chief Inspector looked into a face more impossible to read except that it was very agitated under its composure.

She was trembling slightly as she stood there before them. Doris saw it too.

"We can't talk in here. It's not decent somehow. Come into the morning-room, Olive, and tell us what you are really after."

They followed her out. Even Byrd, after a second's hesitation, went too.

In the morning-room Grace was sitting with her face white and drawn.

"Olive is looking for something," Doris said to her, "and we all want to help her find it."

Grace hardly seemed to hear.

Olive, too, made no reply for a minute.

"Sit down," Doris ordered in her peremptory way.

Olive sank on to the arm of a chair but her face was contracted and closed.

"I believe she's after the treasure!" Byrd put in with a discordant half-laugh.

For a moment Olive did not answer, then she looked at him.

"Yes," she said then, "or rather for an account of where it is to be found."

"Oh, come!" he protested. "I was only joking. Of course there's no treasure at The Causeway. If you've mislaid some of his letters to you, if you wait till things are straightened out they'll turn up of themselves."

Olive did not condescend to look at him, she stared dully in front of her. But she was not apathetic, Pointer felt sure of that. Rather was she in that wrought-up mood in which a man does not care what happens, what dangers he is running into. Though, ordinarily, he judged that this young woman would be more than usually circumspect. She looked to him the kind to weigh, as a rule, every word she said before saying it, let alone every action.She walked on out of the room, and as Byrd opened the door for her, she said a quick word in his ear. He followed her, and Jackson too found that he had to fetch something from the hall at the same time. Doris sat on in amazement. "So that was why she wanted Dick to buy The Causeway," she finally said, "but how silly! Hidden treasure! Grace, can you believe it?"

Grace did not look up.

"About her searching your room this morning?" Pointer asked.

Doris told him that that was only a chance shot, and explained what had really happened. "Though why she's started it all up just now—now—to-day," she said under her breath, and still looking as though she had found a quite new side of Olive Hill to study, went on up to her own room.

Grace rose and followed her.

The scene was very odd, but of one thing Pointer was sure, and that was that though Olive Hill had accepted the suggestion made half or wholly in jest, by Christopher Byrd, that she was interested in hunting for a possible treasure at The Causeway, it was not true. It was quite a plausible suggestion for a girl without any money who might be presumed to have heard Anthony Revell talk of it, but it was not true. . . . She was after something else. Stamps? But what most interested the astute detective was that she had given him the impression of being on the verge of burning her boats when Christopher had interfered and suggested something at which he himself scoffed a moment later.

Olive had whispered to Byrd to come with her for a moment. Her hand on his arm she pulled him into the dining-room.

"Chris, I'm frightened," she murmured.

She laid her cheek suddenly against his. Her skin was like satin, and smelt like a clove pink.

He pushed her away. "None of that," he whispered roughly. "I don't trust you, darling. I don't like you, love. You may have tricked poor Revell, but you can't hoodwink Christopher Byrd. What you got out of Revell that you've lost I haven't an earthly. Something you've no right to. Mr. Avery knew of it. I say he did!" for she opened her lips to speak. She turned a livid white at his words. He pushed her away. "Don't you suppose I watched your face when that sermon of his got under weigh?" he went on ruthlessly. "You were on hot coals. I think there was a moment when you thought he was going to be plainer still. Pity he wasn't, as things have turned out."

"He had learned that I didn't love Anthony," she said breathlessly. "Grace had told him," there was fury in her low tone, in her eye.

Byrd stared at her in contemptuous silence for a second. Then he gave his short, cutting laugh. "And you think that explains his sermon." He made for the door, but her next words stopped him.

"I'm coming out with you to the Dutch Indies, to Maboa. I've got my hundred pounds ready to pay in, and I'm coming!"

"Your money will be returned to you," he said sharply. "I told you that we take married couples, and engaged couples, but not single women."

"Yes, and I was coming as your wife!" she retorted.

"And two weeks after that was arranged, you were engaged to Revell."

"I told you that I didn't love him! I only got engaged because—because—" her face worked with some dark passion.

"Of the Fettiplaces' treasure?" he asked in derision.

"I got engaged to Anthony to show that I could have him if I wanted him. I never intended to marry him. Never! I was going to marry you!'

Her face was suddenly beseeching—soft—alluring. He refused to look at her, but stared at the carpet as he had stared at the ground once when Mr. Avery had seen them together in the woods.

"What was it that made the rector preach that sermon?" he demanded.

Her face paled. She swallowed, tried to speak, and before she got a word out, he was gone, and had closed the door behind him with something of finality in the very sound.

CHAPTER TEN

Pointer would have been very interested had he been able to overhear the talk between Grace and Doris after Byrd's suggestion of a motive for Olive's search.

"I can't make Olive out," Doris said as the two sisters-in-law reached her sitting-room. "In a way I'm grateful to her for giving me something to think about other than John's terrible end, and my mother's illness. And she does puzzle me! What she's after—I wonder if it is that quite incredible tale of hidden treasure? You know," she motioned Grace to sit beside her on the little couch, and spoke very low, but with the unmistakable look of one glad to talk, "she certainly hunted for something at The Causeway too. I wondered what took her over there so regularly, but one day when I went there myself—Jack thought that Patricia Revell might be there, and I wanted a word with her—I found Olive buried head and shoulders in a boot cupboard. And her face when I opened the door on her! Consternation is too mild a word for it. Evidently she is after that mythical treasure!"

"I wonder!" Grace said musingly. "For I learnt yesterday that she's been in the habit of taking our letters from the postman and bringing them herself up to the house. That isn't explained by hunting for treasure at The Causeway.

"I missed a postal order that should have arrived a week ago," Grace continued. "No, it's quite all right, as a matter of fact, the ' Brownie' in question forgot to post it. But I met Bowles, one of our postmen, as I walked back from evening service last night—yes, I know you find it hard enough to go in the mornings—Well, to go on, I asked Bowles whether there was any chance of the letter I was inquiring about having been overlooked. He got very flustered and finally said that if one had got lost, it was much more likely to be between the rectory gate and its letter-box. But that he hadn't liked to refuse when Olive offered to take them herself to the house. He's getting old and it is a bit of a walk up from the gates—at his age."

"But how? Where was she? When was this?" Doris was all at sea.

"It seems that Olive was always gardening when the postman arrived." Grace spoke with something of Doris's own occasional pungency of tone.

"Gardening by the gates!"

"Those annuals!" breathed Doris. "She begged to be let plant them herself, and look after them herself."

Grace made an acquiescent gesture.

"John thought first she was getting in training for The Causeway gardens, then that she was trying to get over her grief at Anthony's loss," Doris said. "He let her have that corner to play with. But why? And she's neglected the place dreadfully just of late, as I expected she would."

"'Why' is what I say," Grace repeated. "I don't see how hunting for The Causeway's treasure—even supposing she were so silly as to believe that tale—would explain her taking our letters from the postman for nearly a fortnight."

"When did she start doing this?" Then Doris answered herself. "Let me see, she planted out that bed in the last week of May. Just around the time that Anthony died—"

"Just so," agreed Grace. "And from that time on she was always on hand to take any letters from Bowles or Herrick—Bowles says Herrick, the second postman, handed them to her too. And, a fortnight ago, her interest in the flowers stopped.. . ."

Doris sat silent, considering.

"I remembered the way that letter to you from Dick had been mislaid a month ago," went on Grace. "I had handed it to her at once on its arrival, and she told me that she had given it to you immediately. But you didn't get it till you found it for yourself—next day."

"I can't see what interest Olive could have in Dick's letters to me," Doris said slowly. "No, I should be more inclined to think that she has got in touch with some of these diviners—people who claim to be able to locate treasure by a photograph of the place."

There was a short silence.

"That's possible!" Grace spoke in the tone of one who is shown the right word for the Crossword. "I never thought of anything so simple! But if so, then she was still interested in that immediately after Anthony died! I always told you that she didn't care for him, you know."

"Poor Anthony," Doris said with a gesture of pity. "Your eyes were sharper than mine. He loved her so much that I suppose I took it for granted that she loved him too. He never had any doubts about it."

"Possibly he had at the end," Grace said under her breath. She broke off as Doris interrupted to ask if she was sure that Olive's self-imposed duty as postman to the rectory was now a thing of the past.

"Oh, absolutely." Grace spoke with certainty. "And I let Bowles see that it must never happen again. He assured me, and he's a truthful old thing, that it hadn't happened for a fortnight past."

There was silence in the room after that. Then Grace rose.

"I'm glad I told you about it. I meant to at once last night. And your idea of diviners really does explain Olive's actions. But what a heart she must have—apart from Anthony, here's poor John hardly dead—to be able to go into his study and hunt about in it—what was that for, do you suppose?"

Doris made a weary gesture. "Notes on some of his talks of Anthony's grandfather. Or, more likely, plans of The Causeway foundations. John drew some at the time he was interested in tracing the old manor's outbuildings."

She stopped as Fraser came in.

The Chief Constable asked Pointer and Shilling to dine with him that Monday night.

The talk turned exclusively on the rectory puzzle. Ireton fortunately for himself had an unimpeachable alibi for yesterday afternoon and evening. He and his family had gone by train to some relatives at four o'clock, and had only returned at nine this morning. He could not have tampered with the tray, for there had been a Cinderella dance on that had lasted till midnight, and Mr. Ireton had danced indefatigably. That settled, Pointer told about the odd little affair of the necklace that belonged to Lady Revell.

Weir-Opie held up a hand.

"I've had to spend a precious half-hour calming her down," he said, "not that there was much that I could do. Of course, Lady Revell is quite above suspicion, I should say—quite! And her story of having left it in the study on a previous visit explains it, eh?"

Pointer had been talking to Fraser, and the butler had scoffed at the idea that anything had lain for over twenty-four hours undetected behind the window-seat. And the lack of dust bore this out.

"Umph—odd," Weir-Opie allowed, when this was explained, "but, as I say, I really can't see Lady Revell murdering Avery, or having to. Her life is too well known, even before her marriage, for her to have any black secrets, I feel sure. That some one else helped themselves to that necklace, and wore it yesterday to the rectory is more likely"

"Jolly careless thing to do, sir," Shilling put in, "with a striking thing like that."

"True, but one must account for its presence somehow. . . . Odd . . ." and like good Catholics at Meditation, the three sat silent for several minutes considering the one necklace certainly found, and the one necklace possibly missing.

"And what did you think of the Gartsides?" Weir-Opie asked, coming up out of the deeps.

"They seemed to me rather uneasy, sir," Pointer said, and proceeded to pass on what little he had learnt from them, and from Merton, about the articles which they had chosen for their legacy.

"But there's one thing they didn't tell me, of which I feel as sure as Merton seems to, and that is that neither brother nor sister believe for a moment that Mr. Revell really went home because of a toothache," Pointer said with assurance.

"Do you think they knew the real reason then, whatever it was?" Weir-Opie asked instantly. "Or is Merton right—and did Anthony take to flight?"

"There's one thing, sir. The post had evidently reached them before Mr. Revell spoke to them on Thursday morning, because Miss Gartside said that she was reading a letter that had just come, when Mr. Revell stepped into the sitting-room to say that he must leave them till the following afternoon, so that Mr. Revell could have received a letter that morning."

"I asked them that very question before the inquest, and both said they knew of none," Shilling said instantly.

"Probably they didn't know," Pointer agreed. "There may even have been none, if Merton is right in thinking that it was something to do with Miss Gartside. But Mr. Revell's going to his drawing-room at that hour of night strongly suggests a rendezvous."

"Yes, we got that far," Weir-Opie nodded, "but we found no proofs. Whereas the probabilities are that after killing Revell and finding that the stamps they were after weren't at The Causeway—he hadn't been searched as we told you—the murderer, or murderers, knew about the list, and, recognising it in the rector's hands in church on Sunday decided that it must be secured and destroyed after silencing him."

"In short, they murdered the rector, took the stamps, and didn't get the list," summed up Shilling who liked things put briefly, no matter what had to be left out. "Did you hear anything about that wonderful Sicilian stamp from Sir Hubert Witson, sir?"

Weir-Opie looked at him. "Yes," he said finally. "Oh, yes. I wish he had a better alibi for both the times we're interested in, he talked so ravenously about it. Said he had been allowed to see a specimen once in his life in Berlin at the Postal Museum there. It isn't listed among the exhibits, but is kept in the director's private room, and apparently, from the way Witson went on, is chained to the director day and night. I didn't mention it to him as any motive for Avery's death, naturally—"

Both his listeners nodded. It had been agreed between them that, until they learnt that that particular stamp had been located, there must be the greatest secrecy observed about it.

"So Sir Hubert knew about such a stamp," said Shilling, sticking to his point.

Weir-Opie nodded.

"Did he know about Mr. Revell's owning any Sicilian stamps?" Pointer asked.

"He did. Moreover, Sir Hubert himself put forward a chat on stamps as the reason for the rector's late call on him day before yesterday—Saturday. He said that Mr. Avery had rung him up on Saturday afternoon and said that he had had a good many small gifts of stamps made him lately which were now growing quite bulky, and thought it might be as well to consult such a well-known expert about their value and classification. He wanted to start a boys' stamp exchange and sale with a view to rendering some of his clubs more nearly self-supporting. Everybody around here knows it was one of the rector's many dreams that in time his boys might be able to run their clubs entirely unaided. Sir Hubert asked him to drop in at five o'clock on Monday afternoon, but had to phone up later, about half-past eight, and ask him to come then, as he feared trouble with his eyes which might make it impossible for him to inspect the stamps on the Monday. As a matter of fact his eyes are better to-day, he told me," went on Weir-Opie, "but he had had them bad once, and got nervous."

"Did Mr. Avery bring the stamps?" Shilling asked.

"Witson says not. Witson says he only wanted some general information about how such a scheme might be started. But he mentioned the Sicilian stamps among many others, and Witson says he told him about this particular stamp—Witson, by the way, thinks a well-preserved one would be cheap at six thousand. The rector, according to Witson, said that he was afraid his Sicilian stamps contained nothing so thrilling, but he would look at the list which Revell had sent with them."

There was a short silence after the Chief Constable had finished.

"So Sir Hubert Witson rang up the rector last night around half-past eight. That much of course will be on record," Pointer said.

"And where was Sir Hubert last night, sir?" asked the superintendent.

"Again in his bed, Shilling," Weir-Opie said in his dry tone. "You always seem to think it a most suspicious place for people to be found, I know. But I will remind you that I have exactly the same alibi for last night. Presumably Pointer here has no better. And what about yourself?"

Shilling laughed outright. Then his face sobered. "So he knew there was a list of those stamps to be seen," he muttered.

Pointer looked up. "The list which may have contained the name of a very valuable stamp might explain the rector's murder, and the search of his study—the library wasn't searched at all"

"Because he wouldn't keep anything of a secular kind in there," threw in Weir-Opie.

Pointer nodded. He understood as much.

"But," he went on slowly, "I think a message must have accompanied it to cause the rector to stare at it as he did on Sunday in the pulpit, and above all to preach such a sermon as he did."

"Why, the sight of the stamp on the list was surely sufficient?" replied Shilling, surprised.

"Why should a message have had to accompany the list?" Weir-Opie said, passing the liqueur brandy.

"Because on turning it over in my mind, sir, I don't see how Mr. Avery could so instantly appreciate the significance of that stamp on the list, supposing it was there. I mean—"—Pointer found it hard to put his growing dissatisfaction into words—"say I am the rector. I open my Bible, having given out my text with my mind full of my sermon. Opening out my notes, I see that, by mistake, I have picked up a list of stamps instead. I doubt if I would more than glance at the paper. I don't think I would carefully read the list through to the end."

"Ah, but if the valuable one happened to be first on the list!" Weir-Opie objected.

"Even so, sir, even if I saw on it one I knew to be very valuable, I don't think I would connect that stamp's presence with the month-old death of the giver, a death moreover which was thought to be accidental. I don't say that a detective who was certain that Revell had been murdered might not have seen it in that light. But Mr. Avery, with the first sentence of his sermon already half spoken?"

"I see," said Weir-Opie, twirling his cigar round and round like a screw.

And an answering "I see"came from Shilling who laid down the matches. Both voices suggested the opposite.

"Granted it was the list of stamps that he took out of his Bible, and granted even that on it was the name of a very valuable one indeed, there must have been more than that, to have affected the rector as it did. Must have been."

Pointer spoke with certainty. "Even assuming both those first premises to be true, I feel more and more sure that some message must have been written as well."

"Such as 'Showed these stamps to Witson the other day,' eh, sir?" Shilling cast a look at the Chief Constable.

"Or 'Byrd doesn't think them valuable,'" Weir-Opie lit his cigar. "You always tried to connect Byrd with Revell's death, Shilling, only he too claimed to have been in his bed that night."

Pointer did not appear struck with the two suggestions.

"The rector hadn't time in the pulpit to think things over, sir, and put two and two together."

"He stood a long minute with eyes shut after he saw that paper," Weir-Opie reminded the Chief Inspector. "I thought he was praying. He may have been thinking back instead. He was a very quick-witted man, remember, with a finely-trained, really good brain. You think some incriminating —for the murderer—message accompanied the list . . . umph. . . ."

"I do, and yet again there are difficulties," Pointer said finally, lighting up, "about a message accompanying the list."

"That's it!" Weir-Opie liked to chaff Pointer. "That's it! First throw us a rope. Then chop it in two. Then boggle about letting us have even half of it!"

Pointer laughed.

"What difficulties are there about Mr. Revell having written a very suggestive message on the same page as the list?" Shilling wanted to know.

"Why, the paper was kept in the open-topped jar. Again, granted that the rector had never read it, and that's a lot to grant seeing that he had had it for nearly a month—What about Mr. Byrd? He saw the list, so if there was a message he must have seen it too. But he left it apparently."

"True, there is that!" came in tones almost of disappointment from the Chief Constable. "The butler and other servants could have seen it had they wanted to," Pointer continued, "so that whatever it contained that so appalled the rector on Sunday must have been very inconspicuous. Then why did it burst on him, when he read it, like a horrible floodlight—for it did."

"Could he have learnt something on the way to church which altered things?" wondered Weir Opie, thoroughly roused. "But, no, Colonel Grenville is one of his churchwardens, and I had a word with him to-day. He walked into the vestry with him—they were talking about some repairs, and he said that the rector was more cheery than he had seen him since Revell's death, which had been a frightful shock to him, as to every one. Though not within a thousand miles of the shock which his own death is to all of us who ever met him," added Weir-Opie under his breath, "for to know Avery was to love him."

"I confess, sir," Pointer said after a silence, "that I keep turning and twisting the possibilities of that folded paper over and over, and so far quite fruitlessly." He did not add that he was not one of those men who have to have things told to them before they "detect" them. Pointer could reason, and very far indeed at times his reasoning had brought him. He had controlled imagination, without which the cleverest clues are but as useless stones.

And there was another difficulty too about the missing jar, but he did not mention it. It was the most obvious one, though neither the Chief Constable nor his superintendent had yet referred to it.

"There's no proving where any one was that Thursday night Mr. Revell was killed," broke in Shilling. "Even if we had anything on which to hang our suspicions—which we haven't."

"Or had any suspicions to hang on anything if we had it," amended Weir-Opie dryly.

"Any one else besides Miss Hill in love with Mr. Revell?" Pointer asked.

"He was a bit of a flirt," Weir-Opie said cautiously, "as was only natural. Lady Witson's name has been linked with his a good bit. She's a fast young woman. Sir Hubert's a good deal older than she is, and as jealous as only elderly and very ugly men can be. As to an alibi on the night of Revell's death—none. And only half an hour's walk from his house to The Causeway. And he's an active walker."

"Friend of Mr. Revell's?"

"They were on speaking terms, but nothing warmer."

"Whoever shot him, if it wasn't an accident, would have been a supposed friend, one would think," Pointer said. "Some one who could pick up that revolver without causing any suspicion in Mr. Revell's mind."

"Then there's Mrs. Green," put in Shilling. And Pointer was now told all the local gossip about the artist.

Weir-Opie modified the account by saying, "I don't know, no one will ever know how much truth there is in the story of her infatuation. His mother believes it, I think, whereas the rector didn't. And I'm bound to say that Mr. Avery was a very shrewd man. Very hard to fob off with a lie. And there's this on Mrs. Green's side, the servants at The Causeway swear that there was nothing ' wrong'—their word—between her and Revell. And if they didn't think so, there wasn't. Trust house servants to know."

Pointer did not stay late after dinner. Weir-Opie and Shilling had many other things to discuss, and he had brought away with him to read to-night the unfinished chapters of the rector's Notes on Saint Paul. He wanted to hear, as it were, the dead man talking. It kept him awake. Here was detection at its subtlest and best. Like a man bearing a strong light, the rector had moved through his texts, casting that light now forwards now backwards along the path which he had marked out, and Pointer thought that no Scotland Yard sleuth could better him in his amazing skill in putting the hidden two and two together into the right four. Logic and reasoning this of the highest. Pointer turned out his light with a sigh for the brain lost to the world.

He would very much have liked to hear Mr. Avery's explanation of his own end. Which would mean the truth about the missing stamps, the necklace and, above all, the folded paper that he had taken out of his Bible yesterday morning.

CHAPTER ELEVEN

The inquest on the rector was next morning. As he was walking from the police station to it, Pointer heard his name called. A smart car was stopping beside him. A young woman jumped out, and waved to the chauffeur to go on.

"You're the bogey man, aren't you," she said with a display of white teeth. "The Major was talking about you to me. I'm Lady Witson."

Pointer saw a young woman on the right side of thirty, very tall, very thin, with a dress that fitted her as its last leaf does a cigar. She was, if not pretty, well made up, very up to date. He was particularly interested in her. One of Shilling's men had learnt last night that there had been a tremendous quarrel between Sir Hubert and his wife on Saturday, and that the servants all believed the rector's call to have been made for the purpose of reasoning with Lady Witson who, according to them, had taken very ostentatiously to drink since Anthony Revell's death, with whom all the servants believed she had been carrying on a wild flirtation. Both flirtation and drinking, according to them, arose not so much from affection, as from a hope that Sir Hubert if really alarmed would leave The Towers and go back at once to London where Eva-May Witson longed to be.

Pointer thought that Lady Witson looked capable of anything that would further her own plans. The servants had told Shilling's inquirer that they had heard the name of Revell called out once during the half an hour's talk that the rector had had with husband and wife. It had been apparently screamed at her husband by Lady Witson. The maid who had passed on most of this information, if it could be called that, had heard the rector call her firmly to order, as though she had said something that was unpardonable, but the girl claimed that she had shrilled the name again and again before rushing in hysterics—"put-on ones," in her opinion—from the room.

"I hear that Miss Hill has not been called as a witness by the Coroner," Lady Witson said now in a very sharp nasal voice.

"I suppose the Coroner thought that this second death coming so soon after her own personal loss would have been a great shock to her," Pointer suggested.

Lady Witson gave the little screech that she considered a laugh. "A great personal loss it was indeed!" There was mockery in her tone. "If he hadn't had that accident she would have lost him just the same. Anthony Revell never really intended to marry Olive Hill! What happened was that she misunderstood, or pretended to misunderstand, something pretty he said to her, and the rector came in, and Olive asked for his blessing, and there was poor Anthony in the net! And all for the sake of one of his pretty speeches. Once in, he was making the best of it, but that was really why he went rockclimbing for a fortnight. He intended, he told me himself, to write her a most regretful letter, and an explanatory one to the rector, and be off—free—unfettered. That was why she hasn't a ring. He was going to get free—from a distance. He would have been quite ready to flirt with her, of course, but she wanted marriage, equally of course. Poor thing!"

"That's very interesting," Pointer said pleasantly, "and you had it from Mr. Revell himself?"

She nodded importantly, and repeatedly, before she signed to a passing friend in a car, and jumped in. So she had only got down from her own car to be spiteful.

Yet Pointer thought that in the evident spite lay a possible truth. He himself had wondered whether the engagement of Olive Hill and Anthony Revell might not have been engineered by the young woman. She struck him as essentially an intriguer. But even if things had happened as Lady Witson had just suggested, that would neither account for the shooting of Revell, supposing it not to have been accidental, nor for the murder of the rector.

The Chief Constable's car stopped for Pointer, who reported the words of Lady Witson. The Chief Constable made a face.

"Kind of thing she would say," he muttered. "Is she right? Possibly. Revell loved a peaceful life beyond even the love of women. Or else he had a real attachment—it's whispered-by some gossips that it was to this same Lady Witson—for a couple of years before Miss Hill ever appeared on the scene. There was a lot of gossip about it, but some thought that it was started by the lady herself."

"Nothing more likely, I should think," Pointer said with a faint smile. "Anything rather than be ignored is her motto, I fancy."

"There's even a whisper or two beginning to circulate about the night young Revell was shot. Shilling's ears, stretched like drums, have caught it."

Pointer's expression did not change, but the quality of his interest did.

"To the effect that Lady Witson was seen going, or coming—one whisper has it one way, one another —from The Causeway the night Revell returned home. This would explain his return with never a word to his servant or any of his old friends, we all know. But she didn't shoot him!" and the Chief Constable laughed. "She can't shoot, to begin with. Shilling found that out at once. And neither was there any reason for it. She's not the intense kind. I think she's quite fond of her husband really, but thinks he needs a little rousing now and then. I don't say she's wrong. Certainly he never neglects her as he did his first wife. Some men have to feel insecure before they value anything."

"Do you think the rector could have got to hear of the gossip about Lady Witson being there that night?" Pointer asked.

"The last man to learn of it, I should say," was the opinion of the Chief Constable. "And it's only just beginning to spread. No one knows where from, of course."

Pointer was thinking.

"Well?" asked the other as he said nothing. "What do you think of her as the writer of a possible letter giving Revell a rendezvous?"

"I'm wondering how Lady Witson could have induced Mr. Revell to give up two whole days out of a fortnight's climbing. He lost Thursday getting back here, he would have had to lose Friday returning to Derbyshire."

"Yes, and the Gartsides could only stay the two weeks. Saturday—Saturday—Saturday," Shilling threw in. "He's a very junior clerk at Lloyds, and couldn't possibly get his holiday extended."

"And generally one chooses some extra good climb to end with— "—Pointer was a great climber—"something to stretch to the last possible minute. By leaving on Thursday, Revell practically closed the expedition. Possibly there was bad feeling between him and the Gartsides—"

"We could learn of none. Shilling here was very keen on finding that out at once," said Weir-Opie.

"Certainly unless there was trouble between them, or unless Miss Gartside frightened him home, if Lady Witson could get him to so cut short the trip, she must have had a very strong reason to give him. Something very compelling—Would Sir Hubert be likely to start divorce proceedings easily?"

"Ah! He's as jealous as a Turk. But as to divorce—I dunno."

"One would have expected that only Miss Hill would have had the power to get him to come back like that," Pointer was eyeing his polished shoe tips.

"Lady Witson is quite capable of suggesting that she was in a fearful hole if by saying so she could stir up Revell or her husband." Weir-Opie's tone did not suggest any great amount of affection for the lady. "She's a curious type. Must have things swirling around her. Seems to be meat and drink to her."

"Let's hope that the rector wasn't poisoned for want of a thrill," Pointer said dryly, and the other agreed. They were by now at the schoolhouse where the inquest was to be held. Weir-Opie promptly went on ahead for a word with the Coroner.

The inquest was crowded. Pointer himself was present throughout, for there was the one obvious point connected with the missing yellow jar which still puzzled him extremely, and which he hoped might be cleared up at it.

Also, in a murder case, the faces of the people listening to the evidence always interested him. The first person at which he glanced held his eye for a woman whom on Sunday in church the rector's sermon had so shaken. A question to Shilling nearby, and he learnt that, as he thought, she was Mrs. Green. An interesting but ravaged face, Pointer had thought it in church the day before yesterday, now it bore still more marks of grief, yet he had been given to understand that the rector was practically a stranger to her. Queer.

The inquest began.

The Coroner, who had been told that the police wanted all possible information, did his best to ferret out any shreds.

Sir Hubert Witson, a large fat man with sleepy eyes, was called first after the police and medical evidence. He said that the rector called to see him on Saturday evening. Their talk had only to do with a stamps "sale and exchange"for some boys' clubs. The rector had seemed quite his usual self. Witson had a ruthless and mean face, Pointer thought. Superficially good-natured up to a point, but capable of being a very nasty customer once that point were passed. Pointer thought he was telling the truth, as far as it went, but he thought him very determined that it should not go far.

The Coroner next called Lady Witson for a moment. She entirely supported her husband's statement that the rector had merely looked in for a word about his clubs, and bore out unhesitatingly his account of the short chat on stamps that had followed.

Mrs. Richard Avery was called, and described the tray that had been sent in as so often before to the rector on Sunday night. As to the toadstools, different reason. It was she went into that point very carefully and clearly. The rector, she said, was extremely careful about the extract. She went on to repeat what she had already told the police about having gone into the library after her friends had left the house on Sunday evening, and the help in looking up some references that her brother-in-law had asked of her. She had heard his voice in the study, the room below her bedroom, much later—around half-past eleven—when she put out her reading-lamp and fell asleep. She had thought at the time that he was reading a sentence aloud to himself. His voice had sounded quite calm, but she had herself been very sleepy at the time.

Lady Revell, when called, said that owing to her headache she had not walked over to the rectory on Sunday evening as she had at first intended, but had taken a headache powder and gone to bed instead. As to her necklace found under the window seat, she gave the same explanation to the Coroner as to Pointer. The lighter necklace had not been found. Possibly indeed she had lost it on Sunday coming back from church. She had stayed in her room Sunday afternoon writing letters and feeling very much under the weather, and it now looked to her as though she had only taken it for granted that she had laid it on her dressing-table that night.

The inquest went on. Fraser, Mr. Ireton, servants, no one seemed to have anything new to say.

The Coroner finally adjourned for a fortnight, after stressing the fact that owing to the door that led out from the fernery into the garden, any outsider could have been admitted, or for that matter could, theoretically at least, have slipped in on Sunday evening after the tray was brought into the study, and have transferred some of the poisonous toadstool extract to the mushroom ketchup bottle. This could have been done, even with the rector sitting writing in the inner room, for the door between was generally shut, and when deep in his work, he was deaf to what went on around him.

Pointer went for a walk when the proceedings were over. Why had the orange jar been taken away from the rectory study? The inquest had not in the least solved that question. The chief objection to its disappearance did not seem to have occurred to the Major or to Shilling. But Pointer placed himself in the position of the criminal. Granted that he was after the stamps, that he had missed them before when he shot Revell, that he would therefore be all out not to go away empty-handed after a second murder, why should he take away the china jar as well as the stamps? It was roughly a hand high and a span across the top. The lid was china too.

The jar had every fault from the criminal's point of view. It was heavy. It was awkward to carry safely. It was extremely smooth. It was noisy to put down anywhere. It was difficult to hide, impossibly so on the person. It was breakable, and an accident might happen at some most inconvenient time and place. It was most easily identifiable, even at a glance. So much so, that Pointer had at first expected to find it "planted" somewhere. But so far it had not turned up. It seemed to have genuinely accompanied the stamps, and Pointer could not understand why. The thing had no especially valuable qualities of air or watertightness to compensate for its many disadvantages. The stamps were easily taken out. Then why want the cumbersome china jar? What reason had constrained the murderer, the quite

averagely clever murderer, to put up with all its
drawbacks? Pointer worried at the reason, which eluded
him as much now, as on the first moment of learning of
the jar's disappearance. It did not make sense. The
stamps—yes. But the jar—no! A dozen times over, no!

He went to his bed still trying in his mind every
possible combination of circumstances which would
explain the taking of that jar. The strangest small
incident—to his mind—which the case presented, became
the most incomprehensible. It was devoid of all reason, as
far as he could see, and Chief Inspector Pointer saw
further than most men, as well as more quickly and more
clearly. For an hour he lay awake thinking, and at last he
became convinced that there was no reason behind its
absence from the study mantel. That meant that its
taking was accidental, caused by some unplanned
incident. Had it fallen and been broken in taking it
hurriedly off the mantel when the stamps had been stolen
after the death of the rector? Not a speck of broken china
remained. Under the circumstances it must have taken
nerve to have so picked up every particle in that room. . . .
Could there be any reason for so carefully hiding the jar if
it had been broken? Suddenly he saw one.

The rector lay on his couch which faced obliquely
towards fireplace and window. That necklace was found
under the window-sill! What if the rector, discovering
that no bell rang, that his door was locked, knowing that
the windows were too stiff for him to open, had made a
last effort to summon help by flinging the necklace at the
window to break it? And suppose the necklace to have
been lying on the small occasional table that stood near
him? In his weakness, lying on his side, he might easily
have hit the china jar instead . . . and the murderer,
wanting to conceal the fact that the bells were put out of
order, that the doors had been locked, would feel that
broken jar to be far too much of a clue to leave it lying in
bits on the floor. The necklace had dropped out of sight,
but the jar would be buried as near as possible to the

garden door—a trowel and small hand-rake lay on the mushroom table.

He walked swiftly to the rectory, and would have made for the strip of garden outside the fernery door, but for Grace Avery, who, a pile of correspondence beside her on the lawn, sat near it behind a spur of rhododendrons, busily reading, and tearing up papers.

" These are some old papers of last year from my brother's attic store-room," she explained. "They must be gone through, of course. So far I have come on nothing in the least interesting, only old receipts and so on, appeals for help, club reports—that sort of thing. But they must be attended to. There's another couple of hours' work in this lot alone. Tell me, Mr. Pointer, you don't really think that any one intended to poison my brother, do you? It's incredible that any one could want to harm him! Some accident—yes. Though that's hard enough to explain, but not intention?"

So long as it seemed as though the sister had nothing to do with the brother's death, Major Weir Opie thought that there was no reason to tell her of the police certainty of foul play. She, supposedly innocent, would help them as much as she could, without that dreadful knowledge to grieve her still deeper. Yet there was the question of danger. The very grave question. A poisoner undetected is like a deadly snake lying hidden in the grass. One incautious step, and another death may be the result. Pointer therefore contented himself with saying that the whole affair was most mysterious, and that until more was known, it was impossible to rule out any possibility, or any motive for that possibility.

"Any possibility. Any motive . . ." she repeated slowly. "You really think that one shouldn't shut out any quite impossible seeming motive?" Her hands had fallen back inert on her lap, her eyes were wide and looked full of trouble.

"Most certainly not," he said at once and turned to her, waiting. But she said nothing more, only twisted her rings round and round on her fingers.

"If you can think of anything however fantastic or far-fetched, please tell it me," he said then, but she drew a deep breath and shook her head.

"I don't know of anything whatever," she said finally, "or of course I would tell you! Of course I would!"

Seeing that at the moment Grace had no intention of confiding in him, supposing she had anything to confide, Pointer left her to get on with her brother's papers.

But he stepped in for a word with Fraser. Possibly he could, through him, get at what was troubling Miss Avery.

As it happened, the butler met him with very much the same sort of question that Grace had, though couched in different words, and received virtually the same reply.

"We feel sure," Pointer then added, "that there are a lot of apparent trifles which, if we knew of them, might lead to some definite decision. And it's most uncomfortable for every one, as long as we aren't sure of what really did happen to the rector."

"'Uncomfortable,' I don't mind that," Fraser said grimly. "What I mind is the thought of any one murdering the rector and getting away with it. Well, look here, Mr. Chief Inspector, what about—for one trifle—asking Miss Olive what made her listen at the study door twice over on Sunday night as she did. Opened it twice noiselessly as a fly, put a foot in, heard something, and closed it just as silently. Mrs. Richard had just gone to bed, it was gone half-past ten by then. I asked her whether she wanted anything; I thought perhaps she didn't like to disturb the master in the library, and was listening to hear if he was still in there. She jumped as though I had pinched her, and fairly scuttled up the stairs saying something about a book she had wanted but which didn't matter and thanking me for my offer. And Miss Olive isn't one of your thanking sort! Her face, too, looked as though I had given her a rare fright. Funny little trifle that, ain't it, sir? I went off to bed then, but I've wondered—since—what she really was after."

"Did you hear anything from inside the room?" Pointer asked.

"Just the rector walking up and down his study very slowly as though deep in thought."

"I suppose he would often do that?"

"Never knew him to do it before, sir. In the library, yes, now and then. But I never heard him do it before in the study—when alone. No, I never heard him do it there."

"And you think that Miss Olive?"

"I don't know what to think, sir, and that's a fact. It was her air—her manner—that was so odd. Keyed-up and—well—I should call it desperate."

Further questions added nothing to this account.

"And then, there's one more trifle, sir, about another lady altogether. The gardener says that he saw Mrs. Green closing our main gate very carefully behind her latish on Sunday night. About eleven he puts the time at. Mrs. Green has never called here. If she came to the house it was the first time. Higgins always goes home past the front gate."

Fraser was wanted and Pointer stood reflecting on what he had just heard. Miss Hill at the study door . . . Mrs. Green seen leaving the rectory garden... Any collusion between the two women seemed unlikely. But you never knew... He turned.

Olive Hill was coming down the stairs with some letters in her hand.

He had his note-book out, and seemed to be entering some detail.

"Oh, Miss Hill," he turned as though glad to see her. "I'm filling in Sunday night's time-table. Mrs. Richard Avery left the study around half-past ten, you were seen at the study door afterwards going—"

"No," she said instantly, "certainly not! Or I would have told you. I wanted a book from the shelves. But the rector was there, and I didn't like to disturb him. So after I tried twice and heard him moving about each time, I gave it up as a bad job."

Pointer thanked her, wrote in the details as given by her, and went on out again. Round by the side door Grace still sat in front of a garden table. But she was not looking at papers. Her head leaning on one hand, a characteristic pose, she was idly rolling a pencil along the table edge.

She looked up. "About trifles"—she began—"you ought to ask Mrs. Richard, when she comes back, whose voice it was that she heard speaking to the rector close on midnight."

Mrs. Richard Avery was out at the moment.

Pointer did not remind her that Doris had said that she had heard no voice but the rector's own.

"You think she recognised the voice?"

"I do," Grace said firmly. "But I think she counted on the person she heard coming forward and telling you about it herself."

CHAPTER TWELVE

Pointer decided to try that night for the pieces of the orange china jar which he thought might have been broken by the dying rector, and buried by his murderer. Meanwhile, he lit a pipe and went for a brisk walk. That an extremely valuable stamp was in the envelope given by Revell to the rector, was of course possible, and if so, could not be disregarded as a possible motive for Revell's, and for the rector's murder. He ran again over the names of those who had, according to Fraser, seen the stamps and the list. He had had a word with Byrd about them, and the man had seemed quite at his ease as he said that, even if missing, they were of no value except to some one beginning a collection.

But Pointer was not satisfied with the stamp theory, though it could not be disregarded. He wanted something that would explain the return of Revell to his home, and his own death that night, and then another murder—that of the rector after an interval of four weeks. And which would explain also the folded paper, or rather, the sermon which Mr. Avery had preached after seeing the paper. Leaving stamps entirely alone for the moment, what other line of reasoning was there that might lead to the right answer?

Jealousy? Was that the answer to the death of Revell and was some discovery of the identity of the murderer the reason for the rector's death and the accompanying oddities? Sir Hubert Witson was a jealous man from the look of him . . . there was gossip about his wife and Revell . . . she had called out Revell's name during the quarrel which was apparently the real cause of the rector's visit to The Towers last Saturday night. . . .

Something like a cold flame was burning in Pointer's mind. Clear and shining it illuminated whatever he placed before it. A jealous man—but would a jealous man summon Revell home, back to his own neighbourhood? Hardly. But the woman might. If frightened. Or if desirous of a last exercise of power. Certainly a summons from her—a letter from her—something made the flame leap a little higher. A letter written to Revell and found by the rector? But after four weeks? And then the flame played on Revell's car used by the rector for the first time late on Saturday. What about a letter written to Revell summoning him home most urgently, dropped by him in the car, no, rather, folded by him, which had inadvertently slipped down between two cushions? Pointer saw the rector dropping his matches—or spectacles—groping for them—picking them up, and the folded paper as well, putting the latter in the pocket out of which he thought that it had fallen, the pocket where he carried his notes for his sermon. He saw Mr. Avery when he got home, laying the folded paper in his Bible, opening it out next morning in the pulpit, recognising the writing, reading some damnable words which would be to him like a flash of lightning showing a terrible landscape. Yes, a letter then—written by a woman, not by a man. But not necessarily by Lady Witson. There were other women whose names had been linked with Revell's, and if it was true that Revell had not let Olive know of his return, was it not likely that her name had been used as a bait? The flame was shining very clearly now. Or was it Olive herself? A dreadful sequence would follow this, if a fact. . . . And it was possible, except that she seemed to gain nothing but, on the contrary, to lose so immensely by Revell's death. But Shilling's man had heard her say to Byrd in a frantic whisper that she had never intended to marry Revell. The man had missed much of the talk between the two, but, those words had reached him. If that were really so then Olive might not have lost anything she valued. . . . But to commit a murder there must be a tremendous incentive, an overwhelming gratification of some passion of hate or jealousy or revenge or greed. The flame failed to light on any such motive in Olive Hill, according to the facts as known so far. But it was just after her engagement to Revell that he died—just when, in other words, another woman would have learnt that he was lost to her. Fury and revenge. . . And what if that other woman had used Olive as a screen? Here the flame played on the sermon as though it were print, and certain passages stood out clearer than others. Some one was to come forward—some one was to speak up—the rector would not, Pointer thought, have the criminal in his mind's eye, but an appeal to the writer of a letter summoning Revell to a midnight meeting would fit the sermon. A letter in which, moreover, it had been made to appear without giving any name, as though some one, other than the writer wanted to speak to Revell.

Yes, that would fit. And Olive, as that "some one" would fit too, for Revell would have hastened back for her—to her. She had not lunched or dined at the rectory on Sunday, but gone for a long walk immediately after church, doing without lunch, according to her own statement, and taking tea at a verified place quite four hours' walk away.She had come back about a quarter to nine, and had refused any dinner. Had Olive been named directly in the letter. Pointer believed that the rector would have wanted to see her at once. Apparently he had not done so. From all his actions on Sunday it looked to Pointer as though Mr. Avery had received some message from the writer of the letter putting off the crucial moment of discussion very likely till the next day—Monday. Of the three women in the household, any of them could have stepped in for long enough to do this. Outside of the rectory, of the women who interested Pointer, Lady Witson, Mrs. Green and Miss Gartside could all have had the opportunity, for the rector was out all afternoon.

When it was dusk, Pointer had a careful look at the little stretch of shrubs and periwinkle in question, and when it was quite dark he strapped his torch on his head and began to use the little garden fork lying on the table near the gas-ring. He found what he was after almost at once. Piece by piece he laid the orange tinted china fragments out on to his newspaper. He dug on with added care, for there was the possibility of finding a buried envelope of stamps. For if jealousy was the motive that had killed Revell, and the rector had died lest he should give the murderer up, and if Avery had smashed the jar in an effort to break the window, then the stamps, like the jar, might stand for absolutely nothing in the puzzle, and might really have been, as Byrd had declared them to be, absolutely valueless.

He found no stamps. He was not to learn so soon and so easily whether they stood for anything in the affair or not. Levelling, and lightly smoothing over the soil, replacing the leaves and twigs as he had found them, Pointer slipped out of the garden with a package of broken china under his arm.

Back in his room, he lit his pipe, and gazed out at the stars. There was one person . . . but he stopped himself, and instead of indulging in sheer imagination went back in his mind to what he knew about the death of Anthony Revell. He wished he had been able to see the drawing-room and the body at the time. He decided to go quickly over all the rooms at The Causeway to-morrow morning so as to have a clear idea of the house in his mind, and of what the cellars were like, for though the possibility of hidden treasure was, he thought, very remote, yet it did exist.

The Causeway in conjunction with Anthony Revell led him to think of Mrs. Green. He saw again her face as the rector preached. As with Olive, so with her, he had noted its growing pallor—the look of something like fear in the eyes that never left Mr. Avery's face. Had she gone to the rectory on Sunday night? And if so, more than once?

Immediately after his breakfast, he interviewed Higgins, the gardener, who was quite certain that the lady whom he had seen closing the rectory gate was the artist. Pointer now learned that Higgins had been the gardener at The Flagstaff and had only lost that place when Anthony Revell died.

"The rector's gardener had left to join his son in South Africa," Higgins continued—" and many's the time he'll wish himself back, in my opinion—But it left the place open. And so Mr. Avery, when he heard that I had just got married on the strength of my good wages with Mr. Revell, he offered me the place, and didn't I jump at it too! There's a cottage as goes with it, and the rector he looked after his people he did." Higgins pulled himself up with an effort.

"And where are you going now?" Pointer asked.

"I've asked Mrs. Green to take me on again if she buys The Causeway, as they say she may. If I'd a known that she was a-going to be my next mistress, I don't say as I should have come forward, though there's no harm in a lady leaving the rectory garden on Sunday night."

Pointer agreed and asked him about the incident. Higgins seemed unable to add anything to what Fraser had repeated. Walking home around twentypast eleven, he had passed the rectory, when he had heard the familiar click of its gate, and turning had seen Mrs. Green closing it. She had not appeared to see him but had walked rapidly away in the opposite direction—towards the cottage which she had taken furnished.

"I suppose you've heard, sir," Higgins said as though to change the subject, "that the tombstone for Mr. Anthony's grave has come, and they're setting it up? Don't know whether I likes it or I don't. I'm to supply the flowers though. Mrs. Green's work it is, and she is to have the say about what flowers are to go with it. She wants turf a-top, with side bands of gentians and cyclamen and a line of mountain violas at the foot."

Pointer was not interested in the flowers, but he was in the fact that the artist, whose name was so often in his own mind, because so often mentioned in connection with the dead young man's, had designed the tombstone. Under certain circumstances, it might be a macabre touch.

He went on to the churchyard, which was quite close.

The gravedigger and a couple of stonemasons were just smoothing over the earth. Their task was finished A white stone monument stood at the head of the latest grave in the Revell's plot of ground. It represented a high gate of white marble standing ajar, of very fine work, and of singularly effective proportions.

"But I don't like his name just scratched on that bit of a ticket as it were," said the sexton, who had lingered for a final look. "Just that bit of a block where the hasp of the gate comes—seems poor like to me—like a *Wet Paint* or *Beware of the Dog* sign. Though I don't doubt as it's high and fine art."

He hobbled off for the public-house.

Pointer bent down and read the inscription, which was in small lettering on a little square of marble apparently swinging from the middle of the gate. The lettering set forth that here lay the body of Anthony Hibbart Charlton Revell. Armiger. Born in such a year and died in such a year. With below, in very small characters, on one line, a text from the seventy-fifth psalm ' *For in the hand of the Lord there is a cup and the wine is red.*'

For a long time Pointer stood looking at the inconspicuously placed text. It was a strange one.

He turned away, and made for the cottage where Mrs. Green now lived. He had seen it many times set in a charming, quickly made garden which had been a neglected tangle of grass before she took it over. Now chimney bellflowers bordered the walk up to the house.

They were only tall green tufts at the moment, but golden and flame-coloured snapdragons with an edge of purple stocks ran in waves of splendid colour in front of them.

. . . A riot of Canterbury Bells, single and double, rose, blue, lavender, and ' white, swung at the end of the garden.

One would say that a merry heart lived here. But when Mrs. Green opened the door to him, she looked as though the garden and everything in it were but dust and ashes. If a criminal, she was already beginning to reap the first fruits of the punishment which none escapes.

She showed no surprise at seeing him, but asked him in as though he were a regular visitor. He mentioned that he had just been to the churchyard and seen the tombstone put up to the memory of Mr. Anthony Revell. A very striking work of art he thought it. But he owned, he said, that the text chosen by the family puzzled him.

"I chose it," she replied negligently. "I wanted something short and not too smug. I thought it sounded comforting."

Pointer permitted himself to look surprised.

"Don't you think that a cup of good red wine is comforting?" she asked and she showed her teeth in a smile that was like a menace.

"But the text doesn't say that it is a cup of good wine," he replied stolidly, "and the context hardly suggests comfort."

"A Bible reader?" she asked, with what he felt to be an effort at levity.

Pointer somewhat stiffly said that he was.

"Really? I'm not. I just opened a Bible at a venture, and my eye fell on a sentence that would do. The Revells haven't complained. It'll pass muster."

There was a short silence. Pointer wondered, as he had when he first caught sight of it, whether the text referred to Anthony Revell himself, which would mean that the fate that had befallen him was the red wine in the cup. Or whether the text was to be read as a warning to the undiscovered murderer. Either reading might be right. And her way of answering, would do equally for either. For that the words had been chosen with a fierce exactitude to meet some as yet unrevealed position, he was certain.

He next asked her for what purpose she had called on the rector yesterday, mentioning that she had been seen and recognised, when leaving the garden.

She fingered a light net curtain.

"I had got as far as the front steps—nearly—she said now soberly, "when I decided to think it over. You see, I had been told that you can always say to-morrow what you haven't said to-day, but that you can never unsay to-morrow, what you have said to-day. It's not true. For I can never tell him now."

"Tell him what, Mrs. Green?" Pointer asked bluntly.

"That Anthony Revell came back late that Thursday night because of a message from Olive Hill asking him to meet her there on a very urgent matter." Mrs. Green went on to explain that, thinking The Causeway to be shut up, she had yielded to a sudden whim on that same evening to paint it by the moonlight which chanced to be amazingly bright. She was making a swift sketch when she heard steps on the gravel and saw Anthony coming quickly up to the front door. On her calling to him, and suggesting that she come in with him and that they have supper together before she should return to The Flagstaff, he had told her that that would be quite impossible as he had hurried back in order to have a very private and urgent word with some one. She had instantly named Olive Hill, and he had not denied it, though he had insisted on her keeping what she had stumbled on to herself. She had left on that.

"And why did you not tell the police of this when they were inquiring into Mr. Revell's death?" he asked her gravely.

"It wasn't a real inquiry," she said evasively. "They were certain that it was an accident."

"And you're not?"

"No. Not at all certain," she said in a curiously strangled voice. Looking at her he saw the tremendous effort it was costing her to say as much. It was disturbing. The Chief Inspector was rarely wrong in his mental labels, and he did not think that it was love that was the reason for the strain under which she was labouring. It was rather that of an accomplice who had keyed himself up to tell a part of some crime which, if fully known, would be his own ruin too. He waited, not daring to speak. One incautious word on his part might seal up lips that were half hesitant, half determined to speak. He would not even look at her, but played with his gloves, he who never fidgeted.

But when she kept silence he said very quietly, "And why did you intend to tell the rector?"

Her eyes leapt for a flash to his, and then fell away abruptly. He felt the struggle in her. And knew it as fear for herself pulling against a desire to let herself go, let out something bitter, vengeful, or perhaps merely just. Again he waited in a tense silence, his eyes on his shoes.

"I'll tell you," came in a sort of croak from her as she swung far forward in her chair. "Yes, I'll tell you." There was once more that note of caution struggling with deep passion. "The rector preached a sermon yesterday. It showed—" She stopped. He had to fairly hold himself in his seat in an attitude of polite interest. "It showed that in some way he knew that Olive Hill had been to The Causeway. How I can't imagine, but he knew! He knew too that some one else in the congregation was aware of this. He was right. I was. His sermon was spoken to me. To me!" Quite unconsciously she rose and stood, one hand pressed to her breast, one clenching and unclenching at her side in a very extremity of fear. Something long pent-up was rushing to get out, but her instinct of self-preservation was holding it back. Why? It was a most important query. "That was why I went to the rectory yesterday evening," she said, now drawing a deep breath.

And Pointer did not believe her. She had gone—yes—perhaps in response to the sermon—perhaps stirred by it in quite another way than she was representing. It might be true that she had not gone into the house, but if so that was because the same fear of consequences to herself that was in her at this moment had last night stopped her feet when nearly on the threshold of the rectory, had turned them round, and led them away. From danger?

"I meant to tell him that he was right, that I had known about Olive's letter to Anthony. But I decided to wait—and now I can't ask him what he knew, and what I had better do, so I have decided to be frank with you."

Pointer thanked her without irony.

"We are very interested in Mr. Revell's death," he went on slowly with an apparently casual glance, "because, for certain reasons we are inclined to link up his death with the rector's."

"Ah!" she said in a quick gasp, "I was afraid of that—that—dreadful possibility! You think he taxed her with it—to her face—and that—" She stopped as though there were no need to finish. As indeed there was not.

"We think he may have come on some evidence which looked as though Mr. Revell's death was not an accident, and that he was silenced to prevent him following up the trail, or to prevent him insisting on the guilty person going with the truth to the police."

"He would have done just that. He would have insisted on the truth being told, come what may!" she said fiercely.

"You knew him well?" Pointer was aware that, on the contrary, Mrs. Green had rarely met the rector. Apparently she had carefully avoided him.

"I know the type well. My—" She broke off abruptly.

"But I confess I find it difficult to imagine any reason why Miss Hill should have shot Mr. Revell," Pointer said. "That is what you're suggesting, isn't it?"

"I know she did shoot him," Mrs. Green said between set teeth. "As to a reason—there must be one, of course. I wondered whether he had found out something about her—about her past, and that she was wild at the idea of it becoming known—"

"As far as is known, her past is quite ordinary," Pointer replied.

"But perhaps not as far as Anthony knew it—at the last," Mrs. Green now said. "I have no idea of what he learnt about her, but I feel as certain that she killed him as I do that I am sitting here."

"Well, leaving a possible connection between the two deaths on one side, we had already decided that the probabilities were that Mr. Revell was summoned home by some one who had the right to summon him. Or, to put it better, whose summons he would not disregard, whether from fear of the consequences, or from affection. Now, about the exact words in which Mr. Revell spoke of having heard from Miss Hill—"

Pointer was not satisfied with the result of his questions. It panned out to a very indefinite mass of what she understood Anthony Revell to have said, rather than what she could repeat clearly and definitely. His way— the police way—of leaving a subject and then returning to it under another guise, tripped her up constantly. She did not twice repeat Revell's words alike. He asked her finally why this was, and she said, with an effect of frankness, that she herself had been under a good deal of emotion at the unexpected meeting. She had parted from Anthony Revell in some heat when she had left The Causeway, and in the unexpected pleasure of seeing him so soon again, she had not remembered their talk word for word.

It was a very possible explanation, but it hampered him none the less. It reduced her certainty that Olive Hill came to The Causeway to a belief—possibly—that she was coming, and that she was the reason for Anthony's return.

Pointer drew out his pocket diary and turned its leaves for a moment.

"The trouble is," he now said gravely, "that your whole evidence is of no value, because of one initial misstatement. A fundamental one."

Her face, against her will, against her best efforts to the contrary, turned a livid white. "What do you mean?" she asked haughtily with lips that were stiff.

"You say the moonlight was so bright that you decided to sketch the house, and that that was why you were still there at midnight. But there was no moon whatever on the Thursday night in question."

She stared out of the window at the garden which she had made such a mockery of brightness and gaiety.

Then she sighed wearily, and it was a curious sigh. It was quite unconscious, he believed, and it was—unexpectedly—that of a woman putting on a cloak of which she was heartily weary, or taking up again a burden which she thought that she had laid down for good. It interested the Chief Inspector.

"I see," she said dully. "I wouldn't make a good criminal, I'm too careless. Well, the truth is that I went to The Causeway for sentimental reasons—entirely. I thought I should have it all to myself."

"So you were in the house when you met Mr. Revell? Not outside in the garden?"

"I was on my way home when I met Mr. Revell."

"A very lonely road for a lady to be out in at midnight," Pointer said to that. And a sudden spark seemed to leap up in his mind. That revolver taken by Anthony Revell from his bedroom drawer—Pointer had already thought it possible that Revell had fetched it to lend to some one—a lady probably—who was nervous, or who had said that she was—of walking a very lonely stretch alone. And there was another small point that did not disagree with this idea. Pointer knew the full height of Revell, and his sitting height to an inch. He was a little too tall for a woman to have fixed the shot in any usual position. But the flight of the bullet had been too level to have been fired even by a woman if she had been

standing, and Revell sitting. Shilling had thought that
Revell might have been bending down over something on
the table—and if his murderer were a good shot, used to
quick revolver shooting, that was possible. But if a lady—
if the weapon had been brought out for her to take with
her in her return walk . . . Pointer wondered if Revell had
been doing something for her—tying her shoe-string—for
instance? That would have brought his head to just the
right height, and would have given a woman time to lift
the revolver, put it to his ear, and pull the trigger. For
Revell's eyes and hands would—in such a case—have
been occupied with his task. Mrs. Green wore very smart
little tie shoes he noticed, so did most of the other women
around. But Olive Hill, so far as Pointer had seen her,
only wore court shoes.

"Did Mr. Revell offer to let you have his revolver for
the way back?" he asked her next.

"I never thought of that!" she said with dilated pupils,
and seemed to shrivel where she sat in her chair. Then
she looked up.

"I've wondered how it happened. He never kept the
revolver downstairs. And it's quite unlike him to have
lain in wait for a housebreaker with a revolver. Even to
threaten him. His way would have been to lock
everything up carefully and then go to bed. I never
thought of his lending it to—the person who shot him."

Pointer said nothing for a moment. The person who
had shot Anthony Revell might be talking to him. For
that she was on very thin ice and knew it was still
apparent to him. She now showed so white and weak, so
drained by the emotions that warred in her, that he had
to leave. She could barely open the door for him, and as
he turned round at the gate, he saw her holding on to the
lintel. He thought that she made a half-start after him,
but if so, she checked herself and managed to turn her
movement into a faint wave of her hand.

CHAPTER THIRTEEN

Pointer walked away through a very pretty woodside, and for once he, who knew the sound of every bird in every season, heard nothing of the thrush in the thicket, nor the skylark far overhead. All that he had been told by Mrs. Green suggested a murder in which valuable stamps had no part. A murder caused by passions that have swept the world long before stamps were in use, passions that had raged in the caves of the troglodytes.

It rather looked as though Mrs. Green had been the murderer. There was a woman—not the artist —one of whose actions had seemed to Pointer to indicate her as very possibly the double murderess, but he never let a mere opinion influence his judgment. From what he had heard of her infatuation for Anthony Revell, from what she had now told him, Mrs. Green must be very suspect.

Whether guilty or not, she was trying to throw suspicion on Olive Hill. Not very cleverly. But then Pointer did not consider Mrs. Green a clever woman. She had not even made out a case for the visit of Olive Hill to The Causeway on that fatal Thursday night. He said as much to the Chief Constable and Shilling at the police station.

"If Byrd were the murderer," Weir-Opie commented, then Miss Hill was there, and Mrs. Green was only the first of three visitors that Revell had that night."

"And of course Miss Hill herself is out of the running, because of what she stood to lose." Shilling was glad that she was out of it. He was a romantic soul. "Even if stamps were at the bottom of the two murders—and I still think them a very promising trail—even so, Revell's fortune was eighty thousand pounds, not to speak of The Causeway. No stamps would bring her in that much."

"Of course if it were Byrd," went on Weir-Opie, who was just getting under way—"say the revolver was taken for the reason that Shilling first maintained at the inquest, but no housebreaker shows up, and Miss Hill arrives. The revolver lies forgotten on a side-table. Byrd comes in—she would have had to pass his cottage to go from the rectory to The Causeway—"

"Which means pass under his bedroom window," Shilling threw in.

Weir-Opie nodded. "Just so. He follows her. She gets away. Byrd shoots Revell in a passion of fury. Humph." The Major seemed to hold his sketch up at arm's length and look at it, with growing doubts. "Don't think much of that idea," he said at last.

"Byrd has never lost his head, his long narrow head, over Miss Hill, in my opinion. He isn't the type," muttered Shilling.

"What do you say, Pointer?" asked Weir-Opie.

"One of my objections to him is that he seemed to like the rector's sermon," was the quaint reply. "He looked for all the world like the chairman of a debating society listening to a really good piece of special pleading—when he wasn't staring at Miss Hill, and with anything but a lover's eye."

"Do you think Olive Hill turned up at The Causeway, found Revell dead and didn't dare give the alarm because of not wanting it to be known that she was there at that hour of the night?" asked the Major.

"I doubt it," Pointer said slowly. "A genuine appointment would have very much cramped the real murderer, who, according to Mrs. Green, would have been told by Revell that his fiancee was coming. And a murderer likes to have plenty of time for unforeseen emergencies."

"Unless he has an elaborate alibi and is working to schedule," put in Shilling.

"But if it had been intended to ask for the loan of a revolver, ample time would have been a necessity," the

Chief Inspector pointed out. "The murderer could not time the offer and the production of the weapon to a minute."

"True. If Miss Hill were expected, minutes would count." Weir-Opie lit his pipe. "She might have arrived before her time. As you say, a thought to rattle the best of murderers! So you think?"

"On the whole it looks to me, sir, as though Revell had been summoned home by a spurious message, a false appointment with Miss Hill. And if, as it seems likely, the trap had been baited by the murderer with her name, he, or she, would have known that they had the rest of the night before them."

"He or she," repeated Weir-Opie, "which, I wonder?"

"If a man," Shilling put in, "it would boil down to two, wouldn't it—Byrd, and Sir Hubert Witson."

"You're forgetting Gilbert Revell, aren't you?" Pointer asked. "I grant he's in a place apart, because, though he stands to benefit most by Anthony Revell's death, men rarely murder their elder brothers, however much to their financial advantage it may be."

"Nor does he look the part?" Weir-Opie said. "You saw him on Sunday."

"I grant you he doesn't, sir."

"Which theoretically means nothing at all, as we all know," Weir-Opie said sarcastically, "but which, in point of fact, means a lot more than opportunity and profit and all the rest of it."

They then passed on to Byrd and Sir Hubert with the stamps as a motive, or with jealousy as a second possible motive.

Mrs. Green sat awhile at the open window trying to steady her nerves after Pointer had left her. She had not blundered, she felt sure. She had not let slip any word which might have been fatal. But the effort at caution which he had discerned had left her spent, and after a little she put on her hat and walked down to Anthony's grave. She stood looking at her own design for a full minute, murmuring under her breath between her clenched teeth: "And the wine is poured out and has to be drunk." For a second she bent lower, as though she would have liked to throw herself down full length on that narrow stretch of earth. But she straightened up, and turning away with a look in her eyes that made the sexton say to a young gravedigger with him, "The right flower for that grave would be Love lies bleeding. Why, these days, with her grieving, she looks older than her ladyship."

Mrs. Green walked on aimlessly for a while. Then at a cross-road, she turned and looked over at the chimneys of The Causeway.

She had decided to buy the place if only to have the right to keep Olive Hill from wandering over it at will. She walked on. Ahead of her, she caught sight of a tall graceful figure. Only one woman around here moved with that mixture of ease and vigour.She quickened her steps. In a way, she could have wished it had been any one but Mrs. Avery, for the happiness that had radiated from Doris of late was hard to bear, when you knew that never would that look shine in your own eyes again, or flush your cheek any more. Otherwise, besides being attracted by her beauty, Mrs. Green liked Doris, her wide, intelligent brow, her calm dignified air, and if her manner was a shade overbearing, her infrequent smile was enchanting. Doris Avery, Mrs. Green thought, was a woman born to make herself felt—unlike Grace Avery. Given a wider sphere, as now seemed likely from the tales about her husband's altered fortunes, and Doris might make a name for herself.

As she hurried forward to catch her up, Mrs. Green saw Grace Avery also turning into the lane. Mrs. Green decided to give the two sisters-in-law time to exchange their own private news, and then she would have a word with them both, for what she wanted to say was for the two of them. As she watched them walking on ahead, she thought how little she knew the dead rector's sister. As a rule, Mrs. Green summed people up very quickly and, if not always accurately, at least clearly. But she felt by no means certain that she had yet met the real Grace Avery. The very pleasant, quiet, wellread, well-bred outside might extend all the way, or it might not. She could not tell.

She had heard that at one time Anthony was supposed to have been very much attracted to Grace, but personally she had never heard him mention her. Grace, she noticed, had a slower step than Doris, but she covered the ground as quickly. Her fair head with its closely trimmed hair was held as erect as her sister-in-law's. Some people complained of her unresponsiveness, but she had intelligent eyes, grey and clear, and very firm lips. Even her brother's death seemed to have left no trace on her composed, fair face as she turned it now and then to Doris. Mrs. Green thought that in looks she was very like the rector, but that she lacked his charm.

She called to the two women and, turning, they waited for her to come up.

She wasted no time in greetings or small talk.

"The police now believe that Anthony was murdered, and that there is a connection between his death and that of the rector," she blurted out in a fierce voice.

Doris and Grace stared at her appalled.

"Connection? Anthony and the rector? What in the world has happened?" Doris demanded, as Grace looked too horrified to speak.

"Mr. Pointer thinks that the rector learnt of something about Anthony's death, and that that was why he was poisoned."

There followed a pause of absolute consternation. All three women were very pale.

"Was *that* what he meant by Sunday's sermon?" Grace asked under her breath. "That splendid but very searching sermon?"

The last vestiges of colour faded from Mrs. Green's face. She looked suddenly old and broken, and something of the fear which Pointer had read into her gaze came back to her eyes. It was as though, defenceless, she looked at some danger coming towards her.

"John's sermon?" Doris asked now in an utterly bewildered tone. "What on earth have sermons to do with this? This is awful!"

"So was John's sermon—to the guilty," Grace said with conviction.

"It's nothing to do with any sermon," Mrs. Green said shortly. "There's something I told the police that I must tell you both. That's why I caught up with you. Anthony came back to The Causeway that Thursday because of a letter from Olive Hill. She had written him that she had something very urgent to say to him. She had an interview with him there—that night."

Grace jumped. Doris looked as though the fence beside them had hit her in the eye. Then she slowly turned to Mrs. Green with a very critical look on her face. "Forgive my plain speaking, but is this your imagination? You're a bitter enemy of Olive's, we all know. Or have you some private information?"

Mrs. Green told her what she had told the Chief Inspector, and Doris's questions were almost as much to the point as those of the Chief Inspector had been. Mrs. Green answered them as fully.

"I've said nothing about it except to Mr. Pointer," she added, "and I shan't speak of it to any one else. But as things are, you and Miss Avery ought to know—what the police think—where they are looking for the criminal— the double criminal. For they think Mr. Avery found Miss Hill's letter, and because he found it—"

"Oh, impossible!" came from both her hearers in tones of sheer horror.

"He may have learned what I have all along thought was possible, that Olive had a talk with Anthony that night," Grace suggested. Slow in action, she was often far too impulsive in her speech. The opposite of Doris, who could be impulsive enough in action, yet who rarely spoke without due thought. "And that she told Anthony that she didn't love him. Anthony, in the shock of learning that, might have shot himself. But that's a very different notion from this ghastly idea of the police."

"Your idea is nonsense," Mrs. Green spoke quite vehemently. "She ran after him. She stalked him as though she were a hunter, and he a chamois."

"That's quite a mistaken notion of yours," Doris now said coldly, "as I happen to know. Anthony was desperately in love with Olive. Long before she would look at him, he used to rave about her to me. Not a word of these ideas about Olive must get about, Mrs. Green, as you yourself realise. She may have gone to see Anthony that Thursday night, and been foolish enough to say nothing about it, but as for her having shot him—or having harmed my brother-in-law. That's absolutely and utterly out of the question! It really sounds—mad —to me."

Doris's eye was a very clear warning to the artist as to what position she, Mrs. Richard Avery, and Miss Avery would take in the matter. And with that, they took a very frigid leave of Mrs. Green.

"That's a very dangerous woman," Doris said slowly, as the sisters-in-law walked on together. "She means mischief. She's out for Olive's blood. Mark my words."

Grace hardly heard her. White-faced, she was almost stumbling. Doris noticing this, drew her to a stile near them, and the two sat down for a moment.

"What awful thing has come to us?" Grace asked, her eyes wild. "I could have married, more than once, Doris, and I wouldn't, because I hate emotion. I hate to be stirred to the depths. And now here is this awful thing that has us in its grip. Anthony supposed to have been murdered! And John, dearest John, to have been murdered because of it! And we in the midst of it—"

There fell a short silence.

"You know," Doris said suddenly, "the idea that Olive shot Anthony is ridiculous. I don't believe the police think that for a moment. Mrs. Green would like them to, no doubt. Anthony was a windfall for Olive such as she could never hope for again. Of course she didn't kill him—and of course he wasn't shot—except accidentally by himself—poor man."

"If they don't think she shot him and, as you say, she had no motive whatever to, then—according to this awful idea Mrs. Green told us about, of their believing that there is a link between his death and John's—they can't suspect her of killing John either." Grace was groping from impossible nightmare horrors to the comparatively bearable.

"Of course they don't," Doris said in a tone of finality. "Though between ourselves, Grace, I think she may have written to Anthony to meet her on Thursday for a private talk. That much of Mrs. Green's tale I believe. Chiefly because of something John said to me while I was looking up those references for him. Something about a letter he had found and burnt—and about Olive, and Anthony, and The Causeway. He said he wanted a talk with her the first thing Monday morning. He asked whether I thought her, as he did, the kind to do better when given ample time for reflection. I agreed with him, though at the time I hadn't an idea what it was all about. I can't give you the exact words that he said, partly I was busy hunting for a footnote, partly I had come in with a letter from Dick that I wanted to show him, partly too, I think that Jack was rather obscure himself."

"Do you think it was her to whom he talked later that night, for I've always had an idea you recognised two voices? Not just his alone." Grace looked apologetically at Doris. "As a matter of fact, I as good as told Mr. Pointer that you might add something to what you had told him about that, when he pressed me for further details."

Doris looked anything but pleased at having her hand forced.

"Yes, I did hear some one besides John," she finally said. "Don't ask me whom just yet. I'll tell you later. Now about Olive. I don't think she ought to leave the rectory as things are. Not at once."

"But—do you really want her as your secretary?" asked Grace.

"Richard doesn't," Doris confessed under her breath, "but having taken Olive on, it would be brutal—just now, to send her away. It would mean throwing her to the dogs. As long as we stand by her, people won't readily believe anything dreadful. But I think we must know more. I'm going to have a talk with her as soon as I see her."

"Perhaps you're right," Grace said after a pause, "you often are."

"Not about her engagement to Anthony meaning happiness for them both," Doris spoke sombrely. "Oh, Grace, if only the calendar could be put back by two months or so! But now, about Olive's leaving the rectory—we know that she didn't have anything to do with either death, no matter what Mrs. Green says. And we agree that the police can't suspect Olive of doing away with a marvellous *parti*. It's very possible that she had nothing to do with Anthony's return to The Causeway. Shall we walk on now?"

"A very dreadful thought has struck me"—Grace rose slowly—"but first, I must tell you something about Olive which I kept back." She went on to speak of the losses which she was certain had been connected with the girl.

Doris stiffened. "And you let me take her on?" Her tone spoke volumes.

"It was a frightfully awkward position," Grace said apologetically. "What could I do? Just then, when she had had such a frightful shock? I had no proofs, as the police would say. I could trust you to notice at once if—well—if her pilfering started again. John thought she ought to be given a chance. But what I want to say now is this: If Anthony had ever learnt of her dreadful failing "she stopped, and looked in what seemed dismay at her companion.

"He couldn't have learnt about it, surely, and have shot himself on that account? Or"—she grasped Doris's arm convulsively, her usually calm eyes distended with excitement—"or, it's not possible, is it "—her voice shook—" that Olive thought he was going to let Mr. Byrd know about it and—and—"—she paused—" I think Olive would be capable of anything to keep Mr. Byrd from ever learning—"

"You think?" Doris asked in a low voice, as Grace stopped abruptly.

"The awful thought which has just come to me, is whether Olive, who knew nothing of firearms, might not have, in a fury if she thought there was a possibility of Anthony giving her away to Byrd, picked up the revolver, and had an accident with it."

"And what about John?" Doris asked in her cool, incisive tones. "The police think the two deaths were linked. Do you think Olive had an accident with the toadstool extract, too?"

As Grace looked too appalled to speak, Doris continued:

"I feel sure that there was no connection between the two deaths. All the same, you've suggested the one and only possible reason which might have accounted for Olive, if beside herself—" she did not finish the sentence, and they turned in at the rectory gate.

Doris found Olive in her sitting-room busy replying to letters of condolence. Doris did not glance at them.

"Look here, Olive, my rooms have had everything in the way of get-at-able papers shifted. Now, don't say it's the police, they put them back better. What are you hunting for all over the house?"

There was a fiery and determined look in Doris's eye that matched the tone in her voice.

Olive drew a deep breath. Just then Grace opened the
door, saw the two together, and made as though to step
out again, but Doris asked her to come in and sit down.

"Well?" She turned to Olive peremptorily.

"The hidden treasure," Olive said at last. "You both
laugh at it, and I didn't mean to pry among your papers,
but I'm sure it's in existence in The Causeway, or rather
under The Causeway. I once saw a plan the rector had,
showing how the foundations ran. And then, in an old
book of his, I found some drawings belonging to Anthony's
grandfather, giving as nearly as possible the position of
the treasure. And his drawings fitted the real foundations
marvellously. I told Mr. Avery about it, and he agreed
with me that it was odd. He added that he had another
old paper somewhere, one which Anthony's grandfather
had found, a copy of a really old paper dated around the
middle of the fifteenth century, and said he would look for
it and show it me, since I was interested."

"But you've only been hunting for papers in the
library since John's death," Grace said thoughtfully.

"Because Mr. Avery had promised to look for that
particular paper and show it me."

Grace said nothing, but she gave Olive a very long
look.

"And why should *I* have the paper, or papers?" Doris
asked crisply.

"You and Grace, both of you, took a lot of the rector's
papers to look through," Olive explained.

Doris looked less resentful, she even nodded, as
though acknowledging that as a fair explanation.

Grace slipped away. Doris waited till the door was
shut again.

"I have a very difficult thing to say to you," she said
then. "Mrs. Green tells me that the police are dissatisfied
with the finding about Anthony's death. They think he
was shot intentionally, and she has told them that you
were at The Causeway the night that Anthony died."

"It's not true!" came in a loud, firm voice from Olive. "She would like to say I shot him, I know. I've known from the first that she has only stayed on in the neighbourhood for some such reason. But I wasn't there that night. I knew nothing about his coming to The Causeway!"

"And you didn't write to him to meet you there?"

"Certainly not. As I say, I knew nothing whatever about his coming home that night."

"Then I must believe you. Well, there's nothing for it but to be patient, and endure."

Doris gave a sigh, and went in search of Grace.

"Olive denies absolutely that she was at The Causeway the night that Anthony was shot," she said. "I think she's telling the truth. John must have been mistaken, but it looks as though Mrs. Green had been talking to him that night."

"It does," Grace said. "And now, what do we do?"

"Nothing." Doris spoke firmly. "The thing is too big for me—for us—to meddle with. If Dick were here, I should be guided entirely by what he would wish, but he can't get here for another month at the earliest. I'm afraid of blundering again." Grace had never heard proud, confident Doris avow as much. "I've warned Olive what to expect, and the thing must run its course, but I'm afraid of Mrs. Green. I hope Olive will be careful of herself. The person who killed Anthony is, according to the police, the person who poisoned John. And strictly between ourselves, Grace, I think it looks as though it must have been Mrs. Green herself, for it was her voice that I heard in the study."

CHAPTER FOURTEEN

An hour later Pointer, who was at the rectory in order
to look through some papers, was able to ask Doris about
the voice heard by her in the rectory study last Sunday.
She said at once that it had been that of Mrs. Green. He
asked her why she had not told him sooner. Doris
explained that she was not sure herself until Mrs. Green
had stopped and talked to them to-day. Certain
intonations were so unmistakable that she was now
prepared to swear to her certainty that Mrs. Green had
been in the room beneath her own, talking to her brother-
in-law.

"And there's another thing, Mr. Pointer. That letter
of mine from my husband that you found hidden away
under the lining-paper of one of the drawers in the
library, do you remember?"

Pointer said that he did.

"Any one but Mrs. Green would have known it was
mine, they would have recognised the handwriting. But
Mrs. Green wouldn't know it. Nor know that the rector
never kept anything but religious papers in there."

"By 'any one' you mean Miss Hill?" Pointer asked.

"Well—yes. Miss Hill or any other intimate of the
family."

Pointer too thought, as Doris insisted, that it was far
more logical to suspect Mrs. Green than Miss Hill,
Anthony Revell's fiancee. He did not tell her that Lady
Witson had just startled Shilling by asserting that if the
two deaths were linked, the rector had shot Revell
himself, and then taken poison in remorse.

When she left him, as Olive was out on one of her
long walks, he had another look over some of the books in
the locked study and library. So far, nothing had been

found. And if the criminal had been Mrs. Green, then he did not think that anything would be found, for she was not in the least interested in the rooms of the rectory. If she had poisoned the rector for the sake of the folded paper, then, after hunting wildly and ever more desperately that same night, she had found it and destroyed it. Yet she looked to him like a soul in torment. Not, he thought, because of something done that could never be undone, but from some dread of the future. But she stayed on in the neighbourhood. He had wondered many times why she seemed unable to tear herself away from the place.

"It's my belief," Shilling said, "that she stays in the neighbourhood from devotion to Revell's memory—or remorse," he 'added, pulling at his moustache.

"On the other hand it may really be because she finds the neighbourhood paintable," Weir-Opie objected. "Just as I always thought it spoke for her interest in her paintings at The Causeway rather than in Revell himself, that she turned up there immediately after she heard of his death, not to weep over his body—it hadn't been taken away yet—but to varnish her paintings. They were finished, bar that. Now, that's the craftsman's spirit, rather than the lover's! The room had had all the furniture moved out of it, so it was of no interest to us. She was allowed to lock herself in there, and varnish away. Why lock herself in? Oh, that was on account of wanting no dust made by people moving about."

Pointer walked up to The Causeway which had already acquired the forlorn look of an unoccupied house. Jamieson was polishing the brasses on the door. Pointer had already had several talks with him, none of which had thrown any light on Revell's death. As for the existence of hidden treasure, Jamieson could only say that certainly Mr. Revell had never talked of it, and no unauthorised person had tried to gain an entrance to the house since his death. While of those who had a right to enter, only Miss Hill had asked to be left alone to go where she pleased.

"Had her pleasure ever taken her into the smoking-room where the painted panels are?" Pointer asked.

No, he was told that Miss Hill had never asked him for that particular key. When she had finished the varnishing which had brought her to The Causeway, Mrs. Green had handed the key to Jamieson and asked him to keep the room locked until the varnish should be bone dry.

Pointer had it unlocked now. He looked with interest at the room as he stepped in. It was a large one and quite empty, bare even of a carpet. A shoulder-high panelling ran around it, broken only by the three windows and the big fireplace. Over the latter, an oval painting was inset in the wood. Other paintings were similarly set into all the top panels on the three walls. Each picture only separated from its neighbour by the upright of wood.

"There's work for you!" said Jamieson with respect, "but, of course, she thought it was her own house she was painting. That's sure. Though as I told the Major, there was no goings-on here. She worshipped the ground he walked on, right enough, and she hated Miss Hill worse than cold boiled veal. And fine rows she and the master had over her, but that was all. And if you had seen as much of Mrs. Green as I did, why, you wouldn't expect anything else."

Pointer nodded. He was examining the paintings one by one, taking his time over each. Yes, as he thought. Not one of them had been varnished. Not one!

"Did it take Mrs. Green long to varnish these?" he asked casually.

"All of two hours," Jamieson said. "Which shows that she hadn't lost her head over him as some try to make out. He was lying dead in the drawingroom at the very time."

"Had you seen the paintings before they were varnished?"

Jamieson had not. Mrs. Green kept the door locked when away from the house. "It's my belief that that's why she's buying the house," Jamieson went on, glad to have some one to talk to. "She always steps in for a glance at them whenever she comes. Or rather she did, until she decided to buy the place. Since then, she's just told me to keep the room locked, which I have. Yes," he rambled on, "I've had a word on the quiet that the house is as good as sold to her." Though what a widow lady wanted such an inconvenient barn of a place for, puzzled him. Pointer and he agreed that when it came to sentiment, however, women lost their heads. "Why, even her ladyship won't ever come into the house," Jamieson added, "and to one who knew on what bad terms she and the master were it does seem funny. But she told me herself that she couldn't bear to set foot in it."

Pointer said that he had been told that there had been a talk of offering the place to Miss Hill.

Jamieson sagely said that talk was easy, but when it came to actually signing things people felt differently.

Pointer agreed, and asked if he could keep the key for a little while. Jamieson had no objection, and after half an hour spent in the room by himself, the Chief Inspector locked the door and took the next train up to town.

He had telephoned to a Mr. Joyce before he went.

Mr. Joyce was an artist who owed Pointer more than he could ever repay, and who assured him that he would gladly spare the time for a run down to The Causeway and for a look at some paintings there.

"It's this way, sir," Pointer explained, as he drove him from his home in Richmond, "these paintings were finished, and then put into their places in the wainscoting. Well, I believe that some one, apparently the artist herself, has painted other scenes over them. Here and there she has smeared the woodwork with brush marks. The central painting at the moment represents a break in the clouds and shows a group of pines with heather hills in the background."

"Bonny Scotland?"

"The pines are Arolla pines," Pointer said dubiously.

Each basied himself with his papers until The Causeway was reached. There Pointer led the other at once to the study and unlocking the door, locked it again after them. He had brought some clean rags, and a bottle of spirit and white turps with him. But first of all the artist had a general look about him.

"Clever work, but very swift," was his verdict.

"Any information?"

"Used one palette, and one brush throughout. Mixed no colours. All are as they came from the tubes."

"How long would it take, do you think, Mr. Joyce?"

"Around an hour and a half. Her hand shook a good deal. Does she drink?"

Pointer had not heard that she did.

Then Pointer set to work with rag and bottle, the artist helping him. As they cleared the first inset, the R.A. raised his sandy eyebrows.

"I say! What's this! This is really good, you know. Really good!"

Mr. Joyce went round purring like a cat. Finally, when Pointer had finished cleaning the paint off the last, the centre picture, Joyce stood back and surveyed it and the walls around it. The centre showed now a charming view of an old belfry rising from a sea of green, with grey roofs, a red spire, far-away bits of deep blue water, and a distant line of mountains, one of which was snow covered.

Joyce looked at them all very narrowly. He seemed puzzled.

"An artist painted these all right. That's certain. There's splendid work in every one of them. These weren't painted in two hours! Yet there's no composition here. No design. Wonder why not? Wonder why she chose to paint with such photographic exactness? How can I tell they're exact when I don't know the places?" He smiled at Pointer's question. "Bless you, their accuracy hits you in the eye. She hasn't altered one roof-tile, I'll swear, and why such an artist should have left her foregrounds, and backgrounds, and middle distances like that, is a puzzle. They're not pictures at all! Just magnificently reproduced, unselected masses of objects. And now what?"

Now entered Weston, a local constable, and a very good photographer. He had, at Pointer's request, been at work, taking photographs of each picture on the walls, and had brought them with him enlarged and numbered. Pointer asked him to take most careful pictures of the paintings as they now were—the under paintings, the real pictures. He hoped by studying them to understand the significance of their presence in the study here.

The photographs as a whole, and in detail, taken, Weston hurried away to develop and enlarge the results of his Leica, and Pointer, thanking Mr. Joyce, saw him off back to town. Then he walked over to The Flagstaff with the key of The Causeway smoking-room in his pocket. He asked for Gilbert Revell. Gilbert was not under suspicion at all. He had two authentic alibis for the nights which interested the police, at places far removed from the neighbourhood. He had been away a great deal lately and Pointer had only seen him a couple of times. He had found him as he looked, and as was his reputation—a very simple, unpretentious, rather indolent young man who was retiring from a First Division Clerkship at the Admiralty as soon as it could be arranged.

He wanted to see the world, he said, and was deep in yacht designs when Pointer was shown in.

Pointer asked if he might be allowed one room at The Causeway for the present, in which to keep records of the evidence taken at the time of Anthony Revell's death. If Mr. Revell would allow him the use of, say, the smoking-room and let him keep the key for the present, he, Pointer, would be much obliged.

Gilbert came out instantly from the merits of auxiliary steam engines versus oil engines, and blinked at him.

"I don't understand," he said sharply.

"I can't explain more fully," Pointer said regretfully, "and even this much is in absolute confidence. We're not satisfied about Mr. Avery's death, and some inquiries made at the time of your brother's death look as though they might turn out to be of use to us. If we could keep some of our notes at The Causeway, it would save a great deal of going to and fro."

"Really? Oh, in that case, certainly use the smoking-room for the time being, though I don't know how long the permission can stand, for Mrs. Green is thinking of buying the house—at a ridiculous price it's true, but it's none so easy to sell those sized houses nowadays, so Mr. Smith tells us."

Pointer agreed that it wasn't.

"You don't think—" Gilbert hesitated for a second, then pushed on. "Take one of these cigars, Chief Inspector, I'm awfully glad you've called."

"I hoped to find Mrs. Green here," Pointer said as he thanked his host and took a cigar.

"Mrs. Green? She hasn't been near us for weeks," Gilbert said easily, following suit.

Pointer knew as much, and it had puzzled him. By all accounts Mrs. Green and Lady Revell had been good friends—until the death of Anthony Revell. Though no one but Pointer appeared to have noticed the time when the two women seemed to part, and its possible significance.

"I wanted to ask you if there's any truth in the latest rumour," Gilbert went on, "that you're looking into my brother's death? My mother is quite upset."

"Frankly, Mr. Revell," Pointer said with genuine regret, meeting the young's man's distressed eyes, "we are."

"Good God!" Gilbert's tanned face paled a little. "You don't think—you haven't found anything—I mean, why do you think his death had anything to do with the rector's? They say you do."

"The other way round. We are wondering whether the rector hadn't come on something, a letter we imagine, which threw a new light on Mr. Anthony Revell's death."

"A new light," repeated Gilbert in an appalled voice, "what sort of a new light?"

"We rather think that possibly Mr. Revell returned in answer to a letter," Pointer said, "and was shot, either by the writer or by some one who knew that Mr. Revell would be at his home that night. And we think the rector may have stumbled on the letter itself, or on some piece of writing, which made him think that Mr. Revell had been deliberately killed. We think he showed his knowledge, and was poisoned to prevent his coming to us with the information, possibly with the letter which we think he had found."

Gilbert had let his cigar go out, his face was dead white now.

"What a—" he stopped. "How awful! Good God! And what have you to go on?"

"Precious little," Pointer could have said, "chiefly Mr. Avery's sermon." But he only shook his head and looked very wise.

Gilbert had jumped to his feet, and, his hands thrust deep in the pockets of his plus-fours was walking up and down the rug, keeping to it as though it were bounded by precipices.

"Who told you that we were linking the two deaths?" Pointer asked.

"It's all over the place. But Byrd was the one who actually told me. We were going off on an expedition together. Of course this knocks it on the head."

"Mr. Byrd will have to sail without you?" Pointer suggested easily.

"He won't hear of it. Till this dreadful business is cleared up. My mother has gone to her room. I blurted it out rather too bluntly. She swears you're all wrong. That my brother's death was sheerest accident, as it surely must have been!" But he looked interrogatively at the detective officer who said nothing.

Gilbert again swerved on his rug to avoid the parquet.

"You think it was jealousy?" he asked in a low voice. "Some woman who didn't want him to marry Miss Hill?"

"On the whole we do, but there are alternatives," Pointer said. He did not mind how many people knew about the letter which he believed had decoyed Anthony Revell to his death. A letter which was either still at the rectory, or not in existence any more.

In the former case, except in their own respective rooms, no search went on without an unobtrusive but keen eye being kept on the searcher and the article searched. As for the rest, Pointer wanted all the help that he could get. Anthony Revell might have stopped for petrol nearby, might have let drop a word at the pump which might be of use. Nothing was of greater help in big inquiries than the small items brought in singly and diffidently, which added up to unexpected totals. In Latin countries the police were often misled by imagination playing the part of memory, but not with the English countryside. What they said they had seen or heard, they had. But the stamps which still might be the explanation of the two deaths were quite another matter. Absolute silence about them was still Pointer's order. If a valuable stamp or stamps had played a part in the double tragedy, there would be no chance whatever of finding it or them if the police were even suspected of an interest in philately.

Gilbert stumped up and down his little island, now raging at the credulity of the police who could not bear to have a simple but intelligible accident remain a pure mischance, but must needs see it through official eyes as a horrible crime. After all, he claimed, men threw over girls, even fiancees, every day of the year without being shot for it. "You know what Mrs. Green is saying?" he stopped his short walk to ask. "That Anthony had thought better of his engagement, and wrote and tried to

get out of it. Came back on the Thursday to see Miss Hill
on the Friday, and was shot. She doesn't say by whom. No
need to. Lady Witson said it first, I believe, but Mrs.
Green had adopted it this morning as her idea too, so I'm
told."

"What does Mr. Byrd say about that idea?" Pointer
asked with real interest.

Gilbert looked surprised at the question.

"Byrd? I don't think he's commented on it. He's the
sort who likes to listen more than to take the floor. But as
Miss Hill wants to come with us and try for a fresh life
under fairer opportunities, it seems beastly unfair on her,
to me. She's a gentle sort of little thing who'd be grieved
no end if she had an idea of how poisonous some tongues
are. She was crying the other day when I overtook her
near The Causeway. Her life's blighted enough as it is,
without this cruelty shown to her. I think people ought to
try and make it up to her."

Gilbert spoke warmly, with a flash of honest anger in
his blue eyes.

Pointer nodded with a speculative look at him. Had
Miss Hill cared for the younger brother, rather than for
Byrd, as Shilling thought? It would alter a good deal, if
so. In that case, she would have lost nothing by the death
of the elder brother. Nothing at all. On the contrary.
Something about Gilbert's face suggested that she would
have an unusually generous young man to deal with.

The photographs of Anthony, which was all that
Pointer had to go by, showed a man who might, he
thought, in time have grown to be somewhat of a
domestic tyrant. Possibly his early possession of wealth
had done it, but there were lines around mouth and eyes
that spoke of great self-will, and a disposition to take
sacrifices on the part of those near him for granted, if not
to expect them. Pointer did not think that Anthony Revell
would have made ultra-generous settlements on any
dowerless girl; or indeed have been generous at all in
money matters.

"What we can't find out," he now said confidentially, "is where the rector spent the most of Sunday afternoon. At the rectory they seem to think he spent the time at some almshouses to which he went as usual. But he shortened his customary saying that he would spend an hour on Monday with the old folk to make up for it. It's not the first time he had had to alter his hours, but it was unusual. And as I say, we can't trace the next four hours. He left the rectory at two. He was at the almshouses by a quarter to three, and left there at a quarter past. He got back to the rectory by a quarter past seven. But where he went to in the meanwhile—"

"That's very important, surely?" Gilbert said.

Pointer replied that it might turn out to be so. It would all depend. If he spent it with a brother clergyman, or at the Bishop's Palace, for instance, it might not have much significance.

Gilbert grinned an agreement, and then, thanking him for letting him keep the key of The Causeway smoking-room, Pointer rose to go. But at the door he turned with another question.

"Is Mrs. Green paying the whole purchase price of The Causeway in cash?"

"Yes. That's why we're letting it go for a song. Why?"

"Just wanted to get an idea of her financial standing," he said vaguely, but he drove on to the solicitor's office and was franker.

"There may be nothing in it, but we've struck something rather odd connected with Mrs. Green," he said to old Mr. Smith. "I can't be more explicit till I know more, but I should mark time about the deeds of the house, if I were you."

"Umph," said Mr. Smith dubiously, "I don't know about that, Chief Inspector. Hurry them up, more likely. She hasn't put down any deposit yet. What's sold is sold. 'Money has no smell,'" he quoted. "You're trying to prove that she murdered Anthony Revell, I suppose. Well, Chief Inspector, as the Coroner who sat on the inquest on young Revell, I should think you're wrong, but for your record. What have you got to go on, eh?"

"You'll hear it all in good time, sir. But don't say I didn't warn you off Mrs. Green. You looked up her financial standing, I suppose?"

Mr. Smith shook his polished head on which his hair grew like close-clipped grass on the slopes of a glacis. "Nothing to look up. She's paying in cash—bankers' draft. Good enough, eh?"

"To stop all questions? Quite," Pointer said dryly and hurried away.

Curious how lacking in background Mrs. Green seemed to be. She claimed to be the only child of a Dublin doctor whose wife had died when she was born. She was absolutely without relatives, she said, even her husband's people had quite died out. He was a London solicitor who had died thirty years ago, one year after their marriage. Left a very young widow, she had spent her life chiefly abroad, except for this last year when she had tried to stop in North Ireland, but found the climate too harsh for her.

None of her statements could be proved or disproved. And she was paying cash down for The Causeway, so that that transaction too was of no help in finding out her past.

"Well," Weir-Opie said in some surprise, "it's interesting—very. But what does it prove? Eh?"

"That's the riddle, sir," Pointer said, while Shilling looked very profound.

"Why did she paint all those pictures in the first place, if she was going to paint them all out?" the superintendent asked finally.

"Exactly," Pointer spoke crisply. "Apparently Revell's death turned things that before it had been harmless, into dangerous things, things that must be hidden. Or else the idea was that the police mustn't see the paintings."

"Bad as that?" Shilling asked with a look of shocked interest.

Pointer had to laugh. "Not for any ordinary reason, Shilling. That's the puzzle."

"You think that was why she locked herself into that room at once?" the Major asked.

"I can't read the overpainting in any other way, sir, but that the originals must not be seen."

"But they had been seen." Shilling saw that this was just what the Chief Inspector was maintaining, and stopped himself.

"Exactly, by Mr. Revell's friends. Apparently only the police was the danger."

"She nattered us!" Weir-Opie said sardonically,

"Look here," Shilling's tone was quite excited, they were all dining again with the Chief Constable, and the coffee was on the table, "were the original pictures signs to a gang? A sort of painted cipher? Did they conceal a secret?"

"Clues to The Causeway treasure?" Weir-Opie asked with a smile. "I never heard of its existence before these last days, but every one is asking me about it now, as though its existence were an established fact. Smith rang me up just before dinner to know if that was why you wanted him to go slow over the sale to Mrs. Green. Was that really why?"

"No, sir. Only I thought that in a general way he might find it better to go slow until the facts about the lady were clearer. But if he thinks there's a question of letting a treasure go cheap, he won't need any more warnings."

But were the pictures clues, do you think?" persisted Shilling, adding sagely, "They must have had *some* meaning."

"If they were merely meant as signs, clues, ciphers," Pointers said slowly, "I don't quite see why she took such pains over them. Here are the enlarged photographs of them."

The Chief Constable looked at them with interest, so did Shilling, whose face was more puzzled when he laid them down, than when he took them up. Then he had another suggestion to make. "Perhaps they were painted so well to prevent their being taken away or changed by Revell?"

That was a possibility which had struck Pointer too. "Joyce told me that the colours chosen for these, the originals, were all of them 'unalterable' as he calls them. They won't fade with time or light. And they are painted on metal."

"Of course," Pointer said after an interval, "her absolute change of, shall we call it plan, seems at first sight to exonerate Mrs. Green from any share in Revell's death."

"You mean it caught her out," Shilling said. "It does look that way."

"But it might only mean," Pointer went on to say, "that something unexpected, unforeseen, of which we know nothing, had intervened, which had made the paintings not merely useless but dangerous."

"Dangerous, umph . . ." meditated the Chief Constable.

"I've thought ever since I saw her, ever since the rector's last sermon, that is, that Mrs. Green lives in dread of some one or something. The latter I should say, since she does not seem in the least nervous about living alone in a cottage, but for a gardener near by." Pointer again had a long look at the pictures. "Another funny thing is, that she claims never to have been in Switzerland. I asked her about each country in turn when she said that she had lived on the continent a great deal."

"Well? Why should she have been to Switzerland?" asked Superintendent Shilling, but the Chief Constable's eyes told Pointer that he understood.

"Revell didn't know it," Weir-Opie said now. "He always went to Norway and Sweden for skiing and tobogganing, and to Holland for skating. But I can see why you wondered that Mrs. Green didn't own to knowing Switzerland well. These here"—he pointed with his pipe stem—"are certainly Swiss."

"Just so, sir. Unmistakable Swiss chalets, aren't they. And besides"—Pointer knew the country well. He was a great climber.—"these are Gentians. And here are St. Bruno lilies, and mountain roses and the little wild violas you find everywhere in the summer. And that's glacier water in those brooks. That snow too on the one white-capped mountain is what people call 'eternal,' or I've never trodden it."

"Switzerland," murmured Shilling, eyeing the pictures again. "All of them?"

"Every one."

"If you know the country, can't you make a guess as to the place?" Shilling asked hopefully. 'It ought to be easy," Pointer agreed, "though as a matter of fact I've never seen these particular scenes. Have you, sir?"

Weir-Opie had not.

Pointer said he would take the photographs back with him and study them a bit. Then the talk drifted to other points of this most perplexing case.Pointer learnt that Mrs. Richard Avery had just had a sudden summons to her mother in Tunbridge Wells, who again was reported to be dying.

"Apart from affection, the old lady's said to be quite well off, and not to have made a will yet. So I suppose none of her children care to be away when she asks for them," suggested the Chief Constable.

Doris had notified him of her departure, since she had not been able to get into touch with Pointer.

Then the talk turned to other local matters, and Pointer went back to the rooms that he had at the police station. Seating himself at the table there, he spread out the photographs of the under-paintings and looked carefully at them. He hoped to be able to locate some of the places that they represented. At any rate that of the central panel should be easy to find.

CHAPTER FIFTEEN

The belfry in it rose from what was clearly part of a cathedral. A quaint red spire rose to one side. Old tiled roofs, showing among green trees, sloped unevenly down to a great blue lake far below, a vast lake that spread beyond the picture's limits, with a range of mountains on the other side. Where in Switzerland was there a cathedral town perched high above a big lake with such a range of mountains beyond it?

Geneva was too flat. Besides, in the painting there was only one far-off, tiny, snow-covered tip to be seen, not the whole Mont-Blanc range. Basle has no such lake. Neither has Berne. Zurich runs up to no such heights, has no such mountains facing it. Then he thought of Lausanne. A town where he had never been. A large town—on a lake, the Lake of Geneva—with a cathedral. If so, that one snow mountain could be the extreme tip of Mont Blanc. Early next morning, he dropped in at the offices of the Swiss Federal Railways in town, and satisfied himself that he was right, that that central painting could only stand for the capital of Canton Vaud.

From the railway's guide-books and folders, he even recognised the belfry and the quaint red spire standing to one side on a lower level as that of the Church of Saint Francois.

Why was Lausanne chosen for the largest painting? Why had it and, according to Joyce, all the other paintings too been done with such meticulous accuracy? Why did all the pictures have to be obliterated? That was the crux to which he always came back. Or rather the double crux, the careful painting first, and then the concealment of what had been done with so much labour.

Pointer flew to Lausanne on the following day, after leaving word to watch the little knot of people in whom he was interested night and day, especially Olive Hill. Arrived at the Blecherette aerodrome, he took a taxi, and told the chauffeur to drive him for an hour or so through the town, so as to give him a general idea of the place. The man was intelligent, and Pointer stopped him once or twice and made a note of where they were, so certain was he that he was passing near some view recorded in one or other of the smaller pictures.

As for the cathedral belfry and the spire of Saint Francois, he had already greeted them as old friends from the aeroplane.

Incidentally, he was amazed at the beauty of the city spreading over its hills of Pully, and Chailly, along the ridge of Mon Repos up to the Chalet de Gobet, and sloping down to the lovely shore of Ouchy and the great Park of Denantou. He felt as though the drive alone was worth the journey, though a chamois seemed to have designed some of the rises and dips of the streets.

Pointef placed Lausanne—in summer at any rate—far ahead of Naples for sheer beauty of situation and for wonderful range of colours. He had already got from the Swiss Railways the name of the best Lausanne photographer, a firm that had been there for seventy years. He drove to the shop and bought several photographs. Then he asked if he could have a word with a member of the firm itself. The youngish man who was serving him told him that he himself was one of the junior partners, that the photographs just bought were all his own work or that of his elder brother, his father and uncles devoted themselves more to the make and sale of photographic appliances. Pointer then showed him the photographs of the under-paintings at The Causeway, explaining that the pictures had been found painted on the walls of a country house in England, and that he had come to Lausanne for the express purpose of finding out what places they represented.

The first one which the young Swiss picked up, was
the central view. "That's our cathedral and that's the
spire of St. Francois Church, but it was painted at least
twenty years ago. That view is now spoiled by the big
Federal Bank put up at that time. And I know where this
one was painted from—the exact spot. It's a view of the
town from the *Square de l'University*, as it was at least
twenty years ago."

"You can't date it nearer than that?"

"I'll ask Gustav."

A moment later his elder brother came in and bent
over the photograph. "Parbleu, Henri, here's a bit of the
Academie, as it was before the roof was altered, and that
was done years ago."

The two brothers bent over the photographs. No one
else was in the shop and all the world loves to solve a
puzzle. In the end they were able to date the central
picture for Pointer with certainty as "painted thirty years
ago."

Their father came in and added his confirmatory
vote. Then the rest of the photographs were studied one
by one, located, and dated. There were only four of which
they were not sure, beyond the certainty that they were
painted somewhere in the Canton Vaud, as was shown by
the cattle and by the shape of the cow-bells. None of them
were of the French side of the Lake.

The curious thing was that all the dates of the
paintings ran from between thirty years ago to the
present time, and that the paintings ran consecutively
along the walls, the oldest to the left of the centre
painting, the most recent being the painting of *Place St.
Frangois* that joined it on the right of the fireplace.

The oldest of the little paintings, which dated back to
the same time as the central painting, was not of
Lausanne, but of a little place near it on the lake called
Morgen, where there was now a large horticultural
college. The parish church of Morgen figured four times
in all among the paintings, each at an interval of ten

years. Thirty years ago—twenty years ago—ten years ago—and present time. Of the cathedral there was only the large centre one and a small one done about ten years later. The photographers were enchanted with the paintings, father and sons vying with each other to point out this or that now vanished landmark.

But as to who could have executed the work, none of them could give a guess. Pointer found to his surprise that it was going to be very difficult to find out anything about a Mrs. Green. For two days, he visited the heads of the various art schools without learning of any artist who could possibly be her. As for the name itself dropped casually, it meant nothing to these good Lausannois. On the fourth day, Pointer decided to try Morgen. He had been told that another of the landscapes was of the mountains as seen from there, a view that was now blocked by the college, and had certainly been painted, so the elder Carrard maintained, from the parsonage garden itself.

Pointer had a private investigator, well known for his work at Geneva, look up the question of the parsons of Morgen while he was trying to find out about Mrs. Green. He learnt that the present incumbent, Doctor Desvernois, was eighty-three years old, a fine scholar and a great authority on Swiss dialects. His wife, a Swiss lady, was still living.

The only son of the marriage had been professor of phonetics at the Lausanne University. He had married a Miss Walker while very young. She was entered in the records as of Birmingham, England, and at the time of the marriage had been a student at Lausanne too. Her present age was fifty-three. Pointer asked for all possible information about this younger Madame Desvernois. There did not seem much to learn. She had had six children. Two girls, now grown up, had married very well indeed. One son had been killed with his father some twenty years ago while mountain climbing. The bodies had both been recovered and were buried at Morgen. An earlier son had been still-born. The two younger children had died, and been buried, in Zurich. More than this, the town records could not tell. Pointer felt that he must continue the search himself. The first step was to go out to Morgen, a pretty place, and send in his card to the lady of the house asking permission to sketch the mountains as seen from the garden.

Out came Madame Desvernois herself, a charming old lady who deplored the shrinkage of what had once been a lovely view. "In the old days, my daughter-in-law painted it many a time," she added. Pointer started his pencil sketch. He was an extremely accurate draughtsman, though no artist.

Pointer was always shocked at the liberties that real artists took with views, moving trees, and changing river banks, with incredible casualness.

Madame Desvernois sat down and named some of the mountains before them. Pointer brought the talk around to her daughter-in-law's work. Would she allow him to see, from it, what the view had once been?

The old lady promptly took him in and showed him, in the main hall, a length of framed watercolours. Two of them were identical with two views that Pointer had seen done in oils at The Causeway, and of which he had the photographs in his pocket. He asked if he might be allowed to ask the artist a question about the way in which she secured a certain afterglow effect? He was told that young Madame Desvernois was in England at the moment. "She is English. This is her picture," she added in a rush of smiling indiscretion, pointing to a framed photograph near the staircase.

Pointer looked at the face of Mrs. Green, but young— and gay. "A very young lady—" he murmured.

Madame laughed. "Would one not say so? Yet she is already a grandmother. There might be ways of explaining that, but not in her case. She never has, and I think she will never look anywhere near her real age."

The woman whom Pointer had seen had looked every day of fifty-three.

And then Madame led Pointer out again and begged him to draw or paint from any part of the garden or orchard that he liked. Could he draw the parsonage itself, he asked. It was old and very picturesque. Certainly he could, and with that Pointer had to set to work.

As Pointer sharpened his pencils he wished that he could sharpen his wits at the same time and as easily. What was the link between this little place on the Lake of Geneva and The Causeway? Why did it figure in four paintings at intervals of ten years or so. All of them painted in summer he had noticed, just as, excepting for the circular painting, all the views of Lausanne were of the autumn, spring, or winter. Why had Madame Francois Desvernois changed her name to Green, and gone half across Europe to paint these home scenes on the study walls of a young man who had been afterwards found shot dead in his drawing-room. And why had the artist, on her death, covered up her work with what had seemed such desperate speed? Also, she was no longer English, but Swiss, by marriage, yet she had not registered as an alien. The penalty for not doing so is very unpleasant. Why had she risked it?

She had apparently never met Revell before seeing him at The Flagstaff. Or had she? Were both he and she acting the parts of strangers? If so, what was the secret link? Apparently she belonged to a most blameless section of society, yet she had gone under an assumed name—Pointer went the full circle again. Why were the pictures chiefly old? There were no dates on them. Did they represent dates, and were the dates ciphers? But that would presuppose an accomplice who knew the old Lausanne, and the old parsonage here at Morgen. . . .

Pointer put his things together, glad of the excuse of a sharp shower. Back at Lausanne he arranged for a wireless to Scotland Yard asking—in cipher—some questions about the passport of Madame Francois

Desvernois, adding her maiden name. He got the answer within a couple of hours. From it he learnt that she had landed in Dover two days before she appeared at The Flagstaff. The Chief Constable was sure that she and Lady Revell were strangers. Pointer asked him by cable many questions about the Revells in the hope that one of them might lead him out of the fog. Only one reply interested him, though he could not see that it had any significance.

Lady Revell had had three children. The first, a girl, had been prematurely born in Paris at Neuilly, after a motor accident, and had only lived a few hours. Lady Revell's life had been despaired of, but she had finally, though very slowly recovered. Then came the information that so interested Pointer. That was that Anthony, the second child, had been born at Evian les Bains. Now Evian is a smart French watering-place on the Lake of Geneva, exactly opposite from Lausanne, and steamers ply all afternoon long in summer between the two. So Anthony had been born on the lake that figured so often in the pictures. Yet not one of them was of Evian or its surroundings. Pointer established that fact from direct questions to the Lausanne photographers who had a branch at Evian to which they went in August.

He returned to the parsonage garden of Morgen. Madame Desvernois, who had taken a fancy to him, came out again and told him little facts about the scene before him which would have interested him greatly at any other time, but which he now looked on merely as possible stepping-stones to inquiries about her English daughter-in-law. He was able to inspect her paintings in the hall a second time. He lingered over them, and finally said that he hoped that if she had any children, they had inherited their mother's great gift, for he considered these paintings the work of a very remarkable artist, he said.

Madame Desvernois's worn, but still pretty, face lightened. "She is indeed," she said warmly, "and very different would have been the lot of her children but for that gift. She had no idea of it when she married my son. She painted for pleasure to be sure, but she intended to be a teacher of languages. It was only after his death"— she described a fatal accident in the mountains—"that she felt she had to do something. She gave shows of her pictures at Lausanne, at Berne, and finally at Zurich. Selling, oh so few, and for such low prices! But at Zurich she heard of the Cantonal prize for the best original designs for Swiss lace curtains. She sent in some designs, and with that success—for she won it—she found her real metier. You may have heard of the Schweitzer Atelier in Zurich that turns out all the best designs for lace curtains of every kind? It is my daughter-in-law's. She has her work promised for years ahead. She is well-to-do now, and all as the result of her talents."

Pointer talked on. He saw no light yet, but light was certainly to be found, shining behind the cloud of mystery, of that he felt sure.

"I will show you the portrait that she painted of my son when they married. I think it a wonderful piece of work." And Madame Desvernois led Pointer into her own sitting-room. There, over the mantel, was a painting of Francois Desvernois, at which Pointer gazed long and intently.

And as he gazed, the light grew clearer and clearer. He might not be able to prove what he saw in that picture, but he knew that he was reading it aright.

"He is like a young man who died recently in England," he said finally.

"Really?" Madame Desvernois looked sceptical.

"He was the handsomest young man in all the Canton," she said proudly. "So handsome that I used to fear for him. But he had an angel's character. Besides, we were poor, very poor, and I think that may have helped—"

Pointer held out the photograph of Anthony Revell, which had originally had beside it a portrait of Mrs. Green. It was taken from a snapshot procured for him by

Major Weir-Opie before he left England. Madame Desvernois looked at it with interest.

"He is very like the portrait, isn't he?" Pointer said lightly.

"Like?" Madame Desvernois was not sure. "Like? Yes—perhaps—a little—a very little. Yes—there is a distinct resemblance. Yes. I see what you mean. Yes, he is like Francois's son—the one who was killed in that accident. My daughter-in-law had only the one son. Another younger one was stillborn. I never saw him." The old lady liked to talk of her family. "He was born in Lausanne before they had to leave the University. My son had to give up his work," she went on, "that was the black year as we always call it, though my daughter-in-law will never refer to it. The bank failed with all our savings in it, so that we had nothing to help the children when they needed it so badly! That was why the baby was born dead—his mother was in such grief. They came here to us afterwards heart-broken. But heaven helped. Her grandmother left her some money which let them all go to Leysin for two years, where my son was quite, quite cured. Then the Lausanne University asked him to come back to a better post—as Professor of Phonetics, which was his ambition. Oh, yes, the bad year was made good, though Eva—my daughter-in-law will never agree that that was so."

Pointer took his leave saying that he was going on to Zurich and should certainly do himself the pleasure of calling at the Ateliers but for the fact that Madame Francois Desvernois would not be there. They parted quite regretfully, did Pointer and the old lady, after he had been allowed to take some photographs of a couple of the sketches in the hall. They happened to hang on either side of Madame Francois Desvernois's portrait, so that her likeness was taken, too.

Back in Lausanne, he tried to find out who was the doctor or the nurse who had attended Madame Desvernois thirty years ago when her first son had been born. Apparently there had been no doctor. The nurse, a registered midwife, had died some years ago. But her address was entered as of Evian-les-Bains as well as of Lausanne. And, moreover, she had come from Neuilly-sur-Seine—Neuilly, the suburb of Paris, where Lady Revell's little girl had been born. An inquiry of the Neuilly town records, and Pointer learnt that the same woman had nursed Lady Revell then too. Possibly Lady Revell had come to Evian because of her. Here at last was a demonstrable link between Mrs. Green and Lady Revell. It was a vital one, Pointer thought, for he felt certain that Anthony Revell was the son of Professor Francois Desvernois. The professor's young wife, faced with the prospect of still another child to bring up at a time when there must have already been the greatest difficulty about bringing up the two they already had, and faced too with the very sick husband to whom she longed to give a chance of regaining his health in a sanatorium, had, he believed, agreed to sell her baby to Lady Revell if it should be a boy. "the midwife, appealed to by the latter, would be the carrier-out of all the necessary formalities. The trail, it was true, ended in the death of the nurse, but from the locality where she had died, and from the grave where she lay, it looked as though she had been unusually well-to-do for a woman in her position. Her son, too, was a "fonctionaire" it appeared. He had been sent to Lysee. Pointer thought that it looked as though the nurse had been well paid by Lady Revell for her help in substituting Madame Francois Desvernois's child for either a non-existent, or a dead baby.

The former, probably, for further replies to cipher cables told him that Lady Revell's father-in-law had spoken of his intention of leaving his huge fortune to the first grandson to be born him. Of his four children at the time, one was an unmarried woman of fifty, two sons were married but had no children. Admiral, or as he then was, Commodore, Revell's wife, Lady Revell, had no living child, and the doctors doubted whether she could ever have another. It was quite easy to understand that, given a character which would not baulk at the deception and the lies involved, and given the opportunity, Lady Revell had done what she doubtless considered a very clever thing. Her husband had just been sent to a China station. It must have been easy for her to spend the necessary time in quiet places abroad, then go to Evian, ostensibly to have her baby, and come home with a boy, whom she presented to the grandfather, and later to her husband, as Anthony Revell, the first grandson.

Yes, Pointer felt that he had solved the reason for those paintings and their overpainting. The real mother had not forgotten her baby. She had evidently insisted on knowing to whom the child had been handed. Lady Revell, on the other hand, he believed, did not know the mother's name, or had been told a false one by the midwife. Madame Francois Desvernois had gone to London, dropped her own name, and as a Mrs. Green appeared with a good excuse at what she would think was her son's home. She had loved him when she saw him, but she had kept to her bargain, and indeed any revealing of herself was impossible for Anthony Revell's sake.

She had evidently determined though that he should have some reminder of his birthplace. Putting her soul into her work, she had reproduced on his walls, not fairy tales, but the scenes with which he would have been familiar had he lived in his real home. There were some little figures introduced every now and then. Pointer recognised old Madame Desvernois in one. The others, he thought, were probably those of the father, grandfather, and the brother and sisters.

Yes, the paintings were explained, and that exactness in them which Mr. Joyce deplored. What Mrs. Green wanted and had secured, was as close a reproduction as possible to what Anthony would have seen had he remained the little Desvernois of Lausanne.

And explained, too, was her desire to cover them up, when the police were investigating the strange death of the young man. She had feared that they might do just what they had done, and lead the police on to the trail of who Anthony was, or rather who he was not.

He flew home next morning, and in the late afternoon motored out to see the Major.

Weir-Opie listened very silently to what Pointer had to say.

"Well played, Pointer!" he said heartily, when the former had finished. There had been a time when that had been an often-heard shout on the football ground. "To think we had the same chance of noticing that those paintings hadn't been varnished as you had, and didn't realise what it meant! This explains Lady Revell's growing dislike of Anthony, when Gilbert was born twelve years later. She had herself put the cuckoo in the nest and could not now disown it. And now, what of her new position, eh?" Major Weir-Opie said slowly and meaningly.

"Anthony Revell found dead at The Causeway just a few weeks before a wedding would have meant a will cutting out Lady Revell and Gilbert from any likelihood of sharing in a large fortune. No wonder that Lady Revell was quite indifferent as to whom Anthony intended to marry. . . .

"It's hard lines on Gilbert Revell," Weir-Opie said finally as Superintendent Shilling hurried in. The Chief Constable had sent a word over the telephone to him. He heard in a silence that was eloquent what Pointer had learnt at Lausanne.

"Then Gilbert Revell was done out of his grandfather's money by the so-called Anthony! And now Olive Hill has been done out of it—but no, she hasn't been done out of anything but her young man—for the money never was Anthony's by rights."

As far as Anthony and the fortune left him were concerned, Pointer did not think that the position was so simple. For the money left to the so-called Anthony Revell by his equally so-called grandfather had been left him because of the old man's affection for the boy of ten.

Pointer had read the letter that had accompanied the will, a letter kept by Anthony and found docketed by Major Weir-Opie, and knew that between the boy and old Sir Henry Revell had been a strong, deep, affection. True, Sir Henry had thought that he was leaving his money to his only grandson, but it was chiefly because of his love for Anthony that he had left it to him. That was what made the problem so difficult.

"Like you, Pointer, I don't believe Lady Revell knows who Mrs. Green is," Weir-Opie said suddenly out of a cloud of smoke, "for she really believes that she was in love with Anthony. We know now why Mrs. Green hung around the lad as she did. Poor soul! Especially as you say he was very like her husband in looks."

"I shouldn't wonder, sir, if that was why she hasn't let any one see of late the portrait of Anthony Revell which she painted. It may have been much more like his father than like him."

"Yes, but does the real mother suspect the sham mother, and is that why she hangs around the place?" Shilling asked curiously. "Is all her talk against Miss Hill just camouflage? The necklace you found, the one with which you believe that Mr. Avery smashed the jar with stamps in it, becomes immensely important now. Lady Revell denies that she went to the rectory at any time that last Sunday," Pointer said slowly.

It was now Saturday.

"Fraser and the maids deny the possibility that the necklace was left behind on any earlier visit," he continued, "and the dust-free condition of the room supports them. I'd like to have a talk to Mrs. Green first of all. She may know something which she didn't dare tell us, for fear of coming too far forward into the limelight. That fear of hers—that restraining fear—we know now that it was terror of our finding out about her relationship to Anthony Revell—not terror of our learning fresh facts about how he died. I believe no one wants that cleared up more than she does."

"'For in the hand of the Lord there is a cup; and the wine is red,'"quoted Weir-Opie dreamily.

"Red for whom? I don't think she suspects Lady Revell, sir," Pointer replied, "but that may simply be because she daren't. I take it that nothing fresh has turned up in the case?" But Pointer knew that otherwise he would not have been allowed to tell his own tale uninterrupted for so long.

"Nothing. Mrs. Richard Avery returned early this morning. Just in time for the funeral, at which nothing of any interest to you happened, though the whole countryside turned out for it, and Shilling and I were a bit unpopular because the poisoner wasn't behind bolts and bars. Miss Avery asked after you. Whether from personal affection, or because something was stirring in her that would like to get out. I can't say. Miss Hill was at the service, but didn't go to the churchyard. She's looking better."

"Were the Revells there?"

"Oh, certainly. Both of them. So was Mrs. Green."

Mrs. Green also had looked better, Shilling thought, but Lady Revell might have just come back from a health cruise, so marked was the improvement in her looks. "Odd, ain't it?" Shilling wound up "the last thing to expect of the rector's death would have been that it apparently has relieved so many people's anxieties."

"In Lady Revell's case prematurely, I fancy," Weir-Opie said dryly as Pointer rose to go.

"But would any letter of hers to Mr. Anthony, if found by the rector, have shocked him so?" Shilling suddenly struck in. "As his mother, why shouldn't she write asking him to come back? Mr. Avery wouldn't have dreamt of connecting her with her son's death, unless she wrote some threat which would certainly not have brought Mr. Anthony racing home for a talk."

"But if she wrote about some one else—if she used that as a decoy—then the rector's shock would have been that Lady Revell had kept the letter—and the appointment—secret," suggested Weir-Opie. He glanced at Pointer.

"We are agreed that Miss Hill wasn't mentioned in the letter by name, sir," said Pointer as he hurried off.

CHAPTER SIXTEEN

Jamieson opened the front door on the Chief Inspector with obvious pleasure. "I'm glad you have the key of the smoke-room, sir. Rare fuss Mrs. Green had been making. She's proper wild at the police having it."

"That's only natural, seeing that those paintings in there are her work," Pointer said casually. "A lady as could fly off the handle like that for a trifle, isn't one I'm going to serve." Jamieson shook his head in renunciation absolute and complete.

Pointer tipped him in proportion to the hurt to his feelings and went on into the smoking-room himself. He was only just in time, for a car could be heard coming up the drive.

Pointer waited. He heard Jamieson's greeting, and Mrs. Green's inquiry as to whether the police had yet given up the room.

"The Chief Inspector is in it now, madam," Jamieson said with relief in his voice, "waiting to see you about it," with which added embroidery, he opened the door for her.

Mrs. Green took one step inside, and stopped as though a snake were in the room. Jamieson closed the door and went on down the passage. Slowly, as though all her muscles had stiffened with the shock, Mrs. Green turned her head, and looked from the pictures to Pointer, anguish and terror in her eyes. As he said nothing, only bowed stiffly, she stared again at her paintings which faced her as they had been originally, free of the overpaint.

"Yes, we had them cleaned," he said quietly, "but let me get you a chair." He went to the door to return a moment later with a chair of Jamieson's which he placed for Mrs. Green at the farther extremity of the room. "Yes,

Madame Desvernois," he went on gently, "I've just got back from Lausanne and Morgen. I know now who Anthony Revell really was. When and where he was born."

"So the rector left a message behind!" she said in a sort of gasp.

"Not at all. The pictures told me. I saw your paintings in your home at Morgen—I was shown your portrait. Then, too, the dates tallied. Lady Revell in Evian, you just across the lake. The same midwife—who had previously been with Lady ReveH when her child was born in Paris. Your own very great trouble—Lady Revell's doubtless most tempting offer coming just then through the nurse—"

Mrs. Green put out her hand to stop him. "It's true," she said under her breath. "And true also that had my son borne his own name he would be alive to-day." She covered her face, all broken up, with her hands. "Nothing you can say can hurt me like that knowledge."

"How do you mean?" Pointer asked, as though surprised.

"What else did Olive Hill want but the position? The money?"

There was a short silence.

"And now are you going to prove that she shot my boy?" she said in a voice that trembled with excitement. "I will stand whatever comes out about me, if you can prove that."

"Are you sure that it wasn't an accident?" he countered.

Mrs. Green gave a laugh in which there was no merriment.

She sprang to her feet.

"It was all a mistake—my trying to get to know him without his knowing who I was. I thought I had managed it so cleverly coming as Mrs. Green—Lady Revell had never seen me. I am a painter of some merit—she had pictures worth copying. It would rouse no suspicions in her if a Mrs. Green called at The Flagstaff when she happened to be in the village, and asked if she could copy them. I could meet Anthony there—as I did. When I found that he had his own home, and I got him to let me paint some panels for his smoking-room, and stay there while I worked, I thought I was in heaven. As I was at first. Though"—a flush rose and faded in her worn face— "I had purposely made myself look as young as possible— on account of not arousing any suspicions in Lady Revell. And so people—she among others—misunderstood. Even Anthony did, when I warned him against that odious girl. A horrible position," her eyes grew sombre. "Horrible position!" she repeated under her breath. "I never did anything harder than when I let him think me just a jealous middle-aged woman who had fallen in love with him, and didn't want to see another, younger, woman win him away from me. And worse was to come when he got engaged to Olive Hill, and I knew what the future would hold for him, married to her. I realised that I had sold him into bondage." She paused for a moment, her face very white.

Pointer said nothing. He was intensely sorry for her.

"He was a Swiss boy," she went on passionately in French, "a Lausannois boy. He had a right to the simple happy life that our other children had. And because of what I did, he had to live here in another country, with a so-called mother who hated him, and grudged him every piece of luck that came his way. And that girl—How could he but take sham for real affection, he, who had never had any true love that he could remember? I couldn't even put his own name on his grave. He lies there under a false one."

"And the text you chose?" he asked gently.

"The vengeance of God," she said swiftly. There was more in the same strain. Pointer did not try to stop her. He let her breaking heart pour itself out, she, who for so many weeks had had to suffer in silence.

"But the rector learnt the truth about Anthony's birth, and, I feel sure, about his death too," she said finally in a shaken whisper. "How he learnt it I have no idea. He preached that sermon straight at Olive Hill— and at me. He wanted me to tell—however late, the truth which would let justice be done. And now—whatever he knew has been buried with him!" she said almost fiercely.

"Why didn't you immediately on hearing his sermon go and tell him all the truth, and let him use that knowledge as he wanted to?" Pointer asked. "Since you think he had you in his mind when he preached his last sermon?"

Mrs. Green looked at him in pallid shame.

"What of my daughters? What of my father and mother? I can't let them know the truth."

She set her jaw firmly. "Think of the deception of all these years! My people would never understand—never forgive what I did. I've always been afraid it might come to that. But if I am sent to prison for letting Lady Revell foist my son on her family as her own, I shall go as Mrs. Green."

"I hope it won't have to come out," Pointer said, dubiously. If it was Lady Revell who had shot Anthony and poisoned the rector, the whole truth about Anthony's parentage must be told in court.

"But the rector," he went on, "how could he have learnt the truth about your son?"

"That is what I cannot understand," Mrs. Green said. "That was why I turned back when I was half-way to his house on Sunday evening. Yes, the gardener was telling the truth. He did see me leaving the garden then. I was suddenly not sure whether the rector meant—besides Olive Hill—me or Lady Revell? I thought he might have learnt from something she said after Anthony's death about him—that he was not, could not be, her son, and yet not know that he was mine. It's quite possible that she went too far when talking to him, showed too clearly her lack of any love for Anthony. Mr. Avery could be very quick in some matters, I am sure; he was too like my own father for me not to realise that. That was why I met him as little as possible. I always felt that if he saw me and Anthony much together he would guess the truth. And his sermon showed he guessed at least part of it."

There was silence for a few minutes. Pointer asked her if she knew where Lady Revell had been on both nights in which he was interested.

Mrs. Green looked very surprised. She had no idea.

At The Flagstaff, she had slept at the other end of a different wing from Lady Revell's room. And the furnished cottage that she had taken—as she could not tear herself away from the place where her son had—she felt sure—been murdered, was away from The Flagstaff or rectory.

"My own opinion is," she went on sombrely, "that the rector called Olive Hill to account on Sunday afternoon, met her by chance, possibly outside the rectory—I hear that you still do not know how he spent part of the afternoon—and showed his knowledge of what she had done. Mr. Avery would have a very stern side to him. I suspect that he gave her the choice between herself telling the police, or his telling them."

Pointer said nothing for a moment. Then he asked her what reason Olive Hill could have had for shooting Anthony Revell.

"Jealousy of me," Mrs. Green said forlornly. "A quarrel over me. I suppose she said that she never wanted to see me in her house, and he put in some kind word—he was conscious of a strong attraction to me. Though he did not guess its reason."

"But that would hardly explain her shooting a man who was about to raise her from dependence to ease and independence. You know, Mrs. Green, in the mind of any one else, all the facts about you and Mr. Anthony suggest quite another person as the murderer of your son. I wonder you haven't thought so yourself."

"Whom?" she asked fiercely.

"A woman who stood to gain much and lose nothing. Unlike Miss Hill. I am thinking of Lady Revell. You who loved your own boy so dearly will know how strong her resentment might have been at the difference in position, in wealth, between her own, and her supposed child. And if Mr. Anthony should marry, her son—and also she herself—would have probably no chance whatever of inheriting."

"Not Olive Hill!" It was characteristic of her dislike of the girl that it was the possibility of her innocence and not the possible guilt of Lady Revell which was the first thing to strike Mrs. Green. "You think she's not the one?" she repeated. And then, as he did not answer, her mind at last turned to consideration of the one whom he had suggested as being guilty. For a long minute she sat quite still. Then he saw her face turn pale again, as pale as it had when he first spoke her own name.

"If you're right, then it was I who really murdered my son," she said finally in a voice of horror. "As I have felt from the first that I had. Antoine Desvernois didn't stand between any one and a fortune, between any woman's real son and the inheritance which rightly belonged to him. But poor Anthony Revell did."

There followed another pause.

"Olive Hill wrote to him asking him to come back at once and meet her in The Causeway drawing-room at midnight precisely on that dreadful Thursday night." So far she still spoke with certainty. "But you think?"

"I think that Miss Hill's name may have only been used as a decoy," Pointer said. "As yet I can see no reason for thinking that she knew of, let alone had any hand in, his death."

Again there was a silence, then Mrs. Green spoke again, in a tone of stifled horror.

"After she left, you think that Lady Revell came and killed my son? And he's buried in that name—though I made it as small as I dared. And Lady Revell wears black for him!"

Again a pause.

"So it was Lady Revell whom the rector talked to last Sunday afternoon," Mrs. Green went on in a low voice.

Pointer doubted this, but it was possible.

"What he said must have been very definite for her to have done what she did," Mrs. Green went on as though talking to herself. "She has a savage nature, Chief Inspector. I don't mean by that cruel. I don't think that Patricia Revell is cruel at all. But she considers, in some odd way, that laws aren't for her, that anything she does becomes inevitably the best that could have been done in the circumstances. When she does anything wrong she blames the circumstances for having forced her hand."

This was very much Pointer's own view of Lady Revell's character. But he saw many qualifications. The important fact was that his discoveries in Lausanne had drawn a full confession as to Anthony's birth. She went on to explain the intention of the pictures. Just as he had guessed. It was to bring before Anthony Revell the places that he would have seen as a child, as a boy, and as a young man had he stayed where he was born. Mrs. Green had pretended to him that one was the house of the Seven Bears, that another was the home of Red Riding Hood, merely to allay her own nervousness that some one might be struck by their un-English aspects. When she heard of his death, her first thought had not, however been, as Pointer had fancied, fear of discovery. That had seemed to her impossible with only the paintings as a guide, but the determination that what she had meant for her son to enjoy was not for others, especially not for Lady Revell and her son. That was why she had so hurriedly but so completely obliterated the loving work of weeks with a couple of hours' slap-dash strokes.

"Oh, it's been a horrible circle. I couldn't speak. Silence was part of the sale—part of what I had taken that money for. Just as Lady Revell had sworn to love my baby as her own. But the difference is, I kept my word, she broke hers."

"Not at first, I understand," Pointer said gently.
Mrs. Green gave a weary sigh. "No, not at first," she
agreed. "She meant to keep it. But—of course, when she
had a child of her own—everything was different. She
believed when she bought Antoine that she could never
have another baby. But fate knew better."

Pointer asked her one more question bearing on her
story. Her portrait of Anthony Revell, had it been a
failure?

She was surprised at the question, but not
apparently disturbed.

In some odd way, the longer I worked at it the more it
turned into a portrait of his father. At last it was too
unlike, and yet too like, Anthony for me to dare to show it
to any one. I have had it boxed up and sent to Zurich."

As for the paintings Pointer told her he would be
much obliged if she did nothing about them for the
present. He had no right to ask this, as he had not taken
formal charge of them as "exhibits," and in fact it
mattered very little what became of them. The
photographs which he had had initialled by Mr. Joyce
could be produced in court if need be, and sworn to by
three witnesses. But it was the facts to which they had
led him, not the paintings in themselves which were of
interest.

As to her stay in England under another name, he
sketched the steps he would take on her behalf so as to
immediately regularise this. She had only been here four
months in all.

When he left her, he went to see Superintendent
Shilling. The Chief Constable was up in town. Shilling
was immensely relieved to hear that Mrs. Green was not
going to prove troublesome, by which he meant obstinate.

Pointer left with him his notes of the interview, and
went on for a word with Lady Revell. But she was out on
one of those long swift tiring drives to which she had
taken since the death of Anthony.

Mrs. Green only stayed a short time longer at The Causeway. She telephoned to the indignant Mr. Smith that she was changing her mind about buying the house. She had not definitely promised to take it—as he knew. She would like to think it over for another week yet. The solicitor reminded her of the many slips due to procrastination, of the immense demand for houses of this kind just now, of the fact that the incredible price which the Revels were prepared to accept for an immediate sale might easily be raised any moment—"and so on, and so forth," as he himself expressed it when repeating the conversation to Gilbert. But Mrs. Green only said at the end that she was sorry, but she feared that she had let herself be swept away by a liking for a house which she began to realise was not an easy one to run, and by the charm of a locality which was not proving as paintable as she had at first thought. She did not tell him that she now realised that for her to settle in the locality would be impossible since the police knew her story, even though she had intended but to live there for six months of the year, and in Zurich six months.

She was very shaken by the interview which she had just had. Thankful in a way that the clever Chief Inspector—whose personality had impressed her at her first glance—had discovered the truth. And yet deeply disturbed at the price that she might yet have to pay for that thirty-year old transaction which at the time had seemed so providential. But she had never known a happy day since, or at least, not a happy week. Anthony had been a lovely baby. He had been born at dawn, and for one hour he had lain in the hollow of her arm. Then she had let the nurse take him away in return for what seemed salvation in English bank-notes counted out on her bed. And in the cot where her other children had lain, the cot made ready for the third child—was laid the waxen little form of a still-born infant, born during the night to a washerwoman in Ouchy. The nurse had promised to lay it in the coffin of an old lady who would be buried to-day. Instead, she had had the little body with her when she came to Madame Francois Desvernois, just as she had had the money ready. And it had sometimes seemed to the young wife that of all her children none was more constantly with her than little Antoine. She had got the name of the new "mother" from the French woman, and had verified it by a telephone inquiry an hour after the nurse would have reached Evian. More than the name she did not know until she came to England this year, a well-to-do woman, able to take as long a holiday as she wished. At the Revells' town house, located by means of the telephone directory, it was easy to learn the whereabouts of their country house in Surrey. And the rest was as Pointer knew.

Now she asked herself bitterly why she had come. True, she had talked to Anthony, had even kissed him once good-bye, but what little pleasure she had had was woven and striped with bitterness and painful misunderstanding. Regret, unavailing and futile, rent her.

CHAPTER SEVENTEEN

Pointer walked back the short distance to the rectory, and asked for Miss Avery. She was engaged for the moment, and he went on into the study. It was his conviction that Mr. Avery when he felt himself ill, when he found the door locked, when no bell rang, had left some writing for the police. But so far not the most diligent search had found anything of the sort. So there were possibly two missing papers—the folded paper opened by the rector in the pulpit, and a posthumous message left by the dying man for the police. But though he looked for the latter he had not much hope of ever coming on it. Finally, after another intensive search of the wallpaper behind a bookshelf, he stood looking at his shoes, lost in reverie.

Pointer thought that the shooting of Revell had not been a prepared crime. It had been a very dangerous one. It had, to his mind, every mark of some swift decision, some sudden urgency. Lady Revell would have had time to plan something much safer. Yet it was possible that reflection had shown her no better way to get rid of Anthony than the one taken. After all, even if a criminal, she was not a practised criminal.

He had spoken to Mrs. Green as though Olive Hill were out of the range of suspicion, but that was not really the case. Mrs. Green herself—yes. In her case Pointer did not think that she need any longer be considered suspect. She had nothing to gain by the murder of her son, a son whom she evidently had loved very dearly. But the motive of jealousy still existed as one of the most likely reasons for Anthony Revell's death, though Mrs. Green no longer fitted in. Lady Revell logically took Mrs. Green's place. But both women, and if another suspect, Lady

Witson were included—all three women had shown themselves as absolutely unconcerned about any papers at the rectory.

Yet Pointer felt that he was not doing the murdered rector justice if he had not tried in his last hour to find some really safe hiding-place for the paper that he had opened in the pulpit. Unlike any statement of Mr. Avery's own, it—Pointer believed—was tantamount to proof of the wilful murder of Anthony—in the eyes of the criminal. Would the poisoner, flustered, hurried, terrified of detection, have been able to find what a really clever man had hidden? Pointer felt that he could trust Mr. Avery to have set the searcher a stiff proposition. There was a safe in the rector's bedroom, but Avery had not been able to get to it after his supper. Though Pointer was beginning to think that the new rector might have put the paper into safety before that. The bedroom, too, like the attic, had been hunted as for an indispensable needle . . . From the way in which the study had been searched by the criminal, Pointer was sure that Mr. Avery had shown—or read—the folded paper to him or her, who had promptly, Pointer believed, given some specious explanation which would not hold water if tested, but which had apparently allayed Mr. Avery's doubts for the moment. The calmness of the writing on St. Paul left by the dead rector, and the hearty supper taken, made Pointer sure that an explanation, rather than a confession, had taken place.

Mrs. Green still believed that Olive Hill had been the writer of the note bringing Anthony back. From what Anthony appeared to have said to Mrs. Green, he had expected to meet his fiancee in the drawingroom. But Pointer thought that Mrs. Green might have quite misunderstood the hurried, and doubtless irritable, words spoken by the surprised Anthony, when he found her hovering around his front door that Thursday night. Pointer saw no reason to think that Miss Hill had been near The Causeway on the night in question, but as he thought it very likely that some veiled reference to her had been used to get Anthony back so swiftly, therefore any specious explanation made to Mr. Avery on Sunday night would probably have been a shelving of all responsibility on to her. A responsibility which she would certainly repudiate at the first question put to her by the rector.

Miss Avery came in at that moment, and, looking very troubled, asked Pointer to sit down, as she had a very painful thing to say to him.

Grace prefaced the talk by saying that she had no idea how it could interest the police, but she had decided at the funeral of her brother to do as Pointer had asked her, and pass on any information in her possession, however far-fetched it might seem, and with that, she told him about her doubts of Miss Hill's honesty. He listened very attentively. He knew what apparently Miss Avery did not, that Miss Hill wanted to join Mr. Byrd's band of pioneers, and that in order to do so, she would have to pay into a common fund a hundred pounds. Money which Mr. Byrd gave a guarantee to repay should the expedition not start within three months of the time set.

In the questions that followed, he learnt from Grace of her own wild idea as to what might have really happened at The Causeway.

He asked if he could see Miss Hill, but learnt that she had been fetched by Gilbert Revell for a drive as he thought that she looked ill. "That's why I let you drag out of me my horrible nightmare fear of how Anthony may have died," she added meaningly. Then she had to leave him. But first she asked him whether he could wait for Doris, who would be in almost at once, and who also very much wanted a word with the Chief Inspector. Pointer decided to wait. A last question of Grace brought the answer that she still had no faintest idea of where her brother had spent the hours, yet unaccounted for on last Saturday and Sunday afternoon. After hearing which,

Pointer put in some work on the library floor. As he searched for every loose board and cranny, he thought over what he had just learnt about Miss Hill. It might explain a small puzzle within the infinitely larger one.

On the table on which the rector's supper-tray had stood last Sunday, the police had found a small carved wooden box about the length and depth of a middle finger, and the breadth of three. It had a hinged top and was quite empty. One corner had been deeply and recently dented, and there was a newly made mark on the woodwork at the side of the window which seemed to fit the dented corner.

Fraser said that he had first noticed the box when he brought in the supper tray. It was then on the table at the head of the couch, and therefore close to the door leading into the hall. No one seemed to have ever seen it until Miss Hill, on being shown it, immediately claimed it as hers. She said that she must have left it by accident in the study when she stepped in during the afternoon. She had not missed it, she said, as it was just an empty little box which she had at some time or other taken down to the morning-room, and which on Sunday she had at last meant to take back to her bedroom. She spoke with a certain tense affectation of carelessness, but Pointer had felt sure that something about it had both moved and perplexed her greatly—just at first. For that reason, he had not yet returned it to her. She had not tried to take it away from the study table, often though she had been in there. Nor did she seem to pay it any further attention. Yet what had puzzled people even for a short time without their speaking of it, always interested the Chief Inspector.

It was odd that two articles—a necklace and a box— neither of which belonged to the study, should have been found there in the morning, though only one had been seen in the room on the night before. What Grace Avery had told him might account for that, and for the puzzled feeling which he felt sure Olive Hill had suppressed with some difficulty when he had first let her handle the box on the Monday morning, for it was possible that Olive had taken Lady Revell's necklace. It was just the kind of trinket to which, in her own case, Grace Avery suspected that Olive had helped herself more than once.

It now seemed likely that the necklace had been inside the box when Fraser had noticed it—closed—on the little occasional table by the head of the couch. If so, the rector, flinging the box at the window in a last effort to get air, and to summon help, could have unknowingly flung the chain of crystals as well. The necklace might have slithered out of sight under the window seat. And the murderer, picking up the broken china jar, had probably set the box that had broken it down on the nearest table.

It was the emptiness of the box—if Pointer was right in his guesses—which had puzzled Olive when he showed it to her on the Monday. But what had brought the box with the necklace inside it to the study on Sunday night? Pointer thought of Olive's face—and the rector's sermon— and believed that he understood. Understood, too, what had made her hover around the door listening to see if the rector had not yet gone, until she had given it up for the moment, and perforce gone on to her bedroom. It was a small additional point in favour of the argument that it was not she who had poisoned the rector, that the box had been left in the room. Olive would have certainly hunted for the necklace, which she alone, Pointer thought, would know had been inside it. Yet once she knew that the necklace that she had placed in it had been picked up, the box would have no further interest for her.

He must question her about it, of course, but she would equally of course deny it, and her denial would not alter matters. The point for him was, that Lady Revell might conceivably be speaking the truth when she said that the necklace could not have been left by her at the rectory last Sunday night. It looked as though Olive had thought that the rector's sermon was directed at her, which meant that her alleged habit of pilfering was a fact, so she believed that Mr. Avery had been adjuring her to come forward and speak up—own up Pointer thought that Olive, really moved, might have taken the only thing which she had not yet disposed of—Lady Revell's crystal necklace, put it in a little box, and gone with it in her hand to the rector who had had no time for her—at the moment—and that Olive, determined to burn her boats, had left the little box on a table in the study, the table standing nearest to the door, at the head of the couch. Then, Pointer surmised, had come reaction. She had wanted to get the box back, but each time that Fraser had seen her hovering round the study door and trying to slip in unnoticed, the rector had made some movement that had told her that the room was not empty, and finally she had gone to bed, sure that she could get it back in the morning. He might be wrong, of course, but the mere fact that he might be right, altered Lady Revell's position. The necklace had seemed a most damning piece of circumstantial evidence against her. It was quite valueless now.

Fraser came in with a telephone message. Mrs. Richard Avery would not be able to get back under an hour. Pointer decided not to wait. Shilling hoped to have something of interest to tell him by that time, and Pointer wanted to hear it. It concerned Sir Hubert Witson.

As he walked to the police station, there to get to work on some papers, Pointer met Byrd and stopped for a word with him. Byrd, to the surprise of the village, had attended the rector's funeral. He was looking very grave, Pointer thought, and at a word from himself, Byrd fell into step beside him, as the two turned towards the open country.

Byrd seemed in a softened mood for once.

"A good man gone," he said tersely. "Yes. Thanks to a poisoner," the detective officer agreed.

"It still seems incredible—that—to me," Byrd said.

"Why so?" Pointer wanted to know. "He had stumbled on some truth about Anthony Revell's death, we think. That being so, no high character would save him. You heard him preach last Sunday, didn't you?"

Byrd seemed to stiffen. "Yes," he said curtly.

"So you think he was referring to Revell's death? I happen to know that he wasn't. He wanted to get some one to come forward and speak up—own up—well, he was hardly likely to expect any one to hang themselves, was he? As a matter of fact, he said that he hoped he had inspired some one with courage. Hardly fits a murderer, eh?" Byrd finished with a scoffing little smile.

"So on Sunday afternoon he talked to you about his sermon of the morning?" Pointer asked quite casually, himself under his breath.

"He did," he said finally. "And now what?"

"Why didn't you tell us sooner? You know that we have been trying our hardest to find out where he spent some hours on Saturday and Sunday afternoon."

Byrd said nothing for a moment. He shot his lower jaw out, and opened and closed it once or twice, as though to see if it would work in that position.

"Well, as I let my tongue get too long, I may as well tell you that he spent both afternoons at my cottage talking to me. At my request. At least the Saturday was at my request, the Sunday was his own idea. He was waiting at my cottage for me when I got there."

"You talked about?" Pointer said as Byrd fell silent.

"Souls," Byrd said. "Heaven," he added crossly. "Future life," he threw in from between clenched teeth. "Teaching of the church," he wound up fiercely.

Pointer said nothing for a moment.

"Why should I have told you?" Byrd demanded."What business of yours was it that I was interested in such things. Fact is, Revell's death was rather a shock. Unexpected. Unexplained. Made one think. I asked Mr. Avery to drop in on Saturday for a talk. He came at two and talked till five. He got me to give him my objections to religion, and took them seriatim. He dropped in on the Sunday to finish. He didn't finish then either, as a matter of fact. By the way, if you want proof"—Byrd gave his sarcastic smile—" he dropped some sermon headings when he sat in my arm-chair on the Saturday. I didn't find the paper till Tuesday. Here it is—but I want to keep it—I liked the rector. He—well, he was genuine. I wish I'd talked to him more—when I had the chance."

He stopped, and took out a pocket-book. From it he extracted a paper folded in four, lengthways.

Pointer caught his breath. Even he, with his sharp eyes, thought for one instant that it was the identical sheet of note-paper at which he had seen the rector staring with distended eyes last Sunday. Then he saw on it a series of some eight lines like a poem in the rector's beautiful writing. They were key sentences for the sequence of his sermon, beginning with *Reverence for knowledge among the Jews.*

He turned it over, but Byrd put out his hand.

"I'd rather you didn't read it, they were meant for Mr. Avery's eyes, when he should call again."

Pointer had seen all that he wanted to. The back was covered with Byrd's neat but stiff writing; and such words as Priestcraft. Freewill. Cruelty a law of nature—and so on, figured largely in it. He handed back the paper reluctantly.

"I suppose I couldn't be allowed to keep it locked away," he asked with real earnestness, but Byrd, as he knew that he would, shook his head decisively.

"Then please keep it carefully," Pointer said, and Byrd nodded.

"I shall. It's a souvenir. But it'll be where you can't get at it to read it out in court"—and with that he put his pocket-book away.

"You got in late for his sermon on Sunday morning, didn't you?" Pointer asked casually.

"Not late, no. He had only just begun it. Why?"

Pointer did not tell him.

"What was Mr. Avery like on the Sunday afternoon?" he asked instead, watching him as he did so. "Absent-minded?"

"Not he! He gave his whole mind, and a damned good mind it was too, to the points I had raised. They took some answering."

"He didn't refer to anything else that was troubling him?"

"You're thinking of that sermon of his? No, he might have been thinking of it though, when he said that when you had an insoluble problem on hand, it was a good thing to leave milling it over, and turn instead to some work in which you could forget it and all other puzzles."

Pointer questioned Byrd closely. He set concealed traps for him. But Byrd stood all tests. Apparently, therefore, the unaccounted-for time of the rector could have had no bearing on his end. Pointer had a notion that Byrd knew, or thought he knew, at whom the sermon was aimed, but, if so, he refused to acknowledge it, and from some of his answers, Pointer by no means saw eye to eye with him on the matter. Finally Byrd shot him a quizzical glance.

"Never give up? Eh? Never know when you're beaten? What a man! Wish you were sailing with us."

"Mr. Gilbert Revell and Miss Hill are going with you, I understand?"

"Neither," Byrd said briefly. "We can't take her, and his mother doesn't want him to go."

"But Miss Hill is counting on going," Pointer expostulated.

"She's mis-counted, then," Byrd said. "We don't want single women."

"Perhaps she'll marry Mr. Revell, and both will come along after all," Pointer said, as though it were a soothing idea. Certainly Byrd did not appear to feel hit. He seemed to think that he had gone as far with the other as he cared to, and dropped off with a nod, to walk back to the railway station and there wait for a train in from the nearest town. Olive Hill was one of those who got down. Byrd joined her outside the station.

She gave him a cool greeting. He returned it in kind.

"Look here, Olive. Mrs. Green was talking the other night—up at the Revells'; Gilbert nearly hit her, he said. She thinks you shot Anthony as well as the rector. What about it?"

Olive said nothing. Apparently the suggestion bored her.

"Can't you muzzle her?" he asked.

"When I find out, and prove who did the murders, then she'll stop. I shall yet. And soon too." Olive spoke confidently. "When does the expedition sail? In another month, isn't it? Well, I shall have cleared things up by then."

"You're not coming!" he snapped. His face was dark.

"I shall pay in my hundred, and this time it'll stay in," she retorted.

"It's because of that money I don't want you to come," he said sullenly but firmly. "You've brought it on yourself—so listen, then. You no more got that hundred honestly than I could lay my hands—honestly—on a thousand. You told me in the beginning that you had saved just four pounds towards the—"

"And have you never heard of a hundred-to-one bet coming off?" she asked, her face suddenly pinched. "What about Flamenco and the Derby?"

"You didn't bet on Flamenco," he said with certainty.

She turned on him, her face scarlet, but he stopped her with his glance—penetrating—contemptuous.

"Very well, since you want to hear it all, you shall! I saw you pinch that crystal necklace out of Lady Revell's bedroom. I was on her balcony getting an aerial right for Gilbert. I saw you slip in last Saturday, and go to a little cabinet on her dressingtable, thrust your hand into a drawer and pull out a necklace which you dropped into your handbag, and then you were out of the room again like a flash."

Olive was facing him panting, her hands clenched at
her sides. She passed her tongue over her dry lips. "And
you! you! Who always said that we ought to take from the
rich what they didn't need? Who said that if they
wouldn't share willingly, they ought to be forced to hand
over? But it's not true! I fetched the necklace for Lady
Revell who had forgotten to put it on. Where are your
eyes? She'd worn it all that afternoon."

Byrd looked taken aback. His glance faltered. Then
rallied.

"Then what did last Sunday's sermon mean? Avery
knew about those beads. And you knew that he knew!"

For a second she faced him hardly. Then:

"Yes," she said with a genuine little gasp. "And yet
when I stepped in after dinner to tell him, explain, he
wouldn't hear a word. Told me to come to him next day,
fairly shut me up as though it didn't matter. Looked at
me as though he didn't know what I meant when I asked
him how he knew "She paused for a moment then went
on fiercely. "It was your own words I followed. I needed it
to make up the hundred. I want to go and find the
island!" Her face began to break I up. "I never took
anything really valuable, anything they prized. And as
soon as I got the hundred together I was going to stop.
Even so, I was going to return that necklace at the first
opportunity, as I wanted to tell Mr. Avery. What Mrs.
Green says doesn't matter—but this—is this going to part
us?" she asked.

"Doesn't matter what Mrs. Green says!" He preferred
to keep to the first part of the sentence. "My dear girl, you
may be able to keep the necklace part dark, but
Anthony's and the rector's murder? Good God! If you can
sit down under an accusation like that!"

"You wait!" she retorted. "I have one piece of proof—
of part of what happened. And in time I'll have the full
proof. You wait!" With that she turned, and left him
standing there.

CHAPTER EIGHTEEN

Shilling and the Chief Constable were waiting for Pointer.

"What d'you make of this?" the superintendent asked eagerly. "Sir Hubert Witson has paid the Gartsides a cheque—value unknown—for some of the stamps in Anthony Revell's album. Now what's the betting that those stamps weren't originally in the envelope handed by Mr. Anthony to the rector?"

"Did you see the stamp album that they chose as one of their legacies?" Pointer asked. The news was certainly of importance.

"I did. It's a haphazard affair. Under ' Italian Stamps' comes a couple of bare places where they claim they found these that they've sold to Sir Hubert. Sir Hubert swears the same. If you ask me, I think people were a bit hasty in abolishing torture. It's the only way sometimes. A trifle of a squeeze, now, or a tight press, or a little peeling, and Sir Hubert and the Gartsides mightn't be snapping their fingers at us."

Shilling spoke with heat, Pointer only laughed. He knew the superintendent for one of the kindest of men.

"Well?" Shilling asked disconsolately. "Nothing to prove anything! What has your afternoon brought you?"

Pointer told them what he had learnt from Miss Avery.

"So Lady Revell may be telling the truth," was Weir-Opie's comment. "In fact, seems to be—and Miss Hill—"the Chief Constable made a face.

"Well, Pointer, Shilling and I will occupy ourselves with the difficulties of our arson case, and leave simple matters like the rectory mystery to you. Another ten minutes is sure to solve it."

Pointer smiled a trifle wryly. "I wish the rector had helped us a bit more," he said. "I think he tried to . . ."

"You know, we never had anything but their own word for where the Gartsides were all day and night on Thursday and Friday," Shilling struck in. "They claim they were walking and sleeping out under their tent, and so on. They had their tinned food with them, biscuits, bully beef, milk, tea, and so on. They say they bought bread and fruit from farmers, but we couldn't prove whether they did or not. It looks to me as though they might have followed Revell back to The Causeway."

"We always did know that was a possibility," Weir-Opie was balancing a pencil on his forefinger.

"But we couldn't prove it!" ended Shilling. "No more than we can now."

Pointer was only listening with half his mind.

Weir-Opie looked at him questioningly.

"You've had an idea from the first," he said as he had said once before.

Pointer only discussed the stamp theory a little longer, and then left them. He had to go up to town that evening to be present at a discussion of a case with which he had previously had some connection.

The discussion prolonged itself over the Sunday, and it was not till Monday noon that he was free to return to his rooms near the rectory. Before he left, he asked Superintendent Shilling to have his men on duty redouble their vigilance. He was worried about Olive Hill. If he were wrong, and she was guilty she was in no danger. But if she were not guilty, then she was far too eager in her search of the rectory rooms to be safe.

He had a very serious talk with her on the matter, but Olive listened with a mulish look on her closed-in face. A look that said that she would have nothing to do with the police. That she wanted no protection, and no suggestions.

"I'm going up to town for a short time," he said finally, and I want to give you two final words of warning."

Her eyes met his on that, interested but very selfconfident.

"First of all—give up looking for papers. They're dangerous. And I don't think you'll be misled by the form in which I have to give it—beware of anything to do with Mrs. Green." He spoke very seriously. "Anything to do with her, mind. Any place where she is. Anything with which she might, however distantly, be connected." He gave her a long look, but Olive's eyes again said that she felt herself eminently capable of looking after herself. It was an expression which would have surprised Gilbert Revell, who had only seen its opposite.

Pointer left her with a feeling that she had already decided on some course of action, and that he had wasted his breath. He could only hope that whatever she had in mind did not clash with what he had just said. On the whole, he thought not. There had been no defiance, no opposition in her eye. He believed that she knew her danger, but he was uneasy. Very.

He might have been still more disquieted could he have seen Olive after his talk with her, attacking a *Daily Telegraph* with scissors. She was cutting words out, and laying them in sequence on a table beside her. That done, she pasted them on a sheet of cheaplooking paper torn out of a copy book. They made a paragraph which ran: "I have found a letter which may interest you among the effects of a late client who died from an accident with his revolver. The letter is one summoning him back to his home. The price for it will be a thousand pounds in one pound notes. If you insert in the Morning Wire's Personal column on Monday 'By Promise Bound,' I will write and suggest a place in town for the transaction." Any words which could not be found in their entirety she built up of separate letters.

The task done, she washed her hands, carefully addressed the envelope, an affair which seemed to take her a long time, and then, folding up the paper, took it out with her, and slipped the letter into her bag. She posted it at the nearest pillar-box to Mr. Smith's office, then she walked back through the woods. In one open glade she seemed to have an accident while lighting a cigarette, and set the paper she had with her on fire. Gilbert came on it while she was beating out the flames. He told her how thoughtful she was not to let it lie smouldering, a menace to the underwood. Olive explained that she hated thoughtlessness of any kind, which was but a form of selfishness, and asked him if it were true that he had really given up his idea of going with Byrd.

Gilbert had, very much to his regret, he said, but his new duties would not let him absent himself for an indeterminate time just now. Olive agreed that one's duty must come first. He was still hoping that Byrd could put his ideas into execution, he said. He still intended to pay one thousand towards the expedition's expenses; unfortunately, death duties would not let him pay Byrd the other thousand that he had promised, and which would have let the little expedition start with sufficient funds to buy an island site when found. But as she also knew Byrd was advertising for a chairman, and would doubtless find some one to come forward and advance the money, especially as the chairman would have very much of a say about the place when selected.

Olive asked some very intelligent questions as to just what the donor of the second thousand could expect in the way of directing the expedition.

Gilbert explained Byrd's views as to what would be the fair thing to offer, and Olive seemed quite interested in them too. But then, Olive was a girl who was interested in so many things, Gilbert thought. He was very chagrined that his mother no longer seemed to feel the affection for her that she had shown on her engagement to Anthony. Just lately he had found it

better not to talk of her much, not to press for the offer to
her of a yearly allowance. That was that pestilential Mrs.
Green's doing, he knew. She had talked his mother quite
out of her earlier and more generous mood. But he
himself, as soon as the estate was settled up, would have
a word with his solicitors and see what could be done. An
annuity of three hundred would not cripple him, but, if
the veriest trifle to what she would have had, would at
least keep her from poverty.

Olive and he had a delightful talk. He thought what a
pleasure it was nowadays to meet a girl so simple, so
straightforward, so friendly. And she had charm, a charm
which wound itself around your heart. He was not sure
whether it came from the glance, timid and yet
interested, of those large dark eyes, or whether it lay in
her shy smile. No wonder Anthony had fallen in love with
her. Olive had confessed that Mrs. Green was right in
thinking that she had never really loved Anthony. She
knew that now, but she had thought that she had at the
time. After all, Gilbert reflected, a little country mouse
like Olive would not at first be able to tell the difference
between love and mere friendship. She had never told
him what had made her realise this, only giving him one
of her heart-stirring smiles and changing the subject with
a little, very fetching sigh.

He walked back with her to the rectory and Grace,
who met them on the steps, looked perturbed, he thought,
even through the marks of grief that her face had shown
at the funeral.

On Monday morning, Olive was down early, and had
a look at the Morning Wire. She found By Promise Bound
almost at once, but there was a message following it
which ran "Cannot get to town this week. Suggest
painter's cottage at three to-day. Telephone or telegraph
'yes' if you can meet me there."

Olive thought this over. She knew what cottage was
meant. It was shut up at the moment. Mrs. Green was up
in town arranging an exhibition of her paintings. After

careful thought, Olive went out for her usual walk. She stepped into a telephone-box and rang up the apartment house in Mayfair where Mrs. Green had taken rooms. Grace Avery had the number and the key of the cottage in her room, as the artist was not sure whether she would not want to send back some of the pictures which she had taken with her, and if so, Grace had promised to see to their safe disposal..

Mrs. Green was in, and told her that she would not be back till the end of next week. She said that she was glad that Grace had telephoned to ask how she was getting on, as she was leaving her rooms at once and going to a hotel. She did not care for the service where she was. She gave her new number to what she believed was Grace, who hung up at once. Olive's interest was over. She would not be disturbed at the cottage, which was all that she cared to know. It was a good hour's drive to London.

Stepping to the letter-box, she now dropped in an envelope exactly like the one that had contained the printed message. Inside was another cut-out message which ran: "I shall send an old nurse with the letter to the cottage at three sharp. Hand her the money but, as she is deaf, please do not speak to her. She has been given a false, but quite satisfactory, explanation of what she is to do. You will let her count the money, and she will then hand you the letter. Should she not be back by three-thirty, something very unpleasant would result. I have taken every precaution."

After Olive's return to the rectory, she ate a good breakfast, then she caught the nine-thirty train up to town and with a small blouse-case—empty apparently— went by bus to Swan and Edgar's at Piccadilly Circus.

At half-past two, a stout, handsome, blackhaired, very much painted-up lady who looked like a foreigner with her thick eyebrows meeting over her rather humped, thickly-powdered nose came up the garden path of Mrs.

Green's cottage. She stopped at sight of the gardener who was at work on a flowerbed.

"Alio!" called the foreign-looking lady. Then as he paused in his work, she beckoned to him. "Madame Gr-r-reen she is away, I know, but I am old fr-r-iend. I stay here. She have give me her key. She returning this evening. My luggage it should have come to the station by the tr-rain coming fr-r-om town. You fetch it, eh? Here is my name—Madame Levitsky. You wait and br-ring it, eh? A lar-rge tr-runk and two smaller-r-r ones, eh? You wait for them? I can confide in you, eh? 'Ere is zumzing for-r-r your tr-rouble now. When you br-ring the baggage I pay more, eh?" She handed the man two half-crowns. "You go at once, eh? I want my baggage as soon as it arrive. I will make myself comfor-rtable till she come back this evening," and with that she waddled with flat feet up the steps to the door, which she opened with a key and closed behind her.

The gardener went off at once, the half-crowns jingling merrily in his hand.

Pointer meanwhile had spent a disturbed morning.

The mystery at the rectory had been at the back of his mind all the week-end. He spent a very wakeful Saturday night, with the uncomfortable feeling that his subconscious mind was endeavouring to signal to him. But try as he would, he could not think out what this something could be.

Coming down in the train late on Monday afternoon, he sat with closed eyes. As though he were inspecting film strips, he reviewed wall by wall the room where the rector had been found dead. His subconscious was telling him that he had passed over something as trifling which was important—vital. But what? He started on his mental journey from the door. He spent a long time over the little occasional table by the couch (on which he believed the box containing the necklace had stood), the couch itself with the body of Mr. Avery on it—the mantel on the farther end of which had stood the orange jar containing the stamps, the jar which he had rightly deduced to have been broken and therefore buried. The stamps had either been destroyed in some way, or saved and sold. He stopped a long moment here, but finally he felt sure that he had missed nothing about the jar. Then he passed on to the bookcase where he had found the single, valueless, Italian stamp. The window-seat under which he had found the necklace—the necklace—and so he came to the table with the supper-tray. Item by item he reviewed the things on the tray. And suddenly he jumped up. The dessert-knife—covered with Mr. Avery's fingerprints. Firm and bold prints. Yet the blade showed that the knife had not been used. That at least had been what had been thought up to now.

When the train got in, Pointer went at once to the police station and unlocked the safe. The Superintendent was absent, but the inspector on duty took out for Pointer the box containing the fingerprint photographs; and then the box of "exhibits" themselves. Pointer again had a look at the polished silver blade with its pointed end. Very carefully he ran a finger along the edge. It was no sharper than dessert-knives usually are. He put away the exhibits and studied the photographs of the rector's fingerprints on the handle. It was a heavy handle with a slightly bulbous end. Pointer finally decided that it had been used by Mr. Avery, first for cutting and then for boring into something fairly firm. He memorised the position of the fingerprints, and then replaced the photographs also in the safe. There had been a Stilton cheese on the tray, but it had been crumbled by himself until nothing remained. Everything on the tray had been tested for that paper. Yet the knife had been wiped after use, and by Mr. Avery, as the fingerprints showed.

Pointer's pulses quickened, impassive though his face remained, as he set off for the rectory. He was all out to find where Mr. Avery had hidden the precious, all-important paper which the rector had unfolded in the pulpit, and he believed that at last he had a clue.

Mr. Avery—a clever man—who knew that he had been poisoned—could be trusted to have guessed the reason. He had put his wits to their last earthly task of foiling his poisoners. He had used the knife, and then, lest the marks give the hiding-place away, had wiped the blade.

As he strode along, Pointer again ran over item by item everything in the room and in the library. There was nothing for which such a knife could have been used bar the plaster ceiling, and that was unusually high in both rooms. Nothing . . . nothing. . . so whatever it was on which it had been used must have been taken out of the room. Or had the rector's efforts at a hiding-place failed? Had the poisoner triumphed? He would soon know. But he had a hope that Mr. Avery's brains had been too much for the murderer.

CHAPTER NINETEEN

Fraser opened the door and Pointer asked him where Miss Hill was.

"Out with both the ladies, sir, house-hunting."

Pointer had to leave it at that for the moment. He signed to him to follow him into the morningroom.

"Look here, something is missing from the study, or possibly from the library. Something was taken out on Monday morning before we got here. You feel sure that it couldn't have been by the doctor?"

"Certain," Fraser said after a second's thought. "Quite certain. And *I* took nothing away, not so much as a pin, sir."

"What about the housemaid?"

Pointer knew that Shilling and Weir-Opie had already questioned her and all the servants, and had been satisfied that she had left everything as she found it.

"Nothing, sir," Fraser now said with certainty.

"Must have," Pointer replied with equal certainty. "Could it have been anything that she always took out of a morning? Part of her regular duties which she didn't think of, when questioned?"

"You mean the paper-basket and the plate of apples, sir? They were taken down, of course. The basket I had brought up again untouched for the Chief Constable to find in its usual place when he got here. Nothing had been taken out of it, for the very good reason that there wasn't anything in it. As to the plate of apples, she had to take them away every morning, and I would make them up to the four the rector always liked to find on it, for her to set on the writing-table when the room was finished.

He hadn't touched them that Sunday, for a wonder. All four came down."

"And were eaten later?" Pointer asked casually, but with a tension that would have surprised Fraser had he realised it.

"Not been touched," Fraser said promptly. "No one ever ate them but Mr. Avery. They're in my pantry at the moment, standing on the mantel as they stood on his writing-table. I mean to keep them there as long as they don't go bad."

Pointer asked if he could have them brought to him. He wanted to test them for fingerprints, he said. Therefore it might be as well to bring a knife such as the rector used and a plate with them, so as to look as little noticeable as possible.

Fraser seemed puzzled, but he slipped out to his pantry, coming back almost at once with two glass plates, a large one on which were three apples in a circle, with a fourth poised on top of them, and a small plate with a dessert-knife on it.

Pointer waited until Fraser had reluctantly left the room, then he locked the door, lifted off the top apple and took up one of the three underneath. One by one, he scrutinised them. The third showed him what he was looking for—the all-but-invisible mark of a wedge-shaped piece. He pulled at it carefully. Nothing happened. Using the knife, he prised it loose. The apple had a large hollow centre by nature. In it was something white—paper.

Pointer got it out with the utmost care. It was a very thin envelope which had apparently been covered with gum. Careful and wise, Mr. Avery had feared lest the juice of the fruit might damage that which he had slipped inside, for in the envelope when Pointer now slit it, was a sheet of paper which had once been folded in four, though now it had been compressed into as small a space as possible. Pointer replaced the wedge of apple back in its place, and spreading out the paper with considerable emotion, read the few lines written on it. It was the paper which Mr. Avery had unfolded in the pulpit. As he read he saw that his first guess at the criminal had been right, slight though the fact was on which it had rested. Copying the lines swiftly in his note-book, he slipped envelope and paper into another envelope, closed it, laid it in a book, unlocked the door and sent for Weston, one of his own men who had been left on duty, and whom he had not yet seen since his return from town. To him was given the precious book with an apparently casual word as to whom to hand it to at the police station, but in reality it was a code word which meant that what he carried was much more important than his own life. That he was to see it at once locked into the safe, and then return here with Superintendent Shilling.

Before he hurried off on his motor-cycle, Pointer asked briefly, "Everything here as usual?"

"Yes, sir, except that Miss Hill went up to town by an early train and hasn't got back yet. I telephoned Carter to be on the look-out for her at Paddington. He followed her to Swan and Edgar's in Piccadilly Circus, but she hadn't come out when he phoned me. He didn't see her in the luncheon-room, but he hadn't time to look long, he was afraid of missing her at one of the doors. He's still watching them."

Pointer sent him off, and rang for Fraser. "Did you say Miss Hill is house-hunting?"

"My mistake, sir. I thought the ladies went off together. But Mrs. Richard—Mrs. Avery, I should say—is back and asking for her." Even as he spoke, Doris was hurrying down the stairs to meet them.

"I can't think where Miss Hill is," she said now. "She asked me for the day off until four o'clock. She said she'd be back by then at latest. It's now past five. She's never been late before. I have the oddest feeling that she's in trouble—" Doris looked very anxious. "Miss Avery and I have been out all day house-hunting, you know. We must leave here by the end of the next fortnight. And it's so unlike Miss Hill not to be back, or to send a message"

"Where is Miss Avery?"

Doris looked surprised. "Still looking at impossible places. Why?"

"Has Mrs. Green got back yet?" Pointer asked instead of replying.

Doris looked puzzled. "Not as far as I know."

Pointer was looking at his shoes. Olive Hill should have been back by four o'clock, and was still out. He hoped for the best, but her journey to town suggested that she had refused to leave things alone, that in spite of all that he had said to her she had played with gunpowder. He was afraid that it had blown her up. He had told his men to watch her most carefully, but so few men could be spared just now from town. Carter at Paddington was one of the newest men out from Hendon. Willing enough, clever too, but he lacked practice. And it needs three men to watch the exits of Swan and Edgar's properly. There was also the possibility that Olive had come out in a disguise. She could pick up a bunch of curls in one department, a cloak in another, gloves, spectacles, a hat of a different shape to the one she was wearing, she might even—with her figure—have had an Eton crop, bought a suit "for a brother," and walked out as a young man.

Pointer stepped in one stride to the telephone. A moment later and he was speaking to Shilling.

"Weston is on his way to you with a book. Please wait for him and then come on at once to Mrs. Green's cottage, where Mrs. Avery and I shall wait for you. And—" Here in a rather casual voice came some words in code which petrified the Superintendent.

"Impossible!" Shilling's voice was really appalled. "I mean—well—see about it at once, and come at once, too. It won't take a minute. The Chief's here, by good luck."

Pointer hung up and, after a word with Fraser, ran to his car. Doris hurried after him.

"What makes you ask about Mrs. Green?" She spoke in a low voice. "Miss Hill wouldn't go to her. The two, as one would expect, are at daggers drawn. Besides, Mrs. Green is away."

"I think she may have gone to Mrs. Green's cottage," Pointer said. "Coming? I'll leave word where we have gone in case she comes back here."

"Yes, I'll come. I'm worried. If there is any fresh trouble between them?"

Again he did not reply.

They were off. Both were silent. Doris looked very worried.

You don't think she's in any sort of danger, do you?" she asked suddenly.

Pointer did not reply, but he gave the tap on the arm of the chauffeur which meant "still faster."

The cottage looked quite deserted when they reached it. Pointer called out Miss Hill's name as he ran up the little path to the grey door. His chauffeur followed with Mrs. Avery.

"She's not here! It's shut up!" Doris said in a disappointed voice. "We've wasted our time!"

Pointer had the door open on the instant with a key that did not look at all like a key. Inside the hall he called again. There was no answer. He tried a door beside him. He opened it in a trice. The room was empty. He tried the door on the other side. It was locked, but he opened it. There was a curious, acrid smell in the room. By the table Olive Hill had been sitting. She was now slumped far forward on it. The man with Pointer held Mrs. Avery back. "Don't go in farther, ma'am. She's dead! Shot. Head wound—"

"Let the lady come in, Hogarth," Pointer said. "We need her to identify the body."

Doris, with a chalk-white face, was staring at Olive's dead body, which, all things considered, did not look too dreadful. She had been shot from ear to ear, they found out afterwards.

Pointer told Hogarth the chauffeur to telephone at once for the doctor. "We must know the hour when it

happened," he explained to Mrs. Avery. "Sorry to ask you
to stay, you mustn't touch anything"

"Of course I'll stay," she said. "I don't think I would
like to leave her—now—like this—alone. But where is
Mrs. Green? Oh!" The last was an exclamation, as her
glance fell on something on the floor. It was a revolver.

Pointer marked the place on the carpet with a very
casual stroke of chalk. The position of the revolver did not
matter in the least to him. Then he lifted it and wrapped
it in transparent paper, so as to preserve the fingerprints.

"Though they'll be those of Miss Hill, to a certainty,"
he said to Mrs. Avery as he did so.

"But that's Anthony's revolver!" she gasped,
swallowing hard. "Anthony's initials are on it. See! Mrs.
Green was allowed to keep it after the inquest. She asked
for it, you know. Where is she?" she stared about her.

Again Pointer said nothing. He, too, wondered at the
artist's absence. He had expected to find her here.

The chauffeur came back to say that the doctor would
come instantly. The telephone rang as he was speaking.
Pointer took off the receiver. He had just left word with
Fraser to put any message for him through to the Cottage
till further notice. It was Mr. Smith speaking. Where was
Miss Hill? Did the Chief Inspector know? She wasn't at
the rectory and—

"We've just found her dead—shot—at Mrs. Green's
cottage. Did she leave a message with you?" Pointer
asked. The tone of Mr. Smith's voice had suggested that
wonderful possibility to him.

"Shot!" came in shocked tones. "You mean?"

Pointer did not reply.

"Then I ought to have—has she been dead long?"

"Since three o'clock, I think we shall find," Pointer
replied, "but that's the merest guess. The doctor hasn't
got here yet."

"I'm coming at once. Can you wait for me? I shan't
take five minutes to get to you at the cottage," came in a
shaken voice from the other end. "She left an envelope to

be sent—but I'll—You think—did she—poor girl—did Anthony's death go as deep as that? But where's Mrs. Green? Surely she must be somewhere near. Or how did Olive get in?"

There was a sound of a car driving up to the cottage. It was the doctor. He looked staggered at the sight of the dead girl on the chair. Pointer asked him to tell them how long Miss Hill had been dead. His own guess had been a good one, for the doctor put her death at around three, as nearly as he could tell without an autopsy.

Doris stared at the Chief Inspector.

"But if you knew, why didn't you prevent it?" she asked passionately.

The doctor suggested that he should take Mrs. Avery home, but Pointer explained that Mr. Smith was coming with a very important letter that they both wanted to see.

The doctor had to hurry off, for he had rushed away from a maternity case. As he left, the sound of another car could be heard racing up at a pace for which it was never intended.

It was Mr. Smith. Hatless—all but breathless. He was shown into the room opposite, and at Pointer's suggestion, Mrs. Avery and he joined him there.

"Mrs. Avery! What a shock for you—did you find her? Chief Inspector, I must explain at once. My secretary is usually as careful a woman as lives, but we can all of us be caught napping. A messengerboy stepped in around half-past two o'clock, handed her a letter for me—to be sent in at once. That was impossible, as it happened. I was seeing a client on a very private matter, most unfortunately, so Miss Hibbard put the letter on one side, and I regret to say she forgot it till I was having tea just now when she brought it me. It was addressed to me. I opened it at my leisure, and found inside it this envelope."

Pointer had already read it over Mr. Smith's shoulder. It was in Olive Hill's handwriting. "To be handed to the Chief Inspector or to any other officer at the police station if I have not myself asked for this back by four o'clock." Across one corner was written: "Very important. Only to be handed back to me personally. Or given at once to the police if I am not back at the office to ask for it by four this afternoon."

Pointer opened the envelope and drew out a letter, or rather two letters. For they were in different handwritings.

He read each through. As he did so a car rushed up to the cottage door as though it were leading in a race. In the same instant, so it seemed, the room door opened and Major Weir-Opie, very pale for once, and Superintendent Shilling came in. Behind them two policemen closed the door silently.

"Mrs. Avery," said Shilling, and his voice was not steady even now, "I arrest you for the murder of Anthony Revell, and for the poisoning of the rector, Mr. Avery—"

He paused, as his eyes swept to the figure slumped against the table. One look of interrogation at Pointer, one nod from him, a muttered word from Major Opie, who was bending over the dead girl, and Shilling continued firmly and very clearly: "And for the murder of Miss Hill. Anything you say—" he finished the prescribed formula.

Doris Avery swayed back a fraction of an inch. Her face looked as though cut from marble, except for the eyes, the dreadful eyes that blazed for a second as she swept them around the room in a quite automatic, unconscious effort to find some way of escape. Then she turned to Mr. Smith.

"This is monstrous, Mr. Smith." Her voice was clear and calm, but it had a stony quality to it as though it came from a rigid throat. "There is some hideous mistake here which you will be able to put right for me very easily. Of course I am innocent of these preposterous charges. Of course Mrs. Green is the woman wanted." She shut her white lips together on that. And again she swayed.

The horrified Mr. Smith was at her side in a moment.

"Surely there is a mistake, as she says," he urged quickly. "I certainly think you must let her explain"

Pointer regretted the suggestion. He would have refused, but the Chief Constable, with a very grim look, swung round on the solicitor.

"She can't," he said sternly.

"You can't possibly tell that unless you hear what she has to say." Mr. Smith was for once speaking as a man and friend, and not as a lawyer. He felt certain that some hideous and really ludicrous mistake was being made. Why, he knew Mrs. Richard Avery well, had known her for some years now! The detective officer from the Yard, in spite of his ability which imposed itself on one, had made a bad mistake, because he was a stranger down here. A few words now, and Mrs. Avery might be spared the horror of being taken by the police to the station, there to be charged with the incredible list of deaths and locked up. Mrs. Richard Avery! Charged! Locked up! That must be prevented.

"I had better explain," Doris spoke in a very controlled voice. "I recognise what you have there, Mr. Pointer. It is a letter written by a very foolish woman who bitterly regrets her folly. It's a letter of mine to my husband," she explained courteously to the room at large, "saying that I was leaving him, and was going away with Anthony Revell, and asking him to divorce me as quickly as possible, so that we could marry. It's also a letter for which I paid Olive Hill a thousand pounds half an hour ago, at four o'clock. It was all in one-pound notes. She insisted on my handing over the money first. She had a package all done up—I saw my own writing—and she 'did' me brown!" There was no mistaking the rage in Mrs. Avery's voice. "I had to let her hold on to it. She had a revolver with her. That revolver there. But she swore I should have the letter to-night. I told you, Mr. Pointer, that I had no idea where she was—that I was uneasy, because I wanted you to find her with the money on her, of course! I couldn't tell you what had just happened. I couldn't confess my madness. I could only hope that you might yet get the letter back for me."

Major Weir-Opie looked at her with no softening of his face.

"It won't do, Mrs. Avery. There's more than that. We have also in our possession the letter which you wrote to Mr. Anthony and which brought him back to The Causeway. The letter for which you poisoned Mr. Avery—and which you did not find, for all your searching."

"What letters are these?" asked Mr. Smith, who felt as though the world as he knew it was crashing about him. Mrs. Richard Avery had figured in it as Caesar's wife—only a beautiful one—above and immune from gossip.

"The letter sent to you to forward to the police was one I wrote to my husband just before Anthony got engaged to Olive Hill." Doris made a curious gesture of defeat and weariness. "I wrote in it that he and I had been lovers for over a year. Of course that wasn't true. I had quite misunderstood just ordinary civility, and lost my head. It was Olive Hill he was in love with. I made the mistake other women have made before, and will make again, of thinking that I was the attraction. But, as soon as I had posted it, I learnt the truth, and incidentally the truth about whom I really loved after all—my own husband, not Anthony. When I came home and learnt of the engagement between Olive and Anthony it cured me as though by magic. I thought I would go out of my mind, when I reflected on what I had written. You know Richard, Mr. Smith. You know how he would never forgive or forget such a letter. He would hold it as true, no matter what proof to the contrary he had. I nearly went mad, I think. The news that Anthony had shot himself didn't help me. That letter was on its way. That mad, lying letter. But I was saved after all. I got a cable from Richard showing that he had already started for home before I had posted it. Oh, the relief!" For a second her face mirrored it. "The relief! I wrote to Freddy

Anstruther, his secretary out there, told him that I had just posted a letter to my husband which I now wanted not forwarded to him but returned to me unopened. I didn't care what Freddy thought. I knew he would do as I asked. He's an old friend. He did. I got it—as I thought—and destroyed it. But I begin to see now that I was 'done' there, too, by dear little Mousie. Let me look at that letter you have, Mr. Pointer," she urged. "The letter supposed to be mine, enclosed by Miss Hill in her envelope to Mr. Smith?"

Pointer handed the pages to Major Weir-Opie. He would have nothing to do with this scene. Doris studied it very attentively, also the covering letter from young Freddy Anstruther. Then she turned away. She was proud of her brains, but she had been tricked by Olive Hill. That was, Pointer thought, the sharpest sting for a moment.

"But—but she left it with me with instructions to hand it to the Chief Inspector here—or failing him to the police should she not herself ask for it back by four o'clock." Mr. Smith's brain was beginning to function again. "That showed that she was afraid—of just what has apparently happened." He ended up, and he looked very hard at Mrs. Avery.

"Evidently," Doris agreed, "but not from me. She had asked me to meet her here at four precisely and hand over a thousand pounds in return for that letter. Some one else, probably a confederate, was in the plot with her, and shot her, getting away with the money. It's nowhere to be seen and it certainly isn't on her. It was a bulky wad of notes. I'm perfectly willing to be searched, and have my rooms at the rectory searched." She turned to Pointer, who did not accept the challenge until the Chief Constable turned to him. And then he answered him and him alone.

"They're probably 'planted' somewhere in this house. That's why the Cottage was chosen, I fancy. It's no use Mrs. Avery assuring us that Olive Hill chose this place for the meeting. She did that. Because it was Mrs. Green's. So that when Miss Hill was found dead, it would look like her work, like the crime of a woman who hated Miss Hill. And the letter she came to sell Mrs. Avery wasn't this one. Nor a copy of this one. This was her anchor to windward, she thought. The letter she offered to sell was the letter that brought Mr. Anthony back to The Causeway, and so to his death."

Doris gave a contemptuous laugh.

"That's about as true as the other things that you have been saying!"

"Look here," said Weir-Opie, "this painful scene has gone on long enough. To end it, let me say this, Mrs. Avery, that your letter—the original—is at the police station. It runs"—he opened, his note-book and read— "'Tell the Gartsides you must run up to your dentist in town. Be in The Causeway drawing-room to-morrow night. I will come at twelve, to the minute. The girl you love is in a terrible dilemma. Do not fail us and do not write to her. She will be with me.'"

"Well?" Doris asked quietly. She looked normal again, except for her deadly pallor. "It is true that I wrote that note. But I did not go. Olive went alone. She begged me at the last to let her go by herself. She was a thief—as well as a blackmailer—and some one was threatening her with a prosecution unless she paid back a large sum which they had traced at last to her, and which she had lost at the races. I told Mr. Avery as much on the Sunday night. You see, Mr. Pointer, you are not quite clever enough to understand Olive Hill, just as I was not. As no one was. Certainly not Anthony Revell. But I do not think that she shot Anthony."

"Neither do I," Weir-Opie said, as she paused.

"No, Mrs. Green did that. From jealousy. I was not jealous. She was. I am beginning to think that she instigated Olive to offer me that letter you have—the letter to Anthony—for the thousand pounds so that she could take it from her and Olive would not be in a position to fight back. But Olive did try to fight, and Mrs. Green gladly shot her. Every one knows how she loathed her. She is now, of course, safely in hiding."

CHAPTER 20

"As for Mr. Avery," Doris's even voice continued, "No one poisoned him. What must have happened was that the little that I had to tell him about Olive's trouble so bothered him that he himself made a mistake and filled one of the bottles standing on the shelf—one without a label and without a bell on it, then, still thinking deeply, he must have carried it into his study—and got it mixed with the mushroom ketchup on his tray. No one can say just what happened. But I feel sure, I always have felt sure, that no one poisoned him. It was an accident, pure and simple."

Mr. Smith was looking at her very attentively. Perhaps this was the truth. But he was shaken—badly shaken. . . .

Pointer looked at Doris with his clear passionless gaze. At last he spoke to her.

"There are bloodstains on the soles of your shoes, yet when we got here the blood in the other room was quite dry. Besides, you were not allowed to walk about at all."

Doris's face sagged as she tucked her feet under her chair. She had been sitting with her knees crossed.

Mr. Smith's face was eloquent. One horrified glance before she altered her position, and he had seen the stains of which Pointer spoke. He stood back with a gesture that spoke for itself.

Superintendent Shilling took his place. The two men at the door came forward. A moment more, and Doris Avery was seated between the Superintendent and one of his constables in the car.

Each had an arm linked through one of hers. All three sat in a dreadful silence as the car rushed by a back street to the police station.

In the room at the cottage Mr. Smith passed a hand over his face.

"I cannot undertake her defence," he said in a low voice, as he reached for his hat and, without another word, made for his car. Weir-Opie waited till it had driven off, then he turned to Pointer. "You must tell me later how you arrived at the incredible truth in this affair. Shilling nearly fainted from shock. So the motive had nothing to do with the stamps, nor with the question of Anthony's identity?"

"No, sir. Jealousy. Clear enough," Pointer said. "Mad infatuation for Mr. Anthony. There was a love affair between them which had lasted over a year, according to this letter to her husband."

He stopped. Another police car had arrived, of an odd, covered shape. There was a stretcher inside. Four men with it got out, and two of them, quickly lifting Olive's body on to it, drove off by the way they had come. The other two were to stay behind in the cottage.

Weston came down the short stairs. "The money is there, sir, a thousand pounds in one-pound notes, planted in Mrs. Green's bedroom, as you suggested. Stuffed into the back of the drawer under some clothes. And, as you thought there would be, I found bloodstains on 'em."

Pointer and the Major went up to the room which Mrs. Green used as a bedroom. They took the notes away with them in their own car.

"Mrs. Avery believes in doing things thoroughly," the Chief Constable said dryly.

"Quite so, sir. Mrs. Green was, of course, meant to be found at the cottage with them and the body. Something evidently detained her and spoilt the plan."

"Well, we got at least this out of that harrowing scene with Mrs. Avery," the Major said when back at the station: "we know what her defence will be. I mean about the letter she sent to her husband."

"This other letter to her husband was posted at her own home on the day she returned from her mother's to the rectory." Shilling was studying the postmark. "That first time she went home because of her mother's illness."

Weir-Opie nodded. "As soon as she got back, she heard of his engagement to Miss Hill, and she went mad. I think that murder of Anthony was a *crime passionel* if ever there was one!"

"Especially as just then she must have got the news that Mr. Richard Avery was coming home a wealthy man." Shilling had a capital memory for dates.

"By jove," Weir-Opie said under his breath, "what a position for her! By her own doing, she had lost a wealthy husband for the sake of a chap who had no love for her and was going to marry another woman!"

"Yes, and another woman whom she had put in his way." Pointer slowly lit his pipe. The other two were smoking also. "From what Miss Avery said, and from what Mrs. Avery said, and let drop, I think that some one had begun to comment on Mr. Anthony's visits to the rectory, or attentions to Mrs. Avery."

"I rather think that may have been the rector himself," Weir-Opie rightly guessed. "He looked very troubled about that time."

"Mrs. Avery very likely put forward an entirely fictitious interest on Mr. Revell's part in Miss Hill as a shield," Pointer continued.

"And then she had to go off to her mother's!" Shilling said excitedly, "and leave them together for a fortnight. That was what did it!"

"Just so," Pointer agreed. "When she got back she found that Mr. Anthony really was in love with Miss Hill and, as you say, sir, she found at the same time that her husband, to whom she had just written this damning letter here, was a rich man coming home to enter parliament and give her just the kind of life for which, in a way, she was suited."

"And then as you say she went mad." Weir-Opie spoke with deep regret.

They could not know about the rector's bringing her the news of Anthony Revell's death when she had just opened and read the letter from her husband telling her about their entirely changed fortunes.

To him, as to Grace, she had pretended that the letter was lost, that Olive had never handed it to her, that the tremendous mental upheaval in which he found her was her extravagant grief at its nonarrival. In reality it was the shock of finding that she had lost, as she feared, what she knew she could make into a great position.

Only when she received her husband's wire on the way home from the inquest, and saw how the situation could yet be saved, did her spirits revive, rise to new buoyancy, and float far above the mere shooting of Anthony Revell.

Pointer was continuing the talk:

"She got Mr. Anthony home with that note there, waited with him for a while probably in the drawingroom, got him, I think, to lend her his revolver under plea of not being able to wait longer for Miss Hill, and not liking to go home unprotected. He would want to wait on for Miss Hill who knew nothing of the affair."

"Mrs. Avery, too, was most likely a capital shot with a revolver," Weir-Opie said. "She had spent two years on the Gold Coast when she was first married to Richard Avery."

"I think it possible that she got him to tie her shoelace for her, and shot him straight through the head as he did so. As she didn't ask Mr. Anthony to burn this letter to him, nor look for it apparently at his house, and as none from her were found after his death, I take it for granted that he always destroyed her letters."

"And this one, this all-important one he dropped in the car driving back home," Shilling said, continuing the tale. "It must have got between the cushions, and Mr. Avery found it on Saturday night, as you guessed and, as you thought, mistook it for his sermon notes, and only opened it out in church."

"Odd that Mrs. Avery didn't feel that sermon as a warning," mused Weir-Opie aloud in some surprise.

"I don't think she heard one word of it, sir."

Pointer explained where he believed her thoughts to have been.

"She was very happy just then, as we both noticed that Saturday at dinner. I think she thought that all was going right, when she got the chance to get back—unopened—what she believed was her letter to her husband, but which was evidently a clever copy made by Miss Hill.Then came the thunderbolt of Sunday night when she probably stepped into the study for a casual goodnight, and the rector handed her her letter to Mr. Anthony and asked her to explain what was, she hoped, a dead and buried subject."

"Literally dead and buried!" threw in Shilling, drawing in his breath.

"She had to improvise something instant and efficacious. We know what she did. All but emptied the mushroom ketchup bottle which was on the tray and filled it with the toadstool extract. By the way, I think she had been able to give Mr. Avery a more cheerful suggestion about Miss Hill than the one she made to me. I think it much more likely that she put it on some disinclination of Miss Hill's to be married in such a rush. Then came the dreadful attacks of pain from which he died in at most an hour, the doctor thinks. He knew the truth then, and hid the all-important letter so successfully."

There was a profound silence.

"But Miss Hill—where does she come in?" Weir-Opie asked at last. "Why would she know enough to keep this letter of Mrs. Richard Avery's to her husband, and fob her off with a copy?"

"I think Miss Hill suspected Mrs. Avery of having shot Mr. Anthony from the first. She knew, I am certain, that she was in love with him. She realised, I feel sure, that she was only to be used as a shield later. She

A Resurrected Press Mystery

guessed after a little what it was that Mrs. Avery was hunting for, and hunted for it too. But meanwhile, she evidently got hold of that letter to Mr. Richard Avery, which his secretary had returned unopened to the wife. Miss Hill evidently got that from the post-bag, and enclosed instead in the original envelopes two forgeries. Mrs. Avery was naturally easily deceived as to the genuineness of the letters inside. Probably she barely glanced at them. It would never occur to Mrs. Avery that Olive Hill could outwit her."

"She wouldn't easily suspect what was being done. Who would?" said Weir-Opie.

"Miss Hill kept the original as her safety line, I suppose," Shilling suggested.

"If so, she relied on it too much. Something made her decide to get away. I think Mr. Byrd's expedition. He needs money for that. I fancy she hoped to lend it him and force him to take her along. Anyway, she bluffed a thousand out of Mrs. Avery, pretending that she had found what the other had for a time hunted for so carefully—her letter to Mr. Anthony."

The telephone rang. It was a constable speaking from the rectory, where he had been sent to lock up Mrs. Avery's rooms and stand by the telephone. Mrs. Green had just rung up Miss Hill. Acting on instructions, the constable had explained that she was out at the moment, but he could take the message. Mrs. Green evidently thought it was Fraser speaking, and went on to say that she had tried to rush back to the cottage by a quarter to four, since Miss Hill told her she had some most important news for her. But a serious accident to the motor-bus she was in had prevented it, and she could not possibly be at the cottage before halfpast six. Mrs. Green had hung up on that, and the constable had passed on her message—not to the dead girl, but to the police.

"The message was sent in the name of Olive Hill, of course, but here again she was only used as a decoy," said Pointer.

"Criminals repeating themselves," murmured Shilling sagely.

"Lucky accident," said Weir-Opie. "Not that it would have mattered in the end. Not when we had these letters in our possession."

"When did you suspect Mrs. Richard Avery?"

"When she only searched the library, sir, the one room which I was certain that the murderer hadn't had time to hunt through the night before. And there were so many things that fitted. Her great good looks. Her apparent eagerness to have Mr. Anthony be thought in love with Miss Hill, which would explain—and excuse— his constant visits to the rectory. Also, if the letter to Mr. Anthony came from her, it was easy to understand that he would not write separately to Miss Hill, in the same house. What more natural than her spokeswoman should be Mrs. Avery, the headstrong, violent-passioned woman who shot Mr. Anthony in a fit of fury, and found that-it wasn't to stop there?"

"You foresaw Miss Hill's danger when you left us on Saturday, I understand?"

"Yes, sir. You see, Mrs. Avery wanted Olive Hill out of the way. For many reasons. Hatred of her because she had taken Anthony away. Fear of what she suspected. Fear of her determined hunting at the rectory. But she had to wait for a safe opportunity. Mrs. Green's unconcealed hatred of the young woman was that opportunity. Let Olive Hill be killed somewhere where it looked as though Mrs. Green had done it—and all would be well—"

"She thought!" threw in the Chief Constable.

"Just so, sir, 'she thought!' And Miss Hill was mad enough to disregard your warning. Did she forget it, I wonder?"

"I think she fancied herself clever enough to outwit Mrs. Avery, sir. She had scored a great success when she passed off as Mr. Avery's own, the forged returned letter. I think Miss Hill thought herself to be far the cleverer of the two—and trusted to that. Probably also she thought that, if in a tight place, she would only have to tell Mrs. Avery about the letter sent to Mr. Smith—and she would be safe."

"As she would have had to have been if she had had a chance to get a word in about it," said Shilling. "But how did you feel so sure that Miss Hill had been decoyed to the cottage?"

"When Mrs. Avery told me that she had recognised as Mrs. Green's the voice that she had heard talking to the rector late on the night when he was killed." Pointer lit his pipe. He needed it. The last hour had taken it out of him. "Had she really heard her voice, either she would have recognised it earlier—or not at all."

"Especially as Mrs. Avery knows Mrs. Green well," agreed Weir-Opie, "and she has quick ears. Did she hear any voice at all, do you think?"

"I don't, sir. Neither the rector's, nor any one else's. I think she invented that as a possible loophole for herself should things seem to be closing in a bit. When she told me of having heard Mrs. Green's voice in the room below her own, I guessed that she was preparing her final effort—one which would free her from Miss Hill and Mrs. Green, too. The latter's fondness for Anthony Revell was a constant menace to his murderer. Mrs. Green's cottage was obviously the place to try for at once when Miss Hill was missing. I had hoped—half hoped—to find her alive."

They went on back to the cottage first of all, and there they dug out the nurse's cloak, cap and white hair which Olive had worn when she went to her death. She had not cared very much whether she were recognised or not. As for the disguise which Mrs. Avery had on when she sent off the gardener, part of that was found later in a clearing of the wood, the part which had consisted of a thick dress worn over her usual frock. The wig and false eyebrows and gay ribbon on her plain hat, which Doris had buried farther on, were never found.

Olive had handed to Mrs. Avery another forgery, instead of the latter's own letter. Mrs. Avery, too white hot with fury to recognise it as such, quite unaware of Olive's powers in that line, had snatched it from her, shot her in the same instant and burnt the paper. Then she had taken from Olive the nurse's outer garments and the white "front," which had been bought only a few hours before at Swan and Edgar's, and put on her head the felt hat which she usually wore, and which Doris had brought with her, for she had felt quite sure who the nurse would be. The fur stole which she folded round the dead shoulders was the girl's own, which she had herself worn to the Cottage, and hidden under a cushion while waiting for the blackmailer to walk into the trap.

It had taken the swift Doris very few minutes in the wood to restore her usual appearance, get back to the rectory, and run down to meet Pointer with her worry about Olive's non-appearance. Incidentally she had thought that he would still be away in Town, and that it would be Shilling who would find the dead body, and the artist, and the money, all together at the Cottage.

It was a couple of months later that the three men sat once again discussing the case, this time in the rooms of the Chief Inspector at New Scotland Yard.

Doris Avery had just been found guilty on all three counts, and the jury had only taken a quarter of an hour to bring in their unanimous verdict.

"You've heard about Byrd?" asked Weir-Opie finally. "No? He's joined the Salvation Army. The rector has made a sort of posthumous convert there."

Another short silence followed, it lasted till he broke it to say:

"The 'wine in the cup—was red' enough in all conscience! Is that text on Anthony's grave to stand?"

"Miss Avery, sir, suggests a plain R.I.P. as on Miss Hill's grave. And I understand that Mrs. Green is having these three letters carved on Mr. Revell's monument instead of the text that she had chosen."

There was another silence.

"And of all those who heard the sermon, the one for whom it was really meant didn't pay any attention to it. That's life!" Pointer was thinking aloud.

"But you did," the Chief Constable said promptly. "But for the chance that you heard it, and went over to see the room where the rector died—well, a ruthless criminal would have got off scot free."

"To try her hand at something else of the same kind, most likely," suggested Superintendent Shilling.

THE END

Murder at Bridge

When an afternoon bridge party attended by some of Hamilton's leading citizens ends with the hostess being murdered in her boudoir, Special Investigator Dundee of the District Attorney's office is called in. But one of the attendees is guilty? There are plenty of suspects: the victim's former lover, her current suitor, the retired judge who is being blackmailed, the victim's maid who had been horribly disfigured accidentally by the murdered woman, or any of the women who's husbands had flirted with the victim. Or was she murdered by an outsider whose motive had nothing to do with the town of Hamilton. Find the answer in . . . **Murder at Bridge**

One Drop of Blood

When Dr. Koenig, head of Mayfield Sanitarium is murdered, the District Attorney's Special Investigator, "Bonnie" Dundee must go undercover to find the killer. Were any of the inmates of the asylum insane enough to have committed the crime? Or, was it one of the staff, motivated by jealousy? And what was is the secret in the murdered man's past. Find the answer in . . . **One Drop of Blood**

AVAILABLE FROM RESURRECTED PRESS!

GEMS OF MYSTERY
LOST JEWELS FROM A MORE ELEGANT AGE

Three wonderful tales of mystery from some of the best known writers of the period before the First World War -

A foggy London night, a Russian princess who steals jewels, a corpse; a mysterious murder, an opera singer, and stolen pearls; two young people who crash a masked ball only to find themselves caught up in a daring theft of jewels; these are the subjects of this collection of entertaining tales of love, jewels, and mystery. This collection includes:

- **In the Fog - by Richard Harding Davis's**

- **The Affair at the Hotel Semiramis - by A.E.W. Mason**

- **Hearts and Masks - Harold MacGrath**

AVAILABLE FROM RESURRECTED PRESS!

THE EDWARDIAN DETECTIVES
LITERARY SLEUTHS OF THE EDWARDIAN ERA

The exploits of the great Victorian Detectives, Poe's C. Auguste Dupin, Gaboriau's Lecoq, and most famously, Arthur Conan Doyle's Sherlock Holmes, are well known. But what of those fictional detectives that came after, those of the Edwardian Age? The period between the death of Queen Victoria and the First World War had been called the Golden Age of the detective short story, but how familiar is the modern reader with the sleuths of this era? And such an extraordinary group they were, including in their numbers an unassuming English priest, a blind man, a master of disguises, a lecturer in medical jurisprudence, a noble woman working for Scotland Yard, and a savant so brilliant he was known as "The Thinking Machine."

To introduce readers to these detectives, Resurrected Press has assembled a collection of stories featuring these and other remarkable sleuths in The Edwardian Detectives.

- The Case of Laker, Absconded by Arthur Morrison
- The Fenchurch Street Mystery by Baroness Orczy
- The Crime of the French Café by Nick Carter
- The Man with Nailed Shoes by R Austin Freeman
- The Blue Cross by G. K. Chesterton
- The Case of the Pocket Diary Found in the Snow by Augusta Groner
- The Ninescore Mystery by Baroness Orczy
- The Riddle of the Ninth Finger by Thomas W. Hanshew
- The Knight's Cross Signal Problem by Ernest Bramah

- The Problem of Cell 13 by Jacques Futrelle
- The Conundrum of the Golf Links by Percy James Brebner
- The Silkworms of Florence by Clifford Ashdown
- The Gateway of the Monster by William Hope Hodgson
- The Affair at the Semiramis Hotel by A. E. W. Mason
- The Affair of the Avalanche Bicycle & Tyre Co., LTD by Arthur Morrison

RESURRECTED PRESS CLASSIC MYSTERY CATALOGUE

Journeys into Mystery
Travel and Mystery in a More Elegant Time

The Edwardian Detectives
Literary Sleuths of the Edwardian Era

Gems of Mystery
Lost Jewels from a More Elegant Age

E. C. Bentley
Trent's Last Case: The Woman in Black

Ernest Bramah
Max Carrados Resurrected:
The Detective Stories of Max Carrados

Agatha Christie
The Secret Adversary
The Mysterious Affair at Styles

Octavus Roy Cohen
Midnight

Freeman Wills Croft
The Ponson Case
The Pit Prop Syndicate

J. S. Fletcher
The Herapath Property
The Rayner-Slade Amalgamation
The Chestermarke Instinct
The Paradise Mystery
Dead Men's Money

The Middle of Things
Ravensdene Court
Scarhaven Keep
The Orange-Yellow Diamond
The Middle Temple Murder
The Tallyrand Maxim
The Borough Treasurer
In the Mayor's Parlour
The Saftey Pin

R. Austin Freeman
The Mystery of 31 New Inn from the Dr. Thorndyke
Series
John Thorndyke's Cases from the Dr. Thorndyke
Series
The Red Thumb Mark from The Dr. Thorndyke Series
The Eye of Osiris from The Dr. Thorndyke Series
A Silent Witness from the Dr. John Thorndyke Series
The Cat's Eye from the Dr. John Thorndyke Series
Helen Vardon's Confession: A Dr. John Thorndyke
Story
As a Thief in the Night: A Dr. John Thorndyke Story
Mr. Pottermack's Oversight: A Dr. John Thorndyke
Story
Dr. Thorndyke Intervenes: A Dr. John Thorndyke
Story
The Singing Bone: The Adventures of Dr. Thorndyke
The Stoneware Monkey: A Dr. John Thorndyke Story
The Great Portrait Mystery, and Other Stories: A
Collection of Dr. John Thorndyke and Other Stories
The Penrose Mystery: A Dr. John Thorndyke Story
The Uttermost Farthing: A Savant's Vendetta

Arthur Griffiths
The Passenger From Calais
The Rome Express

Fergus Hume
The Mystery of a Hansom Cab
The Green Mummy
The Silent House
The Secret Passage

Edgar Jepson
The Loudwater Mystery

A. E. W. Mason
At the Villa Rose

A. A. Milne
The Red House Mystery
Baroness Emma Orczy
The Old Man in the Corner

Edgar Allan Poe
The Detective Stories of Edgar Allan Poe

Arthur J. Rees
The Hampstead Mystery
The Shrieking Pit
The Hand In The Dark
The Moon Rock
The Mystery of the Downs

Mary Roberts Rinehart
Sight Unseen and The Confession

Dorothy L. Sayers
Whose Body?

Sir William Magnay
The Hunt Ball Mystery

Mabel and Paul Thorne
The Sheridan Road Mystery

Raoul Whitfield
Death in a Bowl

And much more!
Visit ResurrectedPress.com
for our complete catalogue

About Resurrected Press

A division of Intrepid Ink, LLC, Resurrected Press is dedicated to bringing high quality, vintage books back into publication. See our entire catalogue and find out more at www.ResurrectedPress.com.

About Intrepid Ink, LLC

Intrepid Ink, LLC provides full publishing services to authors of fiction and non-fiction books, eBooks and websites. From editing to formatting, from publishing to marketing, Intrepid Ink gets your creative works into the hands of the people who want to read them. Find out more at www.IntrepidInk.com.